BRASS IN THE BLOOD

BOOK SIX OF THE SADDLEWORTH VAMPIRE SERIES

Brass In The Blood by Angela Blythe

Book 6 of the Saddleworth Vampire Series.

First Edition.

Please contact me for details of future books at http://www.angelablythe.com

Published by Willow Publishers.

Cover Illustration and Design Copyright © 2018 by Dark Grail

https://www.etsy.com/uk/shop/DarkGrail

Other books in the Saddleworth Vampire
Series

Sticky Valves

Silver Banned

Brass Neck

Bold As Brass

Seven Bells

Brass In The Blood

1 Shadows

From above Friarmere the fires could be clearly seen. The two parties that had noticed them were entirely different. The first was Michael who had just exited The Grange and was on his way down to the Primary School.

The other party was considerably larger. A group of eighty vampires and humans stood at the top of the Pennines, gazing down at the fires that were in the centre of Friarmere.

Gary had put forward the idea that one was in the Park and he couldn't have been more right about that. The other was in a large house on Springmeadow Lane.

In there three vampires had been discovered and eliminated efficiently by the human vigilantes.

Joe, Father Philip, Darren, Craig and Carl stood just in the shadows as they watched the house consumed by the warming red and yellow flames. They waited to see if they were needed to push the illegal occupants back inside, these critters were always trying to pull a fast one, so listened for all three dreadful voices as they screamed inside to get out. Darren drummed his fingers on a garden fence. Father Philip stood ready to strike.

Three vampires was a very healthy yield for one house, and the five men were ecstatic that they had been able to get them so early in the night. The vampire vigilantes that had seen them on their way past Maurice's house earlier and had tracked them up there. But now the undead foursome were long gone, back down to the centre of the Village, leaving the humans to do this job. One or another of the vampires was always looking for potential victims. Adam was very good at going unnoticed on the roofs. The only sign sometimes was a little falling snow, when he was above his victim. But that was becoming less of a problem; some areas had none now.

Maurice was on his guard in the Park as usual, and Ernie and Mark would mop up any stragglers in the High Street. They were quickly dealt with by a swift drag into the blackness of the ginnel, where both vampires could dispatch their enemy silently and in private.

The blaze in the Park was due to the vampire vigilantes finally catching up with another pesky bloodsucker. This creature had been hunting a dog. His attention was on the poor beast and not on the four vampires who stalked him. They hadn't even got into position that night when they started to hear the noise of the dog intermittently barking and howling. The bloodsucking creature growling behind him. The four of them watched the chase go into the Park.

This was so easy now for these experienced vampire hunters. Trapping and quickly dispatching their victim, they torched the body close to the river rather than their usual furnace area.

They chose a new area because during the struggle, the vampire had managed to rake his fingernails down Maurice's arm. Mark was worried that if The Master found this dead vampire before they had piled him up with the others at the end of the night, he might smell Maurice under the victim's fingernails and know who had attacked him. So, they had to dispose of him here and now. In the end, this proved fortuitous. They had found an even better and more secluded area to deal with the corpses. Win-win.

While Maurice, Ernie and Mark laid the vampire close to the river, put him under the bushes and set fire to him, Adam took the dog as far away from the centre of Friarmere as he could. The opposite direction to where he thought the vampire children were.

'Go home lad. Find somewhere safe until morning. Nothing is free from danger on the streets of Friarmere at night. You had a lucky escape now. Don't push it and hunker down somewhere,' Adam told him.

The dog seemed to know what he was saying or was just glad to get away from Adam as he put his tail between his legs and pelted off.

Joan thought that she had bitten off more than she could chew. She was exhausted, cold and terrified. Friarmere was low and illuminated prettily in the valley far below them. The two orange fires highlighted the danger that they were in now. They were in a new village, and if she wasn't with the others, she wouldn't know where to start. Joan made sure that she was linking arms with her daughter Lisa, who seemed far more confident about the prospect of this.

The Melden gang seemed to be sticking together a little bit more than they probably should. They were still not as integrated as the others, having been with them for less than twelve hours. Paul, Rachel, Mrs Shuttleworth and her daughter-in-law, Helen stuck together with the others from Melden. They walked in another separate group. Our Doris, a fellow Meldener occasionally gave them a thumbs up. She seemed happy enough with all this. Joan wondered if she was being over pessimistic.

She looked around at the group she was with, the other gang seemed a lot more cheerful and knew a lot more than she did. Maybe everything wasn't as bad as they painted it. *Perhaps she should try and talk to these people more*, she thought. They looked like they were capable of lifting spirits and hers needed a block and tackle for that to happen. She decided to go and talk to Freddie and Brenda. They looked like her kind of people.

Everyone was concerned about just getting over to the other side of the village where they could rest, be warm and have something to eat. They whispered as Wee Renee had made them aware that if eighty people were talking at normal volume all at once, it was bound to attract something nasty. She was already aware of something to the right of them, on the Moors. But for now, it did attack them. Wee Renee did not know if it could move fast or move at all. She considered that it could be two threats in one. But she just kept plodding along. Soon they would be too far away to care. These eighty people had bigger fish to fry.

The Moorston vampires surrounded them, a couple at the front and at each side, with the rest out at the back. They should be able to see anything aggressive on its way, from whatever direction it came. Angela was at the front with another vampire. She did not exactly know the way, so kept looking back at Wee Renee who would point at the direction to walk, when they arrived at junctions.

Tony, Sue and Bob looked down at their Street from above. They could easily make it out, as it ran along the main street up to The Grange, which they were close to now. Their house was three-quarters of the way up, close to Wee Renee's. Sue wondered how her other cats were, if Christine had stolen more of her sequined berets and whether EastEnders was still on series link. Looking across at Bob to see if he was watching his house, she saw that he was. Basil was wrapped around Bob's neck, half in his hood and half out.

Freddie and Brenda were so excited to be home too, of course. They had been away from it much longer than Sue and Tony. Alas, it would not be safe to live alone in their house until all this was over, as it did not have the type of huge gates that Jennifer and Beverly's houses had. Chez Freddie was not a fortress at all.

So, for the moment, they would be in the mill with everyone else, but it was still nice to be in your own Village at what could be the end of your adventure.

Freddie was re-questioning some of the old group about the vampires that were in the school the night they were last there. In particular, the ones that had helped to rescue Carl and Gary.

He knew one was Maurice, his best friend. He was asking Pat about how he acted and what he looked like. Freddie had to prepare himself to meet his friend again and found he was quite nervous about it. But he was so pleased that Maurice had not allowed Norman to take his body, mind and soul.

Rick and Lauren walked hand in hand as they spoke to Jason and Lee about different events and weddings that they had done. Lee would do the music in the daytime; the Brass Band would play in the Church and at the beginning of the reception. In the evening, Jason would take over and do the disco. They were very busy which was not surprising, considering in the area that they lived in, everyone loved a Brass Band.

Jason and Lee hoped to go back to this profitable sideline. In fact, everyone was starting to think about what they would be doing when this was all over, which was a new optimistic mood that they had not dared experience before now.

Michael whistled on his journey down to the Village but stopped when he heard a familiar sound. He could hear the engine of a snowmobile, and from what he could tell, it seemed to be idling and not running around or being revved.

Michael peeked around the corner, looking into what just happened to be the street that Sue, and Wee Renee lived in. Mrs White and Keith were tying another person to the back of the snowmobile.

Blow me, he thought, *it's already happening*! No time for Penelope to go out on the prowl and find them by accident. He had to act now. He quickly turned back and retraced his steps up to The Grange.

As he swung to the left by Christine's house, towards The Grange, he did not see the most interesting happening of the night. If he had looked back up to the top road, to the right of Christine's house, he would have seen the crowd of rescuers on their way to Friarmere. But as it was, he didn't see them or hear them. The sounds were too loud from his laboured breathing and the blood pumping in his ears, as he endeavoured to get help before it was too late.

Angela thought she saw someone disappear down a dirt track opposite the junction on the main road. She was not sure, as she had been looking back at Wee Renee for the next direction. Wee Renee pointed to the left, which would take them down the bank. The wind was getting up, and the trees and bushes were blowing. The shadows changed from minute to minute up here. There were no streetlights, and now there was only a faint moonlight. Angela saw there was nothing there now.

Pat was talking to Wee Renee privately. Trying to keep her voice down. The two of them strode forward, apart from the group a little.

'I mean, Rene we have taken a risk and given a lot of assurances about where they are going to stay and food, but do we know that the people in the mill will still be there? They could have moved out or have been slaughtered!' Pat whispered.

'It's all we can say, isn't it?' Wee Renee said. 'The fact is that we were walking into an unknown situation in Moorston and Melden. We can't say that here. During this fight, we have been here twice before and know that there has been a group keeping their eye on stuff here, at least. Whereas there was no-one in Moorston and Melden. I have the confidence that the Wee Faerie has steered me right and all this will be fine, Pat. Don't worry yourself.'

Wee Renee took a brief glance back at Nigel. He still looked down at his ancestor's locket in his hands, his face a mixture of wonderment and sadness. She felt her heart twinge for him. It was not a good story, but it now had been told, and Nigel had had his mystery solved. More importantly, his poor great-grandmother could finally rest with her husband in Melden.

'I hope you are right chucks,' Pat said, 'because if you aren't, we are right buggered up! We have eighty souls in our care.'

Finally, Wee Renee reached the point Angela had been when she had seen the shadow of Michael. They turned left onto the main road, downwards towards Friarmere. Angela was already fifty feet in front of them. They would carry straight down now, until they turned off to the right, up some steps and onto the donkey path. Even though not many of them spoke, there was still quite a lot of noise with the rustling off the backpacks, the footsteps and the dragging of their sledges.

From a distance, several of them thought they could hear an engine. The sound diminished, as it got further away from them, luckily. For once with a gang of eighty people and several vampires around, Wee Renee thought that if she came across a vampire riding a snowmobile, then it would be *the vampire* that would end up in a pickle.

Michael stormed into The Grange. He did not wait to find someone but shouted *'Penelope!'* at the top of his voice. He was still breathless and could taste pennies in his spit.

Penelope soon ran downstairs. Norman followed her to see what all the fuss was about. She had just been telling him about the previous night and a human being dragged to a pulp through Friarmere by Mrs White and Keith. Norman did not find this quite as distasteful as Penelope thought he would but could see her point. It was quite a waste of a human, as they were getting harder to find and would be far better utilised as natural food for themselves or as a new brother or sister.

He finally agreed that they must put a stop to this for once and for all, as Penelope telling them off and the fear of their Master finding out, had not stopped them last night or would do tonight. This was part of the reason, but he also was going to sort it to stop Penelope going on about it. He couldn't bear women *pecking his head*.

It was then that they had heard Michael shouting and had come to listen to his new tale, which took him nearly five minutes to tell, as he still couldn't breathe.

Norman told Michael to no longer concern himself with this matter. Norman would deal with it, and Michael should keep out of the way so that Mrs White and Keith did not suspect that Michael was the one that had alerted him.

However, when Norman realised that Stuart was still in Moorston with Marcel, and Keith had the other snowmobile, he became even angrier as they would have to track them on foot now to prevent this matter from progressing.

Penelope reminded him that as they were about to *get friendly* upstairs, perhaps he should get dressed before he did this.

After he dressed for the night, which took way too much time as far as his girlfriend was concerned, he and Penelope began to run towards the village, and again missed the eighty people that had turned off onto the donkey path a few seconds before they had run past.

The Wee Faerie watched it all. He made sure that their paths hadn't crossed tonight. It wasn't yet time.

Michael, with a lighter heart, walked down from The Grange and made his way to the school to find Diane. He took comfort that his actions had saved a human or at least put a stop to all this baiting for vampire kids nonsense.

2 Doughnuts

The large group of heroes were well on their way out along the donkey path, towards the mill, when Norman and Penelope reached the High Street in Friarmere. The two vampires heard a snowmobile to their right and immediately looking over they saw that it was, in fact, Stuart and Marcel on their way back from Moorston. They didn't expect to see Norman and Penelope standing in the middle of Friarmere so slowed up, even before they were asked.

'What's going on?' Stuart asked. 'Is there a problem?'

'There certainly is,' Norman said. 'Keith and Mrs White are dragging a human through the village to attract the missing vampire children. This is a total and utter waste. That human could be utilised so much better.' Norman relayed this much more coldly than Penelope cared for, but at least he was intervening, and the job was going to get done.

Marcel who felt a little better after visiting Len's body, got off the snowmobile and said he would like to help. He was *in the mood for a ruckus.*

'Good,' Norman said. Then addressed Stuart. 'Go back up to The Grange and await further instructions.'

Stuart did as he was told and disappeared up the hill. As the sound of his snowmobile diminished, they began to hear the sound of the other one and the screams of the human. They seemed to be at the other end of the village, near St Dominic's Church, where there had been the recent fight. Norman, Marcel and Penelope raced down the High Street to confront Keith and Mrs White.

Above them, Adam watched from the roof of the old Bank, crouching behind the apex of the building. His strawberry blonde hair blew in the breeze. He had heard every word. The Master had a thunderous voice when he was angry. *That was a turn up for the books*, he thought. *It looked like mutiny was afoot, and someone had been a naughty boy.*

Ernie and Mark looked up from the ginnel where they were hiding. Adam pointed downwards to the street and put his finger on his lips to tell them to be quiet. Not only did they see the recently discovered *fit* vampire, Penelope, running down the High Street, but that behind her were two others. Another vampire that must be from Moorston shot past, a young redheaded slim man, along with The Master, surprisingly. They all looked furious, and it was obviously due to the two vampires who had recently driven past less than five minutes previously with a human attached to the back of their snowmobile again.

Mark and Ernie had wondered whether this was the chance to mop up the last of those vampire children if the human's body got dumped in the same place again. They felt that this area was close to the kid's nest, but now that The Master and his two new children were intervening, they thought that maybe that option might not be available.

Along the donkey path, there was a central worn-down track about six feet wide where Joe and the others had made their way forwards and back to the Village for supplies. There was also a recent line of snowmobile tracks, which Wee Renee was quite concerned about. She quickly grabbed Pat and Our Doris and pointed to the tracks. They looked very fresh. Maybe they had arrived just one day too late. She had not expected to see this.

'What if they have found the kids and ate them or captured them again? What are we going to find?' Wee Renee asked, her eyes large, searching her friend's faces for an answer. Pat and Our Doris had no answers; it was in their mind that if the snowmobile had found its way down here for some reason, it went without saying that they would follow the footprints of Joe and the others, which would lead them to the door of the mill. The previously very confident Wee Renee was now a nervous wreck, Pat observed.

Andy, Sally, Terry and Gary kept their eyes trained on the trees. They had been caught out this way the last time and did not know whether all the vampire children had been killed or not. There was one thing for sure; they would not be taking any chances this trip.

Lauren, on the other hand, didn't dare look up at the trees. Her encounter with them had been far too much, and she still expected to see one in every branch.

The group passed the spot where they had killed the other two. The pieces now were only just visible, as the snow had fallen upon them and it looked like they had been moved somehow from the centre of the donkey track. Gary's correct summation of events was that they had been kicked willy-nilly by someone.

The human vigilantes Joe, Carl, Father Philip, Darren and Craig, were in a house near to the Primary School quite high above Friarmere. They knew that up here, it was a hotbed of activity. Up here, on the top half of the hill, there was the School and The Grange where most of the creatures stayed. Most of the other smaller nests were around here too. Tonight, they had tracked a singular vampire up to a bungalow there.

They had yet to go in, and Carl could hear engines in Friarmere. As he looked down at the centre of the Village, he could see a single headlight, which meant it must be a snowmobile in this weather. As Joe had told them of his sinister viewing previously, Carl could only imagine what was going on. He pointed it out to the other four men.

This saddened Joe, but he was also happy that they seemed to be going in the direction away from the mill rather than towards it. It would have been necessary if they had seen it going in that direction, to help the others as quickly as they could and maybe come to the rear of the vampire on the snowmobile, as they attacked the mill. Thank heavens that it wouldn't be necessary.

It might be an idea to find out where they parked those, and discretely in the daytime, put them out of action. Joe thought that disconnecting the fuel line would do the trick.

There was always so much to think about and weigh up. Defending the mill was important, but it could not be denied that burning nests was equally important.

Each death was a strike against Norman. Each death made the mill safer. That situation looked secure for the moment, but he told the others to keep their eye on the matter, as the vampires may still travel up to the mill for their sport later.

Keith was doing doughnuts with the snowmobile outside the Church. The man was dead now, so silently bumped along behind them, making a red circle in the snow. Keith seemed to be constructing a bloody target with his doughnuts.

Excitedly, Mrs White realised it was working. She could see one of them on the roof hiding behind a chimney. She was trying not to look as she thought the child would run away. When they were going around in a circle for about the eighth time they saw three figures running towards them down Friarmere High Street. Three adult figures. As they got closer, Keith and Mrs White recognised one to be The Master, then Penelope and they thought the last one must be the vampire named Marcel, who they were yet to meet due to his isolation, up at The Grange.

'What the hell are you doing?' Norman asked.

'Trying to solve a problem,' said Keith.

'You are causing more of a problem by this idiocy than solving it. Did you catch any the other night by doing this?' The Master queried.

'No,' Keith said, 'but we were rudely interrupted then too.' Keith glared at Penelope. She returned his gaze directly. Keith didn't bother her at all.

'So, you have effectively used three humans now, with no success. Three humans that could have been used for food, or to become part of our great Army. Do you think that is intelligent, Keith?' Norman asked.

'I won't be questioned on my intelligence,' Keith said. 'You have left us high and dry in your grief, and I have had to take on the mantle reluctantly.'

'Yes, I bet you did,' Penelope said.

'So, I have done the best I could. Mrs White came to me with a problem and a solution. I have made that happen. Just by using our initiative. To be fair we had a good time doing it anyway, haven't we Mrs White?' Keith asked.

'Oh yes I've had lots of fun,' Mrs White agreed. However, she could tell that this was probably the last time she would have this kind of fun from the look on The Master's face.

'Unleash that human from your snowmobile Keith, and then we will go back up to The Grange and discuss this further. I will not reprimand you in the street. It is not my style,' Norman said.

Keith was furious, and it was evident to the others that there was going to be an argument, which The Master would win. Keith felt humiliated and for a long time had been annoyed at being told what to do by The Master. Mrs White got off the snowmobile sulkily, and Norman told her she was to make her way back with Penelope and Marcel. He would deal with her in the same fashion when he had finished with Keith.

With Norman driving and Keith riding pillion, they set off back up to The Grange. Mrs White still glanced up at the chimney of the roof she had seen her missing child. Now there were two children. This plan had worked. She was so angry that she could have had two of her *loves* back and The Master, plus these two had spoiled it.

Penelope waited for Mrs White to start walking.

'Better shift your little tush,' Marcel said.

'I'm waiting here,' Mrs White said. 'I think the plan is working. Don't look, but there are two on a roof up there. I think they are going to come down for the blood doughnut. If we are still, maybe we can grab them. Please, couldn't we just hide in the bushes for a minute? Then these deaths *would* mean something.'

'You are talking a load of bollocks,' Penelope said. 'Now start walking, or else we will drag you and tell The Master that you wouldn't do as he said, then you'll be in even more trouble.' Mrs White's semi-deflated in front of them. At last, she had them in her sights, but they wouldn't be safely home with her tonight. Right at this moment, she hated The Master for this. She was also a little concerned that the children didn't look quite right anymore. But maybe that was the lack of moonlight on this cloudy night.

They started walking quickly towards the centre of Friarmere. Marcel kept poking her very harshly in the back, so she tripped a little every so often. He seemed very angry with her for some reason. Marcel had not had an outlet for his revenge and had become bitter and short-tempered. Marcel looked like a coiled spring, and Penelope wondered if he was about to snap. She knew that it would happen if Mrs White pushed it that little bit further. His nostrils flared, and he stared at the back of her head as she walked along.

The vampire kids watched their teacher leave. She had left a tasty human on the ground for them by mistake – or was it? Hmmm … last time this had happened, some of their friends had gone down to feast and had been killed. Killed and burned. They wouldn't be caught out again. The children would follow this group of vampires to make sure they had gone, then come back for their delicious meal in peace. Yes, they still had enough self-preservation to do that.

Maurice from the Park, Adam from the roof of the Bank and Mark and Ernie from the ginnel had seen the snowmobile go back up through the Village, and turn up to The Grange, without the human towed behind it. With just The Master on the back, and what looked like Keith behind him, that meant there were others about. So, they kept in the shadows.

It wasn't long before they saw Mrs White, Penelope and the young man walking quickly through the High Street. Mrs White seemed to be distracted; she looked this way and that. Especially watching the roofs, particularly the last one before the Park. As she slowed to get a better look, the young male vampire angrily jabbed her in the back.

Ernie watched astounded as unexpectedly, Mrs White darted off into the Park entrance as fast as she could. Maurice stepped back, even more into the shadows. The snow fell off the bushes that he was hiding in, but no-one was watching this, as Mrs White had her eyes fixed on the two vampire children that had dropped down from the last roof into Park. And Marcel and Penelope were also not noticing Maurice, as they were watching her. They had not seen the vampire children she chased, and they would not have been interested anyway.

Marcel thought that Mrs White was making a run for it. Not only was he angry with her because he was on such a short fuse, but Marcel did not want Norman to think that he could not perform the first task that he had been asked to do. He ran after her, committing to catch her, whatever the cost. Mrs White was small, female, and in life had been close to fifty years old. Marcel was young, fit, male, and he was also not wearing high heels.

It did not take long for him to catch up. Len's unfulfilled revenge fuelled him, and he launched himself onto her back before she disappeared. As he jumped, she turned and was moving towards the left of the Park where the children had dropped down. She grabbed hold of the tree and tried to swing around it to make a fast corner, still unaware that Marcel was following her. Both were fixed on their own quests.

As he threw his body on top of hers, successfully catching her, his weight pushed her downwards on top of some low branches that had been carefully pruned off to allow the tree to grow.

The living wooden stake went straight through Mrs White, entering through her lower ribs. The entry wound was not near her heart, but as she curved downwards, with Marcel's weight on top of her, the accidental staking continued, and the branch finally hit its mark. Mrs White's heart was speared through with the branch.

Marcel could not have been more shocked. Penelope who had been ten paces behind him had seen exactly what had gone on. He put his hands over his mouth as Mrs Whites corpse dangled over the tree. Adam watched from the roof of the Bank incredulously, his hand over his mouth too.

Penelope joined Marcel as he still watched Mrs White. He was hoping that she would start to struggle and this all wouldn't be real. Then that human Michael could patch her up, make her as good as new. He took hold of Penelope's hand, wishing for the slightest of movement. Mrs White continued to be dead.

'What are we going to do?' Marcel asked.

'I don't know,' Penelope said. 'It was an accident. I thought she was trying to escape.'

'So, did I,' Marcel said, 'that's why I did it. I had to catch her. The first thing Norman asked me to do Penelope, the first thing ... and I balls it up. What would Len think? He wouldn't be proud of me.'

'Let's consider our actions very carefully,' said Penelope. 'Norman is furious now. We don't want to make him any angrier. He has just been going on about a waste of life, and now he will bring this up as well.' Marcel looked at Mrs White in silence. He had no idea of what to do. His mind was utterly blank. He felt rooted to the spot. Right now, he needed Len.

'We need to hide her for now,' Penelope said. 'Probably under the bushes will do. Later, when we have got more time, we can get rid of her corpse.'

'How are we going to do that?' Marcel asked.

'There is an outside chance that we might have to do nothing. Someone is burning corpses. Vampire ones. I think that maybe they would do it for us if we left it over there near the entrance. One disappeared outside the Church the other day, and the ground was scorched. They would probably deal with it. I don't know what else to do. I don't have a lighter myself, do you?' Penelope asked.

'No. Why would I?' Marcel said.

'It's just so typical, I am one of the few vampires that smoke, and my ciggies and lighter are up at The Grange. I'll come back another time, see if she's gone. The thing is, burning is the very best way. I don't have any ways of disposing of her body, apart from ripping her up into little pieces. That would be quite a tell-tale sign if we turn up at The Grange covered in her entrails,' Penelope said.

'I think I'm going to cry. My emotions are all over the place tonight, and now this has happened,' Marcel said.

'Shh Marcel, I'm trying to get you out of this, so I have to have quiet to think. She probably has slight scents of us on her, which she would do as Norman had asked us to bring her back. We will say that she promised that she would come up and now we have no idea where she is, after taking her most of the way. We'll say that she insisted that she had to attend to the other children in the School before she went to see The Master,' Penelope said.

'Yes, he'll buy that. She was all about those vampire kids,' Marcel said.

'We do not have her blood on us, and we need to keep it that way. We'll pull her off this tree carefully, put her out of the way at the side of the path. She might not get seen and not disposed of, but we will have to take that chance. Let's do it now before all this planning means nothing and one of the Friarmere lot see us and tell Norman,' Penelope instructed.

The two vampires pulled Mrs White upwards. It was not difficult to remove her, but it did make a sickly, sucking noise.

Maurice still hid in the bushes near the Park entrance and had heard what they had said. He was going to be discovered. He was sure of it. Maurice wondered what they would make of him. It wouldn't take them long, especially Penelope, he could tell she was a sharp one, to work out that he was one of the ones torching the vampire corpses. Then the question would be asked of why – and if he had any more secrets to tell them.

Luckily, he had Adam to watch over him, who could also signal to Mark and Ernie for assistance. But he didn't really want to do this. He wasn't in the mood to fight vampires tonight, as he felt a little tired. These Moorston lot seemed a competent lot too. They would take some handling.

The four of them had already got one, which had been a bit of a struggle if he was honest. They had to chase him, as he chased the dog. Maurice was hoping for an easy kill, then maybe home for a bag of Monster Snacks. He pressed himself against the wall and closed his eyes, hoping that they would not see him if they could not see the reflection of his eyes back at them. The clothes he wore were already dark, so at least that would not give him away. Maurice hoped he had a guardian angel. One that specialised in good vampires!

Marcel and Penelope dragged Mrs White onto the path but after a bit of discussion, left her just at the side of the bush, so that anyone entering the Park could see her immediately. The hole inside her was enormous, and they could see the snow of the Park ground through the centre of Mrs White.

'That's all we can do,' Penelope said. They were not looking anywhere else, only at Mrs White. If Adam had any breath, he would have held it. If Maurice had reached out, he could have touched the two Moorston vampires; he was that close.

Penelope and Marcel exited the park and slowly began to walk up to The Grange. All the way they discussed exactly what they would say so that they could get their story straight.

The vampire vigilantes were concentrating on this new chain of events. They weren't even thinking about the poor dead human lying outside St. Dominic's Church on his own red doughnut. They had forgotten to take their chance at mopping the last of the little ankle biters up.

The vampire kids hadn't forgotten the man on the red doughnut. They freely feasted. The heat was off them for the night.

Josh and Ben were on the lookout on the upper floor of the mill. It was easy to see any happenings from here, as everything was white and showed up so easily outside. The lower levels were boarded up on the windows, so there was no light visible, to anyone passing. The upper floors had no light, and Joe had forbidden any light up here, whether torch or candlelight. It was guaranteed to give them all away. Josh and Ben had to manage with the moonlight. That was enough.

Also, light would distract them, reflecting back their own image. The fact was that only a little light was needed to be outside when the whole ground was like one luminous paper landscape, the trees like dark pencil sketches against the absolute bleakness.

At first, they wondered what they were seeing. First a single person, two people, then a whole sea of figures came from the end of the donkey path and downwards towards the mill. They relentlessly moved forward; this wasn't a seek and find mission. These figures knew what they wanted and aimed directly for the door of the mill. They knew what was there and they wanted in. Josh's stomach turned over. They had been found. There were vampires on their way here. Who else would be on their way here in the darkness?

'Go downstairs and tell them, Ben. Tell them to be quiet. They might just leave us alone if they can't hear us. Let's hope they can't smell us,' Josh said quietly. He wished Joe was here. He wished someone else had been on duty to see this.

Ben disappeared downstairs, and Josh continued to keep watch. These night visitors did not seem to be getting through the snow very easily. He expected the vampires to be able to negotiate the snow far more gracefully than these people. Some of them looked old, and he could see others were holding hands or linking arms with one another. That didn't ring true for a vampire.

Josh stepped nearer the window, examining them as they got closer. He moved his eyes back to the end of the donkey path as the figures continued to stream out from the dark shelter of the tree-lined tunnel, onto the stark contrast of the white snow.

Josh hoped he was right in what he thought because it seemed like a never-ending procession of people. These outnumbered them, even if Joe was here with the others. Around the edges there appeared to be far more nimble people and he could tell that these figures were female.

As they got closer, there was still not enough light on them, just the darkness of their silhouettes against the white snow. Josh knew that they, in their walking and behaviour were human. He was positive. Behind the first lot, the others still came, and then he foresaw another problem. Where were they all going to go?

He rushed back down the metal stairs behind Ben, who was currently telling them all in a hushed voice that they were under siege. When Josh got there he excitedly rushed past Ben on the stairs, with a giggling laugh, he turned to the rest, to tell them the news.

'Come on. There is a load of humans outside, and we have to let them in. I think they've come for sanctuary. And there are hundreds of them!' Josh said.

Beryl looked at him shocked. This couldn't be happening. It was dark. Surely, humans couldn't be outside wandering about just waiting for vampires to bite them! How did they know they were here? Hundreds of them? Wee Renee had gone with less than twenty. It couldn't be her. Could it?

3 Faint

When Norman got Keith up to The Grange, he asked Keith to sit in his study and wait for him. Norman needed to collect his thoughts. He was so angry that he knew if he didn't calm down, the conversation would end with him probably ripping Keith's head off. At the back of his mind, Norman realised this was part of the stress of losing his brother Len. But at the front, all he saw was red.

When he entered the study, Keith had been stewing in his own juice for a while and now appeared to be very quiet. Keith's anger had all fizzled out; he knew he was here to take his punishment. He wanted it to be quick. Keith realised he was in trouble and was unsure of how far The Master would go. Keith was dreading the next few minutes.

To add to the gravity of the situation, Norman sat back in his leather chair and stared at Keith. This was particularly intimidating as The Master never blinked.

'Whatever possessed you to do that, Keith?' Norman asked.

'She wanted them back. I don't know. It was something to do. It seemed constructive at the time and a good use of a human,' Keith gabbled. 'Now when I look back and see that three have been used up for nothing, I am tending to agree with you. It was a ridiculous idea, and I believe it wasn't even Mrs Whites.'

Keith had said all the right things. The exact things, to keep The Master from killing him. It wasn't in Keith's nature to admit that he was wrong, but this was the only course of action in these circumstances.

There were many vampires that Keith would pit himself against. He would not be foolish enough to think that The Master was one of them.

Norman's shoulders dropped. All the anger drained out of him. No further action would be taken against Keith. He would just have a good old moan at him.

'Thank you for being so honest. And coming to the correct conclusion. Not a moment too soon I might add. I am thinking that I cannot be apart from the rest of you any longer if things are getting left undone, and stupid decisions are being made,' Norman said. Keith kept his eyes trained on his lap. Norman thought this was in shame, but it was because Keith was so angry with his Master and he felt humiliated. Keith felt emasculated.

'Sometimes I wonder who your sire is, Keith. You are more like a child of my sisters than of mine. You ought to have seen the community that my brother Len had made for himself,' The Master said. Keith had and wasn't impressed.

'Penelope and Marcel are testaments to how we could live. I know that I find it difficult to be as virtuous as my brother, I am not made the same. Even without his high standards, I certainly cannot condone what you did tonight. From now on you can make no decisions without discussing it with me, and that is the end of it.' Keith did not like this at all. Norman also took the snowmobile keys off him, which he really did hate.

'Wait!' Beryl said to Josh in a loud whisper.

Beryl and a few of the others, did not know the best way to deal with this. As a rule of thumb, they were never to let anyone in, ever. It was so typical that a vast contingent of vampires or night loving people would descend on them when Joe and his gang were out. Beryl didn't know what to do, and the children seemed to sense that there was a problem and began running around nervously.

Understandably they thought they were under attack and from their experiences, this was not going to end well. As the children were getting nervous and excited, they aggravated Bambi, who could tell something was wrong too and started barking as loud as she could. No use being quiet now.

There was a loud rap on the door, and Beryl did not answer. Then she thought she heard what sounded like Pat's voice, from the other side of the door.

'Open up it's bloody freezing,' Pat shouted.

Beryl's shoulders relaxed, it was their gang back again. She instructed Josh and Ben to pull the large pieces of wood away from the door, and she got ready to greet her friends, a smile on her face. The split second before they opened the doors she realised that she still could have heard Pat's voice, but it could have been coming from a dead Pat! She caught her breath, knowing it must be true, as the first face she saw was an unfamiliar vampire.

Adam had watched Penelope and Marcel disappear up to The Grange. He jumped down from the roof of the Bank to give the all clear to Maurice, who was very relieved to be safe.

'That was too close Adam,' Maurice said.

'Come on, let's have a meeting,' Adam said and began to walk out of the Park. They both wandered over to Mark and Ernie who had not got the foggiest of what was going on in the Park but had just kept themselves hidden. From the noises in there, it sounded pretty bad, and even more intriguing, three vampires had gone into the Park, and only two had come out. Adam relayed the tale.

'So, they thought she was making a run for it, but she was really after two of the kids?' Ernie asked.

'Oh yeah, I could see them easily from where I was, then they dropped down at that end of the Park. They are probably hiding under a bush somewhere,' Adam said.

'Or sitting in a tree,' Maurice said. The four of them looked up at the leafless tree's but saw nothing.

'Them pesky kids strike again,' Adam laughed. Everyone got the joke. He showed them the tree that had impaled Mrs White; then they went over to see Mrs Whites body.

'Ewww, nasty,' Mark said.

'What a massive hole. Marcel got her good and proper,' Ernie said.

'I thought when it happened,' Maurice said, 'that it could so easily happen to us when we are fighting these other vamps. We need to be aware of what upstanding tree branches there are. I never imagined that that was possible. Now I see that the Park is a hazardous place.'

'Oh yes – and railings,' Mark said. 'But at least *they* aren't wooden.'

'Let's get back into position,' said Ernie. 'We've only got one tonight, and that's not even worth coming out for.'

'Me and Adam will drag Mrs White under the bushes. We don't want her giving away our position,' Maurice said.

Joe and his band of vigilantes had completed their singular vampire mission. They kept to the side of the road, close to walls and any vegetation. Craig had heard two snowmobiles go back up recently, and none come back down. Joe said that at least, vehicle wise, the High Street must be clear.

They knew the two areas that the vampire vigilantes were hiding in, and as Adam was always on watch at the top of the Bank, he saw them coming a mile off. Joe looked up at him, and he beckoned them to come forward, as the High Street was clear for them to enter unobserved.

When they had got into the safety of the ginnel, Adam jumped down and took Maurice over to see them.

'How many have you got?' Joe asked them.

'Just one earlier. But then we've had saga. Two of The Master's new vampires rubbed out Mrs White, so that has done some of our work for us,' Mark chuckled.

'That's a shock,' said Carl.

'Not as much as it was for Mrs White,' said Ernie.

'Why did they do it? Are they on our side?' Father Philip said.

'Unlikely,' Maurice said. 'It was an accidental staking.'

'How many have you got tonight?' Mark asked the humans.

'Three earlier and just that one then. But we are still out working, we haven't stopped. We'll get some kip in a couple of hours. Any ideas for some more?' Joe asked.

'I think there might be a couple in the cul-de-sac off Wellmeadow Lane. It's that little street near the School end at the top. You can't miss it. Right at the bottom of there, I think there are some. They were making a right noise a couple of nights ago anyway. Having a party,' Ernie told them.

'Right ok. We'll check it out,' Joe said. 'See you later and good luck.'

'Wait here,' Adam said. 'I'll give you the all clear.' He peeked out of the ginnel, ran across the road, through the Park and up onto the Bank roof. He looked this way and that for a second. He thought he saw something on another roof on the other side of the park. *The vampire kids*, he thought. But they won't stand a chance against five vigilantes, and they don't tell tales either, so he gave the all clear to the gang and off they went.

Beryl stared into the face of Angela, quite clearly a vampire, but smiling. Beryl's legs went weak, and luckily Louise was next to her, who supported her quickly as she let go of the door. The door swung open, and it was revealed that there was indeed a group of vampires standing at the door. Angela and Jackie had insisted that they check out the building first just in case it had become a vampire nest in their absence.

'It's a trick, it's a trick!' Beryl shouted. She tried to shut the door quickly without success. Pat laughed loudly from somewhere, and Wee Renee yelled from somewhere.

'Don't be soft, Beryl!' It all began to get hazy for Beryl. She had admitted a dead Pat and Wee Renee, what could be worse? They were doomed. The rest of the people began to surge through the door. A thousand thoughts ran through Beryl's head. She had let the vampires in, and she reckoned that was much worse than what Father Philip had done. All the children were going to be killed, and everyone in the mill would be lying in wait for Joe and the other four men when they came back in the morning. Beryl would go to hell for this. And what about poor Bambi, what would they do with her?

All this was too much from Beryl, and the next thing blackness descended as she fainted. Everyone else in the mill was also unsure of what was going on. Only the children recognised the people that had entered, whether they were dead or alive. The only adults that knew them were the men that were out and Beryl. No other person in the mill knew what Wee Renee and her gang looked like.

As they surged forward, the vampires who needed no invitation in this public building with no owner, strolled in, clearly saying to the current inhabitants that they meant to stay. The remaining adults that were in the mill took up whatever weapons they had and stood in front of the children, pushing the kids behind them for protection.

'There is no need for that,' shouted Gary. 'Honestly, there is no need. These are good vampires, and we are here to help.' That wasn't what the people had expected them to say, and Louise was trying to drag Beryl out of the way of the door, out of the way of the incoming snowy feet and the possibility that she could be rapidly eaten at any point. Beryl was currently an easy target.

'What the hell is going on?' Louise asked.

'We will explain everything when we get Beryl conscious again, that's the most important thing. And where the bloody hell is Joe?' Pat asked.

Beryl started to come around after a few seconds and at first, was disorientated and wondering what had happened to her. Then she remembered with a bang as a sea of faces looked down at her. Her eyes rolled up again as if to faint.

'Chuck! Pull yourself together!' Pat shouted.

'Aye,' Wee Renee said. 'We need you compos mentis. Snap out of it!'

There was already chaos in the mill even before the door shut. Haggis realised that there was another dog in the room. Bambi realised the same, and also, horrifically for Bambi, a cat!

All the children were running after Haggis and wanting to see their old friend again. Our Doris naturally was shouting *'No weewee'* at the top of her voice

When everybody got inside the mill and shut the door, Ben tapped Beryl on the shoulder.

'Should we put the wood up against the door again?' Ben asked. Beryl studied their faces and knew that this was not, in fact, a vampire invasion. They would have eaten Haggis for a start. She didn't know what it was exactly. But her friends seemed to be as human as her.

'Yes, lock us in,' Beryl said.

The vampires had gone off together and were congregating at the bottom of the steel steps in the corner. They had taken themselves away as a sign that they were not attackers. With Angela at the front, the undead ladies, stood neatly and quietly, watching the situation unfold.

'Who are all these people?' Beryl asked.

'Helpers, heroes, people that are going to assist us. We are going to take our Village back, Beryl,' Wee Renee said.

'I don't understand any of it,' said Beryl. 'Are all these people from Moorston and where have you been for days on end?'

'It's a long story,' Wee Renee said. 'But in a nutshell, a lot of these people are from Moorston, and the vampires are from Moorston, apart from one. It might be hard to comprehend, but they are good vampires. They have helped us, and we have helped them. We work together, and they are going to work with us against Norman Morgan. There are also some people here from Melden to help us. We went there again after we had been to Moorston.'

'Why didn't you come straight back, after you had been to Moorston. We have been so worried about you?' Beryl asked.

'Ah, that's not an easy answer,' said Our Doris.

'No,' Gary informed her. 'The fact was that there were more vampire Masters than we knew. Norman Morgan's brother Len was over in Moorston. All the villagers were happy to be with Len, there was no help to be got. After we had been there a couple of dark days in the falling snow, Norman's sister Anne, who I told you was over in Melden came over and killed him.' There was a gasp from the *audience*, who had been trapped in this mill for days, with no exciting news from the outside world.

'She killed her own brother?' Louise asked.

'Yes, basically that young girl over there,' Gary said, and he pointed to Angela who stood at the front of the vampires, 'is now the new Moorston Mistress.'

'The one with the long dark hair, in a flowery dress?' Josh asked, amazed.

'I know,' Freddie said. 'You could have knocked me down with a feather when I found out too.' He winked at Josh.

'Yes, and she is named Angela. Obviously, they had to avenge their Master, so we all helped them and rescued Freddie from Jennifer's house and the rest from Melden. She is dead now, and one of her vampires has joined us. All the others are gone, but we discovered that Norman was in league with her against her brother and this is why they will help us to do this,' Nigel said. Beryl looked at them all.

'It sounds like you had a lot of dangerous adventures,' Beryl murmured quietly. She still felt quite dizzy.

'Aye,' said Wee Renee that is just the tip of the iceberg, if only you knew.'

'And I have just been here for most of the time looking after kids. Nice and warm - living it up. I feel a right fraud,' said Beryl.

'You were protecting our future generation, Beryl. There couldn't be a more important job,' said Terry.

Bob had wandered over to the group of kids who were now playing with Haggis and Bambi. He was happy to meet the little brown puppy for the first time and began talking to the children that he had made friends with before he had left the mill. One girl who had been extremely fond of Basil put her hands out towards the cat who came forward to be picked up. She cuddled him, burying her face in his fur. Some of the adults relaxed now that it was clear there was no threat. One of the ladies joined the little girl and asked what the cat's name was as she stroked him under his chin.

'Zazil,' the girl said.

'So, are Joe and all the others alive?' Rick asked. 'Have they gone back on vigilante duty?'

'Oh yes, they're all fine. They've only started back recently though. When there were enough survivors found to protect the children. You wouldn't believe the other stuff that has gone on here!' Beryl said.

'We are exhausted actually,' Brenda said. 'I wonder if there is someplace we can just lay down, just for a short while. We've just walked all the way from Melden, and I certainly aren't used to it.'

'Of course, what am I thinking. There is plenty of time to tell you all the gossip and hear every bit of your story,' said Beryl. 'How many of there are you exactly? Just in this small corner of the mill, with all of you in a clump, it feels like there is about two hundred!' Beryl began to laugh.

'There is just over eighty of us,' Wee Renee said, putting her nose up in the air proudly. 'We have various bedding items that we can use. We knew you would not have enough for all of us. If you can just point us to somewhere that we can lay down?'

'Well if we all squash up, we could probably keep on this level,' said Beryl. 'We just have to do take down those pallets, that they have been using for a little football pitch.'

'What about the upstairs?' Wee Renee asked.

'There is only one resident up there, and he is currently out, so you would be welcome to use that floor. I know it's safe on that floor, but a couple of floors above, I believe aren't. There is another matter though. I'm wondering where your erm… special friends will be going because upstairs all the windows aren't boarded up so the sunlight will come in.'

'I will have to think about that. Maybe we have to use those football pitch pallets and one of those tarpaulins outside or something. I will sort it. Don't worry yourself, Beryl,' Wee Renee said. 'Those lot are very resourceful. No Diva's amongst them.'

'I'll tell you what I would like though. A necessity,' Our Doris said.

'What's that?' Beryl said.

'A nice cup of tea, I'm spitting feathers here,' Our Doris informed her.

'Of course,' said Beryl. Turning, she studied the shocked and confused faces of the current inhabitants of the mill. 'Everyone! These are friends and our rescuers. You must have heard Joe talking about Wee Renee going to find help, well here it is. We need to use the play area now as sleeping accommodation for these lovely people. They are tired, and they need to rest. It's the children's bedtime anyway, so while a couple of us make some hot drinks, if we could all come together and get them settled as quickly as possible, that would be grand.'

Ben and Josh took the wood from the door and outside there were several thick tarpaulins that had been previously used for renovations before the funds had run out. The vampires bought them in with a couple more pallets. They moved everything they needed to the second floor, the floor above where Father Philip slept. One side of this was totally fine, and so they thought they would be safe there and just avoid the dangerous area. Under the guidance of Sarah, they made a kind of large cave with a double layer of tarpaulin on all sides. Inside they had 100% darkness. They were pleased with their accommodation.

At the moment, none of the new arrivals had any idea who stayed on the first floor below the vampires. That would be for tomorrow.

Keith had returned to the Primary School on foot. When he walked through the door his face was like thunder. He walked straight past the Head Master's office, which he had been occupying, leaving it for when The Master would return, as he said he would do.

Lynn and Michael were sitting in the foyer of the School in some soft seating that had been used for parents and visitors when the School was normal. They watched him storm past without a word, and Michael could imagine what had gone on.

'What's happened there?' Lynn asked.

'I shouldn't say really,' said Michael. 'It's private. Probably just between The Master and Keith.' Michael tapped the side of his nose as he said it.

'Oh, go on, I won't tell,' said Lynn.

'Well seeing as though you're twisting my arm, I will tell you,' Michael said, making himself more comfortable in the seat. 'He has been a naughty boy with Mrs White.'

'I never saw Keith being like that. He is the last person I would have thought was a ladies man,' Lynn said. 'You do surprise me, Michael. What has that got to do with The Master? They are both adults and free agents. I don't understand.'

'No, I don't mean that way,' said Michael, taking a deep breath, 'heaven knows what that union would be like! He's been taking the snowmobile out and dragging people behind it to catch the vampire kids for Mrs White.'

'So, what!' Lynn said. 'I knew about that.' Michael raised his eyebrows. He was quite shocked at Lynn's approach to the news. *Since Lynn had been turned she was hard-core*, he thought.

'The Master thinks it is a waste. We could be dining on them or adding them to our ranks, using them in lots of other ways, you know,' Michael said. Lynn didn't know what other ways there was but didn't want to appear ignorant so said nothing. 'He has wasted three folk, that's what The Masters annoyed about. Three at least that I know of,' Michael said, touching his nose again. 'There might be a lot more.'

'I do see The Masters point, now you have made me look at it another way,' Lynn said. She nudged Michael. 'He's not gone into the Head Master's office either. Looks like Keith has had his wings clipped good and proper.'

'It's about time too,' Michael said.

'On to much more important matters. How long do you think it will be until Band is back on?' Lynn asked.

When Penelope and Marcel did not return with Mrs White, Norman was quite confused.

'Didn't I tell you to bring her here?' he said.

'Yes Norman, you did, but Mrs White said she had to attend to the vampire children in the school before she could spend plenty of time up here. I got that, it was understandable I thought. I thoroughly admonished her all the way back up to the School, and so did Marcel,' Penelope advised him.

'I was very harsh in particular,' Marcel said.

'Oh, you were, were you?' Norman asked. Marcel nodded and looked at the floor. He did not want to have eye contact with his new vampire Master as he was sure that it would give him away. However, Penelope quite confidently lied to him.

'I think she got the message when you were with Keith … … about how much trouble she was in. We explained to her how bad it was and she came around to our way of thinking. It's up to you Norman if you want to carry on with it but I think you've got enough on your plate and she certainly has got the message,' Penelope assured him, smiling.

'I can guarantee she will not be out looking for them wild vampire kids again, let's just say that,' Marcel said, 'and if she is, you can hold me responsible.'

'You can't say fairer than that now,' Penelope said, and they both turned to each other and nodded firmly once.

Norman looked at them both. What a very strange pair they were. But they were his brother's children, so they were bound to act differently with their different tribal upbringing. He would have to try harder to understand them. After all, he intended to keep them around for a very long time. Tonight, he didn't really know what to say to them.

'Thank you,' Norman said simply and retired to his room.

'Do you think he knows he just got hustled?' Marcel asked her quietly when Norman was well out of earshot.

'Not a chance,' she replied.

4 Conversations

It was only just light when Pat opened her eyes. A few of the children were talking quietly, and at first, she did not know where she was, then she realised and glanced over to where Wee Renee had bedded down.

Pat sat up to make sure, but Wee Renee wasn't in her bed. The sleeping bag was rolled back, and the pillow was empty. Pat looked around the room, turning to every corner. She wasn't anywhere, where could she have gone?

Pat got up as quietly as she could and thought about going up to the first floor. Maybe the single inhabitant had returned, or Wee Renee was beaking out of upstairs windows.

She was about to venture upstairs, her foot on the first metal step, when she heard the unmistakable voice of Wee Renee outside, singing something. She quickly reached for her coat and boots and put them on. Wee Renee had still not finished when Pat put her head outside.

She shut the door quickly behind her to keep in the warmth. There was a light breeze in the morning air, it felt slightly warmer today and had a kind of wet atmosphere about it. Wee Renee still sang and had moved away about twenty feet from Pat. When she got closer, she realised that her friend was belting out a rousing chorus of *Morning Has Broken*. Pat chuckled slightly. That was typical.

A twig snapped under Pats feet, and Wee Renee quickly whirled around to see her best friend.

'Having a sing-song, are you Rene?' Pat asked.

'Yes, I just felt like it. I am really hopeful about today Pat,' Wee Renee said.

'How long have you been up?' Pat asked.

'Oh ages,' Wee Renee said. 'You know me, I'm always up with the cock.'

'That you are,' Pat said

'No-one else came out with you just?' Wee Renee asked, looking past Pat towards the mill door.

'No love, why?' Pat asked.

'I want to confess something,' Wee Renee said.

'Oh, bloody hell. What have you done?' Pat asked.

'I have to say first that it was not my idea, but on the behest of the Wee Faerie,' Wee Renee said.

'Oh, him!' Pat said, 'I know.'

'Well, he came to me the day before we left after we had killed Anne. You know that time I was in the lavatory for ages. I lied. I wasn't constipated,' Wee Renee said. She didn't like lying to her friend, and she knew Pat didn't expect it. She gave her a long look. Her eyes were solemn.

'Go on,' Pat said, rubbing her chin, considering her friends next words.

'He told me, that again the fate of the world was on my shoulders and I had to swing a decision a particular way. The fact is love, that he told me that I had to get hold of that Diary of Anne's and make it look like it was Norman's fault too, or else we wouldn't have got the Moorston lot to come along with us. If I didn't do that, then we couldn't get rid of Norman,' Wee Renee explained.

'I see,' Pat said. 'That doesn't bother me. But I think this Wee Faerie is a bit of a liberty taker. Why can't he do his own dirty work.' Pat shook her head. She thought for a short while. Wee Renee gave her time to let it all sink in. 'So, Norman wasn't against his brother then?'

'It wasn't as clear-cut as I painted it. Let's just say that with different interpretations, it could have gone the other way. Of course, even the writings were from a raving lunatic. I don't think we'll ever know the real truth. It could be exactly as I said. Or it could be exactly the opposite. It was in our interests that I sweetened the pot to that side, you know,' Wee Renee explained.

'I do know. You did right Rene,' Pat said, then dropped her voice to a whisper. 'They owed us anyway.'

'And there was something else he told me. That this will soon be over, but for me, it will continue. There will be other creatures to fight in the future and remember I have to fix all those spectres problems in Moorston,' Wee Renee said. She was very close to Pat, she didn't want everyone hearing in the mill.

'Hmmmm…. the weight of the world,' Pat said.

'And so,' Wee Renee said, 'I want you to help me. What do you think love? Have you enjoyed it this time?'

'Well, probably during this winter I would have been sitting by the fire with my feet up, eating my way through twenty tins of chocolates and enjoying some very good telly. If you had asked me before if I wanted to do this adventure, I would certainly have told you to bugger off and have given you a kick up the arse. But now … … it's strange, I don't want to go back to that life completely. Don't get me wrong I need a bloody good rest and some comfort for a bit, but to know that this was my last excitement in life and it was all just within my reach to go on another perilous quest … … well, of course, I will Rene. That's what I'm saying, I'll join you!' Pat said very happily. Wee Renee hugged her friend.

'I'm glad I don't have to do it on my own. We might be able to get to some of the others on board,' she said. 'Let's wait until all this is over and the dust has settled. Like you say we all need a good rest, but then I'm sure we should be able to call on some of the faithful to help our cause. I don't know how these new adventures will present themselves, but one thing I do know and that is that my friend the Wee Faerie is balls on accurate!' Wee Renee exclaimed.

The two ladies made their way back inside the mill. A few of the others were staring as the door opened, they had not seen anyone go outside, but calmed a little when they saw the Wee Renee emerge from behind it. Beryl was already putting the kettle on for a nice cup of tea. The two women who had come in from the cold took off their coats and boots and made their way over to join Beryl and help with the set-up of the day.

'Morning,' Wee Renee said to Beryl. 'I've just been outside to have a breath of fresh air and a nice singsong to open up my lungs.'

'Oh, I'm glad of that,' Beryl said, 'because after breakfast I hoped that we would have a blow by blow account of your tales and I will tell mine. I think I might shock you are little. Not as much as you will shock me but there is a couple of surprises you don't know about.'

'I'll eat my hat if you top our *frank and beans* story in the tunnel,' Pat said laughing.

'Vile it was,' Our Doris said, who had moved closer to them while testing out if her cowboy boots were dry yet. 'Filthy pig.'

Everyone gradually pulled themselves together and started to have a drink and either cereal or porridge that Beryl, Brenda and Sally constantly made on the four rings of the gas burner that they had.

After breakfast, most of the adults sat cross-legged on the floor to catch up with each other's adventures. The only exceptions to this were Sally, Kathy and Lauren, who re-acquainted themselves with the children that they had looked after in the Church previously. They met Bambi, hearing all about her idiosyncrasies and super-cuteness. Afterwards, the children showed them the toys that they had received from Father Christmas.

Between Gary, Wee Renee, Pat, Our Doris and Freddie they told the former inhabitants of their toils and tribulations, over the past week or so.

During Pat's descriptions, the mill occupants who didn't know her were shocked that her tale was interspersed with so many occurrences of involuntary flatulence.

The eighty or so people that had come over from Melden with her were quite used to Pat, doing this. But the new lot seemed quite taken aback with the constant amount of burping that took place. In fact, to some, it was just as fascinating as their journey and killings.

Beryl listened, amazed. Never in a million years could she have imagined all this.

'You couldn't write it,' Beryl said. She kept nudging Louise, then shaking her head with her mouth open. They had never seen anyone look so shocked, especially about the tunnel, the ghosts and the inside of Anne Morgan.

'Now it's your turn,' Bob said. 'What have we missed out on?'

Beryl summed it up in just a few sentences as she knew there would be questions on at least two or three of the matters that she was about to tell them. So, she gave brief details of the less exciting items.

'Well firstly I agreed to come over here, and on the same day was able to track down quite a lot of other people that you can see here. We have all been here since before Christmas, and we had a lovely day. Joe and his gang have only been going out over the last couple of nights that we have been here. We needed to have more adults here to look after the children. We found Bambi as well in the Park, so he has been a great comfort to the children as they missed Haggis and Basil.'

'Is it a dog or a bitch?' Freddie asked.

'She's a bitch,' said Beryl, 'and a Chihuahua I think, but she was lucky to find us. I don't know how long she would have lasted out there with the cold and those monsters about.' The rest of the people nodded gravely. Anyway, for the next bit of news, there are now a definite group of vampire vigilantes working against Norman Morgan.

'What!' Miles exclaimed.

'Yes, four of them,' Beryl said.

'Is Adam one of them?' Bob asked.

'Yes, that is one of the names I remember them saying. I believe that some of them might have helped you before. I have not met them, but they are killing the bad vampires as well as us,' Beryl informed them.

'Do you know any of the other names, at all?' Jennifer asked.

'I can remember another two of their names, but I can't remember the other one, I'm sorry. Two of the names were Mark and Ernie,' Beryl said, closing her eyes and just about finding the names in her memory banks.

'Ernie and Mark!' Freddie said astounded.

'I bet the other one is Maurice. He was with Adam on that night,' Tony said.

'Yes. It will be Tony. Good old Maurice,' said Freddie. 'Not a bad bone in him.'

'That's it, you're right,' said Beryl. 'Maurice! That's his name, and that's the start of a new story.'

'What's that?' Agnes asked.

'You will be interested in this Gary,' Beryl said. 'Your old prison mate Carl? He killed his wife and then got rescued by these vampire vigilantes, and he stayed at Maurice's house. They looked after him and repaired an injury to his leg!'

'You are kidding,' Pat said. 'My old foil folder friend is still about, is he? Ooh, I am pleased about that.'

'He is,' said Beryl, 'and quite recovered now. He's out tonight with Joe, killing the vampires.'

'Yay!' said Andy.

'And guess who is with them,' Beryl said, she searched their faces with her eyes. Beryl reckoned if she had given them twenty guesses, they still wouldn't have come up with the right name. Even a hundred guesses. 'A recent addition to our fold. Hold on to your hats everyone, Father Philip is here at the mill.'

'Cheeky bastard,' said Pat. 'Didn't I get them both with my boot last time?'

'You do know about him, don't you?' Our Doris asked. 'He's got more faces than the Town Hall clock. And most of them belong to Norman Morgan!'

'He is sorry, and he is fighting it. We all believe him. He's been living in a tent in the quarry since you left. Father Philip is trying his best, and that is why he has gone out killing the vampires with Joe and everyone. He is a different man. I believe he is doing everything in his power to prove that he is on our side and to make up for what he did. We have accepted him, but because the children were quite scared of what had happened previously, he is the current inhabitant of the first floor, I told you about.'

'You could knock me over with a feather,' Wee Renee said. 'Is there anything else we should know?'

'There is one more thing, Beryl said, 'and you may not like it.'

'I didn't like what you told me in your last reveal, don't tell me this part is worse!' Pat said aghast.

'You be the judge of that, Beryl said. 'But the fact is, we have made an unholy bargain with Michael Thompson.'

'What!' Liz screeched. 'I hope you are kidding Beryl.' Beryl shook her head.

'A few days ago, we come across him in the daytime in the middle of Friarmere. He was alone. He told us he knew where we were, and he did. He also knew that you had gone into the tunnel,' Beryl told them, but of course, this was old news to them.

'Oh yes, we saw him there in the mouth of the tunnel before we left,' Danny said.

'Apparently, he hasn't told Norman where we are living. He has told us that, although he has to be there for the moment, Michael knows that we will win, and he is not going to give us away,' Beryl said.

'I bet he is telling every side that they will win,' Liz said.

'He's another *Town Hall clock*,' Our Doris said. 'I have only seen him a couple of times, and I took an instant dislike to him. You know why?'

'Why?' Lee asked.

'Eyes too close together,' Our Doris said. 'And thin lips.'

'Well, that was several days ago, and he has been true to his word because here we are safe and sound. We said that if he did this, and if he took the cure, which we did not tell him the specifics of – just that we had one, that we would speak up for him not to be killed when the time was right, and I think you can't say fairer than that,' Beryl said.

Several people in the old Friarmere Band didn't like this very much at all. It was a shock. But the more they thought about it, if he had not given them away, and was obviously under the thrall, he must be really trying to fight it. But some people would never ever be able to forgive him or even speak to him again.

'That's fine by me anyway,' said Wee Renee. 'If he is trying to change, I think that several people here know that it is tough indeed. Who knows how many times he has been forced to drink his Master's blood. As far as I know, the people infected in our party only had one dose. He has been living amongst them, but he is still trying to do the right thing. I think you can't judge someone unless you walk a mile in their shoes. I say that we should be thankful for his help too. He will probably be more useful to this fight that I can think of. It's worth taking a chance on him, just for that!'

There was a silence amongst all the adults after this comment from Wee Renee. Some of them did not know about Michael Thompson at all, some of them had never met him before, but they had heard that he was Norman Morgan's human spy. Now they had to accept him after this was over. This would take some swallowing, but in time they would do it.

The whole congregation wandered off in their groups. The story that Gary and his gang had told and in return what Beryl had told took a lot of thinking about.

Terry, Liz, Lauren and Our Doris had a small meeting about the infections. Lauren's hand was slowly getting better, but the flesh was white and unhealthy looking. However, the puss had disappeared and so had the smell.

They wondered how much and how long Michael would have to be on the antibiotics for it to work. They didn't even think that they were finished with it. It might be lifelong medication for Michael Thompson.

There was also the matter of Father Philip's infection to think about too. Both of them needed enough so that they felt as good as the infected heroes did now. Terry couldn't imagine, but he thought that if he was going to have to take it after The Master was gone, in this case, Norman Morgan, then everything else should have got back to normal. The world would be open for business again.

In this respect, they could be given a lot stronger antibiotics than he had been able to provide from the Dentist's Surgery. For the most part, at least three of them felt great; Lauren's infection was still a bit recent. So, he was very confident that Michael and Father Philip should make a full recovery in the future.

Agnes had something to say to Wee Renee, who was sitting in the corner with a few of the others from the old Friarmere Band, talking about Father Philip, Michael Thompson and Carl. The people with her were all present on the journey over, so Agnes just came right out with it.

'Wee Renee, as today seems to be a day for disclosures, I have been thinking about what you said last night, and I wondered if you could tell us a bit more about what you saw,' Agnes asked.

'What are you on about, love?' Pat asked. Agnes crouched down, she did not want the children or anyone else who was not there last night to hear this.

'When you said there were things in the trees last night, nothing happened. I didn't see anything, but I know you were right. To be quite honest it didn't half shit me up. What was going on?' Agnes asked.

'Ah yes we are well out of that,' Wee Renee said. 'I wouldn't worry about it if I was you, but the fact is that we are in the Melden Triangle up there on the tops, and there are lots of weird things that even I can't comprehend. If I am brave enough one time I will go and investigate that one.'

'Brave enough!' Freddie exclaimed. 'I hope you are kidding. *You*, after all this, need to be braver to tackle what was in those trees?' Wee Renee nodded slowly.

'I don't know what it was, Freddie,' she said, 'but I've never seen anything like it!' She fell into silence, and the others waited patiently for her to continue. It didn't look like she was going to, so Pat prompted her to carry on.

'You're going to have to spill the beans, Rene,' Pat said. Wee Renee sighed, and her shoulders dropped. She really did have to tell them, it was only fair.

'The trees had arms hanging from them, red arms that ran with blood. It dripped from the fingertips. Like a constant flow. The fingers moved. It was all alive … … and it was dreadful,' Wee Renee said quietly, looking around at their expressions. They were quite speechless. None of them had expected anything like this.

'Like a tree that had living bloody arm fruits?' Bob asked, furrowing his brow.

'Exactly,' Wee Renee said.

'Wow,' Bob said.

'Whatever next,' Our Doris said.

'What was it? A tree that was actually growing them. Or a separate thing inside the tree?' Freddie asked.

'I don't know. And I don't know how we didn't see it before. It must not have been there on the other journeys,' Wee Renee said.

'So, either it's freshly laid fruit on a normal tree, or maybe … … it has travelled there from somewhere else!' Bob said in awe.

'I wish I hadn't asked now,' Agnes said.

'So do I,' said Sue.

5 Greetings

Just after eleven o'clock, there was rustling and rattling near the front door of the mill and in burst Joe and his four vigilante friends. Immediately they saw that there was a massive crowd of fresh humans inside the mill and Joe stared, unaware of what was going on.

At first, he did not recognise anyone and then above the crowd he just about spotted Pat's head, which confirmed to him, that finally, *they* were back.

Bambi had followed Haggis, and they began to bark at the five men entering. Father Philip shut the door behind him. He knew what Haggis meant too, he was going to have to answer some tough questions.

Joe searched the crowd with his eyes but could only still see the top of Pat's head, so decided to save himself a bit of time and effort.

'Wee Renee!' Joe shouted at the top of his voice.

Soon the crowd parted in the middle like the Red Sea and Wee Renee, and a few of the others came forward towards Joe and his gang. There was a round of hugs and kisses as they greeted Joe and found Carl again. Gary walked forward and shook Carl's hand, and then they gave each other a manly hug. No-one would ever know what they had gone through during those long nights at the school. Only they understood each other.

'You don't know how glad I am to see you,' Joe said.

'Likewise,' Wee Renee said. 'We need to fill each other in. However Beryl has given me a good grounding of what is going on here.'

'I'm gasping for a coffee,' Joe said. 'Let's sit down and have a talk about everything.' Beryl rushed to make them all a drink, and several of the Friarmere Band group and the vigilantes took a seat on some pallets to have their debriefing. Rick walked up and shook the hands of his three former vigilante friends, they were glad to see him safe and sound and congratulated him on helping to keep this huge group before them, alive and well.

Father Philip backed away from the crowd and very quietly started to make its way towards the steel steps on the first floor.

'Oy!' Pat shouted at him. 'Not so fast Judas! I think we need to have a word, don't you?' Father Philip shoulders dropped, as he looked back at Pat. This was inevitable, and he was resigned to his fate.

'You stay put until we are all ready,' Pat said, looking at him out of one eye. Father Philip didn't move. Pat's wrath was mighty, he could confirm that.

'There is something else you don't know,' Wee Renee advised the vigilantes. 'We brought a load of vamps with us.' Her eyes darted between the five men's faces. She thought they would be shocked, but of course, they had been working with four vampires in Friarmere too.

'Good ones?' Craig asked. 'Or prisoners?'

'Aye, good ones,' said Wee Renee. 'Seven of them. They are on the second floor now, sleeping in a kind of dark cave they built for themselves. 'I'll tell you all about it in a bit, but the crux of it is, we have help against the Beast of Friarmere.'

'Is it true that Adam and three others have been helping you, Joe?' Bob asked.

'Yes, it is,' Joe said. 'We've even been playing on the PlayStation with them!' Bob laughed loudly at this. Freddie who had not met these men before, apart from Carl, had stood out at the side and watched it all go on. He stood proudly, his hand on his walking stick, taking every word in.

'Excuse me, I wouldn't mind going over to see Maurice, lads. Is he able to be around humans?' Freddie asked. 'I was his best friend before this went down, you see.'

'And me,' Bob said. 'I'd like to go and see Adam.'

'I don't mind taking you over in a bit if you like,' Carl said. 'Until things are all right between everyone again, it's always best if I come as well. I will have a drink and catch up with the news, then I'll take you over if you like. You two should be able to spend a short time with them before we have to get back here before dark. Me and the lads will be out again tonight anyway, and I've had enough kip.'

'I'd like that very much,' said Freddie, then addressing the four other men, 'I'm Freddie by the way,' He shook the hands of Joe, Darren, Craig and reluctantly, Father Philip, who had forgotten that he was still in the bad books with everyone else and had acted on instinct.

'Right, you,' Pat said to Father Philip. 'Got some humble pie to eat, have you?' She sniffed in punctuation.

'We'll go upstairs and get this out of the way. It needs to be done. It's way too noisy for me to think in here and I will have to shout over the racket. That isn't how I want to tell you,' Father Philip said.

'Aye, that's better. I'll get some of the others that will have an interest in this,' Wee Renee said nodding. 'Let's get to the meat of it as quickly as possible.'

In the end, every person who was present that day decided that they wanted to hear what Father Philip had to say. Freddie, Brenda and Gary came upstairs too.

When everyone had followed him upstairs, he stood with the window behind him, looking towards them.

'What would you like me to tell you,' Father Philip said.

'Why you did it? What did you get out of it?' Our Doris asked.

'Why didn't you fight it?' Liz asked.

'My question is, how did he get you to drink his blood?' Wee Renee asked.

'And I want to know how you have spent your time between when we last saw you and now,' Sue said.

'I want to know; how can we trust you again?' Nigel asked.

'Er...that's a lot of stuff. There's nothing I can't answer, but there are things I don't really want to answer, but I will,' Father Philip said.

'Say what? I don't understand,' Bob said.

'You will,' Father Philip sighed. 'I refused the wine, I knew what was in it. But he threatened to hurt some living humans if I didn't. At this point, I didn't know what he was going to ask of me,' Father Philip said.

'Who was he going to hurt, do we know them?' Tony asked.

'Yes. This is the bit I didn't want to answer. I hoped you wouldn't ask.' Father Philip turned his gaze to Gary. 'It was you and Carl, in the classroom. You were both sat against the wall. He showed me through the glass. Carl still doesn't know. I didn't want him to feel guilty in any way,' Father Philip said honestly. Gary nodded and cast his eyes down.

'I bet he knows anyway,' Gary said. 'I understand.' Father Philip sighed. That bit was out. He wasn't bothered about telling all the other stuff. That just concerned him. He really didn't want to make anyone's experience worse. Father Philip knew that by confirming that it *was* them, he had. Sometimes it was hard, to tell the truth.

'So, I took myself off to the Vicarage. That night I was under siege by vampire children. The following day I gathered up all my camping gear and took myself off into isolation at the quarry. I searched my soul for answers over a period of days, and during my time, my physical distance and time spent away from Norman Morgan helped me to regain my resolve. It helped me find my faith again. Made me realise I could be of use again. I just needed one last piece of the puzzle, and that was to spend a night in my Church. Again, I was under siege by, what now was, deformed vampire children. But I was safe inside the Lords House. The next day, I tried to find Joe and his gang after seeing them previously just by chance when I was on a food mission. I was so lucky to find them that first morning, and I have been here ever since. As I need to make up for so much, I volunteered to go out on the vigilante missions, to prove that I have changed.'

'That doesn't answer all our questions. Why didn't you fight it the first time?' Liz asked.

'I tried, but I was under the influence of his blood and surrounded by vampires. Maybe if I wasn't surrounded, or maybe if I wasn't under the influence, I could have fought it. The two factors were overpowering. I know it's still no excuse,' Father Philip said. 'My actions that night could never be explained or forgiven. I was too treacherous. I was too weak.'

'To be fair, *we*, and by that, I mean Liz, Our Doris and myself, only had one of those factors to fight. Not two,' Terry said. 'I understand considering your particular circumstances, it would be far more difficult.'

'Physical proximity to him is so important to it all, I can't explain how much. But I *even* felt more resolve once he ran around to the front of the Church that night. Just that small amount of distance away from me was enough for me to make my brief escape, where I managed to lay above poor Tina and protect her from further damage,' Father Philip said. 'And then afterwards to not follow him - only due to not being close to him or his kind. Luckily for me, he did not seek me out again. He had used me and required me no longer.'

Wee Renee had seen that he had lain there after they had found him. She could not imagine what it must have been like so would not judge him.

'We would like a chat about it, please. Could you go downstairs for a moment,' Wee Renee told Father Philip. He walked quietly away and down the steel steps.

'What do you think?' she asked everyone.

'Must have been bad for him, I think,' Our Doris said.

'I feel guilty. He was right to think I would,' Gary said.

'Bloody hell Gary, it's not your fault, and it's not his. It's bloody sexy Norman. The sexy pig,' Pat said.

'That is something else……. he called him Norman Morgan, not Master. He is well out of his clutches,' Wee Renee said.

'I don't trust him,' Liz said.

'We'll talk about it, Liz. I get it about him. I think he's ok,' Andy said.

'Oh, Andy!' Liz said with an exaggerated sigh.

'I think we give him a chance,' Kathy said.

'Yes. He's been through the mill like all of us,' Terry said.

'Quite literally,' Sally said. There was a little chuckle from a few of them.

'He seems decent to me,' Freddie said.

'Come on then,' Wee Renee said. They walked down the steps, and without a word being spoken, Pat put both thumbs up to Father Philip and they got on with the rest of their morning.

Father Philip still had something on his mind. He was in a moral quandary. But after thinking about it longer, he knew what the right thing to do was. Father Philip walked down the steel steps, located Wee Renee and asked her to join him upstairs alone.

Wee Renee followed him instantly, and not one person saw them go upstairs. When they got as far away from the steel steps as they could so as not to be overheard, he began.

'You have already accepted me back into the fold and thank you for that. I don't have to tell you this to curry favour now. And some would say I shouldn't ever do this … … but after much thought I am,' Father Philip said thoughtfully.

'Oh aye. You fully have my attention, Father,' Wee Renee said.

'Not only was I of use to him, divulging the location of the unconsecrated area of the Church, Norman also used me for another reason,' Father Philip said.

'Oh, heavens no, Father. He didn't!' Wee Renee said, her hands over her mouth, and her eyes enormous.

'No, no. Nothing like that. He used me as a Priest. An advisor. He told me something of his past that he had never told a living soul. Or that is what he told me, and I think that, and his confessions were the truth,' Father Philip said.

'What did he say?' Wee Renee gasped. What could Norman have told Father Philip? If this was something not to shout about how bad was it? Considering all his deeds that were known in the public domain. Acts that he was not ashamed of whatsoever. She had never wanted to know something so badly in all her life.

'When he was younger – a boy, before he was a vampire, his older sister abused him, sexually over many years,' Father Philip said.

'Oh, my Lord!' Wee Renee exclaimed, shaking her head.

'He hated her for that, but he also loved her so much as a sister. He was and still will be in great turmoil, Wee Renee,' Father Philip said.

'Naturally. What a state to be in,' Wee Renee said.

'Do you think it excuses some of his behaviours?' Father Philip asked.

Wee Renee thought that there would be a case for that. An older sister manipulating a younger brother. Indoctrinating him with her ideals. This could get Norman off scot-free if it were known. The Wee Faerie would go berserk if that happened. It would undo all the good work they had done. No, this had to be kept secret.

'There is a lot you don't know, Father Philip. But it doesn't excuse him, no,' Wee Renee said.

'That is fine. I do not wish to know the facts. I just really thought you ought to know out of everyone. I trust your judgement. Maybe I shouldn't have told you – but I wasn't ordained to take or keep confessions from the undead to myself. So, it got out on a technicality, you might say. But it still goes against the grain,' Father Philip said.

'I can see that it would. No, I will tell a select few. Don't concern yourself with it any longer. Rest assured that you have done everything now to show me you have changed,' Wee Renee said, putting her hand on his arm to comfort him. 'Let your mind be calm now, and know we see what you are now, and not then.'

Wee Renee would not be telling anyone about this.

After lunch, Carl said he was ready to take Bob and Freddie over to Maurice's house. He was not sure that Adam was there, he thought that he split his time between staying up at the school and at Maurice's. Bob still wanted to take the chance. Sue and Tony said they would go too as they did not want Bob to be alone with just Freddie and Carl as security. But when Wee Renee and Pat said they wanted to go over and ask Maurice about all his plans and if there was any inside information on Norman, Sue and Tony were happy to trust their son with the two ladies. Carl assured them that was no danger anyway but understood that any parent would feel the same in these unknown circumstances.

As they walked over, Pat told Carl that she was very proud of him for bringing himself to sort Kate out.

'I always knew you had it had it in you,' Pat said.

They walked along in silence for a few seconds, and she did not press him for any details, but it looked like he might tell them a little more about it.

Freddie looked at the trees and tried not to think about how it must have felt to be Carl. It would have been like putting his own beloved Brenda to death. It was horrific. Freddie noticed as he walked his stick went smoothly into the snow. It was no longer frozen. This fact didn't register to be as big a deal as it was, however, because his mind was on Carl's former predicament. They all knew he was going to speak about it, as they had left a beautiful silence open for him, and he used it.

'When I killed her, these worms were coming out of her. Kind of like fat slugs, made of blood, trying to infect me. It was the right thing to do. Even after she was dead, the worms tried to attack me. I got out of the room, and luckily it was daylight, and the sunlight frazzled them up. I went back the other day with Joe, to retrieve my backpack. She is just a pile of dust now, held together by an evening dress and gold sandals. But her hair, her hair is still there. Perfect.'

Freddie closed his eyes. He felt Carl's pain. Carl was still in love with her hair. It had been untouched, so was still his Kate.

'Each day I recover a little. I had to do it, and it was quite clear that it was the right thing to do. There was no coming back for Kate. No human has those things living in them,' Carl said quietly but clearly.

The others said nothing. They could not add insights or clarity. Carl was on his way out of his dark tunnel, and this dreadful occurrence seemed amazingly to have left his mind and sanity unharmed.

In the cold light of day, Friarmere seemed to look the same as it had before Wee Renee and Pat had left it. The buses still blocked the two main entrances and exits, the snow piled high on them. There was a reddish-brown trail through the centre of the Village, which Carl advised them was one of the vampires dragging someone behind a snowmobile. Wee Renee put her hands over her face.

'So, it has got worse then Carl? It's not just the Brass Band shouting their odds?' Wee Renee asked.

'No, the Brass Band haven't been out as much. Maybe it's because of Norman's brother getting murdered. We heard about that from Maurice and the others. Keith announced it outside the school, apparently. Or maybe it is because Christmas is over and there is no carolling to be done,' Carl said.

'So, they are doing this now? Dragging humans through the streets now, are they?' Pat asked. 'The mind boggles.'

'I don't believe it's a lot of them doing it, but yes that has been going on. Don't worry though, Maurice and his gang of vampires, and our old gang of vigilantes have been fighting against them, and slowly we are whittling them down,' Carl said.

When they got to Maurice's house, they could see that there was newspaper over the windows. Freddie was quite nervous about meeting his old friend, but Bob was excited and could not wait. Carl knocked on the door and movement could be heard behind there.

'It's me, Carl, I've brought some friends to see you,' Carl said. The door unlatched and swung open, Maurice moved quickly into his living room away from the daylight. Carl walked straight through into the living room, and Bob, Freddie, Wee Renee, and Pat stood in the hall and shut the door quietly waiting for further introductions. Freddie, Wee Renee and Pat had been here before, and it smelled the same. Mints, tea and old books.

'Hello, lad, who have you brought this time?' Maurice asked. Carl turned his head to the occupants in the hall.

'Come on then,' Carl said to them. Wee Renee entered, followed by Pat. Maurice's face immediately lit up with excitement. The next person to enter was Freddie. Maurice's mouth dropped open, and Freddie smiled.

Without a word, they both approached one another and shook hands.

'My old mate. I'm so happy you're safe,' Maurice said.

'Fancy a pint?' Freddie asked.

'Don't I ever, but I can't blasted have one,' said Maurice laughing.

Bob peeked around the side of the door. He had not heard another voice, but he saw now that Adam sat there, staring at the three pensioners that has seemingly appeared from nowhere.

Adam was astounded at these fresh people coming in. He had briefly seen two of them before when he had helped them up at the school, but he had not seen the man called Freddie before. He knew though that both vampire and human vigilantes had been waiting to hear word from Wee Renee and her gang. The sight of them meant something significant.

He was focussing on the conversation and particularly on Wee Renee. The last person he expected to see enter Maurice's that day was Bob. The moment he saw him, he shouted from his seat in Maurice's armchair, waving the PlayStation controller crazily above him.

'Mate I can't believe it!' Adam exclaimed.

'Neither can I,' said Bob. 'What are you playing?' And just like that the two of them took off from where they had once been. Two living teenagers who enjoyed playing games.

'Well, what it's like to be young again,' Freddie commented, looking at the two of them, confounded at the immediate acceptance and normality of the two boys.

'I'll put the kettle on,' said Maurice and went to make the drinks.

'Anyone else here?' Pat shouted after him.

'No, it's just us two,' Maurice shouted, now from the kitchen. They could hear the clunk and rattle of cups.

'Ernie has to sneak out because of Lynn,' Adam said. 'She is right suspicious, so we had to make up a story that he is working for Mark.'

'We are still talking about our Mark, aren't we? Band Mark?' Freddie asked. 'The percussionist?'

'Yes,' Adam said.

'What's Ernie been doing with him?' Freddie queried.

'Working on the blood farm, you know,' Adam said.

'I don't know really lad,' Freddie said. 'That I have to say. I've been in Melden a few weeks, so out of the loop. But I'm quite intrigued about this blood farm. Tell me more.'

Adam's eyes were fixed on the screen, as were Bobs. His face was absentmindedly concentrating on what he was doing, which meant he would involuntarily spill all the beans honestly. When he was playing games, conversation was not his primary concern.

'He's got some people there. He's selling blood. It's a service, so The Master leaves him alone. But him, and Ernie now, are using it as a cover so they can get on with being a vigilante behind the scenes. He doesn't like what The Master does, you know. But Mark can't help being a bloodsucker. Although the rest of us, we've not been able to do it.' Adam muttered as if it were nothing.

Wee Renee wondered what she was hearing. She sat down on the sofa and collected her thoughts before speaking.

'What do you mean by *do it*?' Wee Renee asked.

'Be a proper vampire, like the rest,' Adam said.

'So, you are saying then that you have still not consumed any human blood?' Wee Renee asked him.

'No, I haven't. At first, The Master wouldn't let me so that I was not tempted to feed on the kids he held prisoner. Now I just don't want to. So Maurice has been showing me what he does, and I have been doing that and its fine,' Adam told them, his eyes still fixed to the screen.

'What does he do, love?' Pat asked glancing at the kitchen.

'Eats liver. He has been eating raw meat all this time, and if it is very bloody and red, it sustains us. Just about stops us from craving humans, which in our heads, we don't want to eat,' Adam advised Pat.

'So, it's just you and Maurice that *hasn't* been eating human flesh?' Wee Renee asked.

'No, Ernie hasn't either. Ernie can't bring himself to do it. He says the thought makes him bilious. Whatever that is. We three have been looking after ourselves, out of Maurice's freezer. Oh, and other freezers too, if we come across them in houses we know now are vacant. But for it to work, we must have it raw, you know. It's not very nice. Well, it's ok if we find best steak,' Adam confided.

'I bet,' Pat said.

'But Mark he was already on the hard stuff. He doesn't bite anyone anymore, he just uses his own blood stocks,' Adam shrugged.

'I don't like the sound of that,' Freddie said. 'That can't be right. What the hell is going on there?'

'Apparently, it's ethically sourced. Those are his words, not mine. I don't know the details,' said Adam. 'I believe that he is doing it all for the right reasons, even though maybe we can't fathom that out.'

'Well I shall be questioning him thoroughly,' Wee Renee said. 'I'm all for him helping us fight Norman, that's wonderful, but I have seen where someone else has been draining humans and feeding on them in Melden. If Mark has any part of that horror, I don't care what he has done for the cause, I'll be staking him!'

'Too right,' Pat said. 'You wouldn't give it credence if you saw it Adam. Even Rene couldn't stomach it!'

'Yeah that's a bad scene to get into,' Bob said, out of the blue, still playing. 'You want to watch him, Adam.'

'He's all right, you'll find out in time honestly. Don't judge him until you know, because he has done loads of good stuff,' Adam said, feeling like he had said far too much about Mark's affairs now.

'Fair enough,' Freddie said.

'Anyway,' Carl said, 'let's talk about other stuff because we only have just over an hour here before we need to get back.' Maurice returned with the drinks and the last few packets of Monster Snacks.

6 Absentee's

Freddie, Bob, Carl, Wee Renee and Pat returned to the mill well before dark. Wee Renee gathered all humans and children together to quietly told them about the Moorston vampires and Sarah. Agnes explained how friendly they were and that no-one was to fear them. In fact, one of them was her very best friend.

The Mistress of them all was named Angela, and she was small and young with long dark hair. She often carried a Hello Kitty backpack, which held her lunch. That is how they would know her. This immediately put them at ease. Angela sounded lovely.

Joe sat listening to all of this, while he rubbed this chin. He was intrigued to meet these new creatures as they sounded quite amusing to him. The children ran off to play, and a few of the adults remained, who had not met the Moorston vampires and Sarah.

'They sound weird to me,' Darren said.

'I trust them if Wee Renee trusts them,' Craig said.

'I can't wait to meet them. More good vampires and they certainly don't sound like they look scary either,' Joe said.

'Are you sure they are up to the task with Norman? They sound a bit lightweight,' Carl asked.

'Ah yes,' Freddie said. 'Do not underestimate them. I did, and boy was I wrong. They look all sweet and innocent, but they certainly pack a punch,' Freddie said.

Agnes said she was going to go upstairs until they awoke, to tell them that they had been pre-introduced and get them up to speed.

Within half an hour, they heard her descending the metal steps and behind her stood the Moorston vampires. Joe was shocked to see the seven undead females, and unless he had been told who was The Mistress, he would never have guessed. Out of all of them, and none were old, he would have guessed that it was a tall woman in her mid-thirties, who wore a calm expression. He was told by Rick that this was, in fact, Sarah, who had once been Anne's vampire and was the only one that was not an original vampire from Moorston.

From Agnes's description, he now recognised Angela as The Mistress. She looked the youngest, smallest and weakest of them all. Joe had learned from meeting Wee Renee however, that small women could be the most powerful.

Angela got halfway down the stairs and then shouted to the humans in the room. She had a surprisingly loud and commanding voice.

'Could I have your attention, please? My name is Angela, and this is Jackie. You'll get to know the others I'm sure. Please do not fear us, we work with and for you. You are our friends, and we will protect you with our lives.' She paused at this moment to let that thought sink in.

'Tonight myself, my friend Jackie and Sarah, plan to go and visit Norman. We do not know how he will react to this, as we have a lot to say to him, in one way or another. I ask that you make sure that you are protected here. However, he will still not know your location. If we must, we will take it to our graves. We will return before morning. I will advise you of everything that has transpired when I return. Please do not worry about asking us any questions, we are happy to answer all of them.' She finished speaking and walked down the stairs. Our Doris stepped towards her.

'Hello love, I believe that there is a group that would like you to escort them over to the village when you go if you don't mind. We knew this was your plan from Agnes, so they have been waiting to meet you and have been able to hold off until darkness, knowing you could give them safe passage. These are the group of people that have been working behind-the-scenes, to get rid of Norman's children,' Our Doris said, gesturing to Joe and his band of men.

'Yes. I am very pleased to meet you. Which one of you is named Joe?' Angela asked. Joe stepped forward and put out his hand.

'Pleased to meet you, Angela, I'm Joe,' he said. 'Should I call you Mistress?'

'I am no human's Mistress. I am only Mistress to these behind me. I do not command you at all. I just wish to work side-by-side with you and protect you of course. You are human and free, I remember that. Hold on to that and enjoy it,' Angela said.

'Thank you, I'm ready to go whenever you are.' Joe said, very pleased with Angela's attitude.

'We'll go now. We'll walk slow so you can keep up,' Angela smirked. Carl laughed loudly and out they went.

As the humans and vampires made their way down the donkey path towards Friarmere, there was a lot of confusion and running about, going on in the Primary School. There had been two notable absentees, and one, in particular, meant that people had to be inconvenienced. The first one was Vincent, Stephen had not noticed the first day that he had been missing, but now after a couple of days, he was wondering where his old fellow spy was.

He wandered around the Primary School looking into various classrooms. Surely Vincent hadn't gone back to his old house. Maybe he was in his mother's house, who lived opposite Sue and Tony. Stephen knew where that was. That was easy to search. He questioned each and every vampire that he came across in the Primary School about Vincent, at least once. Soon everyone was annoyed with him.

'Stop whingeing about Vincent. Either go and find him or shut up,' said Keith. 'No-one's bothered about it.'

'I am!' Stephen insisted.

'You are going on a lot,' Diane said. 'I have to agree.'

'He's got to be somewhere on the Earth, hasn't he?' Stephen said.

'Did he come home the other night?' Diane asked. 'Are you sure?'

'Yes. We were in the village, and Vincent came home, left me on my own. It was late, mind,' Stephen said.

'And then that was it. You haven't seen Vincent since?' Diane asked.

'No,' Stephen said flatly

'Maybe he got lucky,' said Keith. 'He wouldn't want you bursting in on him.'

'Oh, come on Keith. He only has one eye left. The other side is a hole with a tuba mouthpiece jammed in it? I highly doubt it,' Diane said.

Stephen looked at Diane. She still had a central split down her nose, which had not healed, pink office bulldog clips held it together. Stephen looked at Keith who read his mind.

'Some people just aren't fussy, clearly,' Keith said, smirking.

Stephen walked out of the school and decided he would have a sniff around for Vincent. His house was far away, but his mother's house was close so he would try there first.

Within a couple of minutes, he had arrived. He looked over at Sue and Tony's house, which was still dark and empty. A quick glance at Vincent's mother's house, revealed it to be even colder and more inhospitable.

Stephen tried the front door, pushing it open immediately. It must have been left with the latch button pushed up. Inside, Vincent's mother Alice, still lay on the floor, in a kind of praying position. Her knees were bent, her body folded over them. This vision of deep prayer was spoilt by the fact that back of her neck was partly missing having been bitten out, by her own son.

She had never been a vampire and so was rotting in the usual human way. The smell was pretty bad, but that did not bother Stephen. He wondered if deep inside, there was something still good enough to eat and thought *waste not want not*. He would get to Vincent sooner or later, and Vincent wouldn't mind this quick snack on his mother seeing as though he had done with her now. Stephen rolled her over with his boot, exposing the front of her, covered in a blouse and fuzzy cardigan. He ripped these open and saw that she wore a long-line bra, in *café-au-lait*.

He could see that this area was not as spoilt as the rest of her, so knew that this part would be good to eat. Instead of being the mottled black, green colour, of her face and hands, it was just pale yellowish. As was the usual way with Stephen he just plunged his head straight into her creamy abdomen, pushing the *café-au-lait* undergarment aside so he could get to the meat. All thoughts of the missing Vincent were long gone.

The other absentee in the Primary School was not noticed for a while too. This person did not talk a lot to the other vampires as she was always busy, so had not got missed for her own presence exactly, but for her calming influence on its many other inhabitants. This was what revealed her as missing.

There were about fourteen remaining vampire children in the School and they were running wild without their teacher, Mrs White. They thundered around the school, pelting this way and that. All of them were hungry, as she had not brought them a person to eat the previous night, on her way in.

Still very humanly vocal, the imprisoned vampire children were shouting to the adult vampires that they were going to go out and find someone if something wasn't brought into them for their tea. Diane remembered what it was like to keep Sophie full when she was growing up, but these were always hungry. Kids these days.

'When did you last see Mrs White?' Christine asked Keith.

'Last night I last saw her with Penelope and Marcel. They must have got home safe because if all three of them were missing, I'm sure we would have heard about it. Can you imagine if The Master's girlfriend had been attacked! Or his other new favourite,' Keith said bitterly.

'Well she's not here,' Christine said, 'unless she's overslept somewhere.'

'I doubt it,' Diane said. 'That's not like her.'

'No, she does attend to her duties well. Very diligent,' said Keith.

'So, what we have in effect, is that two of us are missing,' Lynn said.

'Stephen could have found Vincent by now,' Christine said.

'Yes, and he might not have either. We are talking about Stephen. I might go and have a snoop around for Mrs White and Vincent myself, and now Stephen is missing too isn't he, as we don't actually know where he is, that's a fact,' Lynn said. The others did not say a thing in reply. They thought that Lynn was paranoid if she already considered Stephen as *missing*. Lynn left them doing nothing and went out into the night.

When Lynn got out of the Primary School, she thought that something smelled very fishy here. She really hoped that this had nothing to do with Ernie. It would just be typical.

Along with Angela, Jackie and Sarah on the trek to Friarmere, there was not only the vigilantes, five from the previous night and Rick who had re-joined his old friends, but most of the group from Friarmere Band had come along with them too. They planned to have a meeting about how this was going to move forward.

They believed, even though Angela and her gang were strong, that there would still not be enough of them to outnumber Norman's horde. They needed everyone else to help to guarantee success.

Their army would consist of Angela's vampires, the vampire vigilantes and a very large contingent of humans, some who had fought several battles.

The members of Friarmere Band plus Agnes, Miles, Lee, Our Doris, Beverly, Terry, Lisa and Joan wanted to meet with the group of vampire vigilantes, to make a plan of action. Carl was going to call for Maurice, and hopefully, he would be there, and the other three would already be with him. If not, Carl would check the two places where they tended to stalk the other vampires.

The rest of the people were as quiet as they could be. The donkey path was damp and misty, only the sound of dripping water could be heard. At first, they could not think of an area where they could meet successfully and where Norman would not sniff them out, then, unfortunately, Pat had the idea that they could meet in the Civic Hall as Norman had dealt with this place a long time ago. They looked forward to some grisly sights.

Carl said he would call for Maurice and the others and if the rest of them could wait in the Civic Hall for them, he would bring them as soon as he could. At least they would be out of the cold.

Angela had been shown The Grange on the previous night when she had been on the tops with the rest of the group from Melden on their journey. The three lady vampires made her way up the hill towards Norman Morgan. The lights were on, and they felt fearless and strong, they had news for him that he would not be expecting.

When they got closer, they noticed that there was another vampire walking in front of them. This was a male vampire charging forwards towards The Grange. It was not Norman.

Angela wanted them to wait for a while, as she did not wish this vampire to discover them and alert Norman before they were there.

When they were at the top of the lane, next to Christine's house, they saw the door open, and the vampire go inside. His face and hands with dark and very strange. Like lumpy porridge.

'Come on, 'Angela said. 'It's our turn now.'

They walked down the dirt track and then crunched over the snowy gravel. Angela knocked loudly on the front door and was surprised when their friend Penelope opened it. She was shocked to see them too and quickly jumped out into the cold, shutting the door behind her.

'Did you do it?' Penelope asked.

'Of course, we did,' Angela said.

'Yeah don't be daft,' Jackie said with a little laugh.

'How's Marcel?' Angela asked.

'Grim,' Penelope said rolling their eyes.

'Other stuff has gone on with him too, that I can't speak about now. Let's just say he got saved by the skin of his teeth!'

'Eek!' Jackie said.

'Why is she here?' Penelope gestured towards Sarah.

'She's with us now. And we trust her,' Jackie said.

'Announce us now, please. Let's do this,' Angela said.

Penelope opened the door and let them into the hall. She walked into Norman's office, and within a few seconds, he exited behind her. The Friarmere Master was clearly shaken to see them there. Especially Sarah. They had caught him unawares. Angela stood with her hands on her hips, Jackie had her arm's folded. Norman could tell they meant business.

'We need to talk,' Angela said.

7 Bodies

Carl found Maurice and Adam in the house, which was the first place he checked. The two vampires were expecting the imminent arrival of Ernie and Mark, and within about fifteen minutes they too had arrived. Maurice had been allowed the happy task of informing Mark and Ernie that Wee Renee and her gang were safe and here to help. They had about eighty humans and seven vampires at their disposal. They had done away with Norman's evil sister, and it was nearly all over. Carl told them the next part, they were to meet Wee Renee and other representatives, including the human vigilantes at the Civic Hall, where plans were to be made between them to end all this.

'Well flap me sideways, I thought it would never happen,' Ernie said dropping down onto Maurice's sofa. 'Lynn won't be pleased about this.'

'Why did you say that? You're not telling her, are you? Please don't. Why would you?' Adam asked astounded.

'Oh no, I'm not that soft. I was just saying … … I don't think they expected this at all. I don't think they thought that Wee Renee could even kill The Master's sister, never mind return here with vengeance on her mind. Plus bring eighty other folk and *good vampires*! It's not heard of!' Ernie exclaimed. His head was in a whirl, and it seemed like a dream.

'Well, it's not that much of a stretch is it?' Carl asked. 'Various brave villagers have joined her because she helped them. And *good vampires*? Well, Friarmere has its share, and they are all in this room.' Carl smiled at them.

'When you put it like that, it makes sense,' Ernie said. 'Plus, Lynn was hopping mad, when The Master said they weren't to be touched if they returned anyway. She's not got over that one yet!'

When the humans entered the Civic Hall, it was freezing. As cold as outside. Before they got into the main hall, when they were just in the entrance hall, they could smell the death and decay just the other side of the door to them. Wee Renee pinched her nostrils, and Bob lifted his scarf over his face.

'It's freezing in here,' Beverly said.

'The heating's probably not been on since it was last used. Do you want me to locate the switch, try and get the radiators on?' Lee asked.

'As much as I would like to say yes, I think not Lee,' Wee Renee said.

'Why? Aren't we going to be here long?' Miles asked.

'I'm not planning to be, no. Just as long as it takes. And to be frank, you weren't here before. There is a lot of cold meat in there that will not benefit from being heated up for a couple of hours if you know what I mean,' Wee Renee said.

'Can't you smell it? I can,' Terry said, always one to comment on smells along with Our Doris.

'Sorry, I didn't realise. I thought it was a bad fart. I thought it was the same as one I smelled on Christmas Day,' Lee said.

'That was one time! And I'd had sprouts!' Pat roared.

It had been nearly a month now since the battle in this place. Many, many bodies lay around the floor in various bit and pieces. There was none that was a whole unit.

It was evident that feeding had occurred long after the night of the battle. There were some horrific sights, and a lot of their chewed bones were strewn around. It a couple of areas it was clear that vampires had sat down for their meal, placing the used bones on the seat beside them. If there was a KFC in Hell it would probably look like this.

Luckily, with the weather conditions, flies had not got in, and the corpses had not had to endure a heatwave. The double doors had been kept shut. But a month, even on an unrefrigerated corpse certainly took its toll. Many bodies were greenish black, the wounds moist and mouldy. Severe leakage had occurred, the juices running out in pools from every cut onto the Civic Hall's nylon carpet. Not to mention the fact that during the attack or just after death, the humans had involuntarily relieved themselves. The place had become a toilet and a home for festering flesh.

The only other thing to be thankful about was that somehow mice and rats had not found their way in here. This would be an ideal place for them to feed and nest undisturbed.

There was not one row of seats that did not have a corpse lying amongst it. The people who had fought that night realised how lucky they were to still be alive. This brought it all back to them. The central aisle was full of them. As Gary looked over the bodies, he realised that not one eyeball had remained in their heads.

No-one would ever know, but Norman had asked Michael to replenish his stocks in the back of the shop about two weeks ago. He had taken a few large food bags down and got to work with two spoons, removing all eyes as instructed. He managed to fill three bags. Michael then made the short walk to the shop and plopped them in the preserving liquor. He gave them a good stir. The Master would be able to play pick and mix with these.

Where the Band had played was entirely free, which was the easiest place to congregate. They inched their way up the aisle. Their shoes sunk into the wet leakages of various types.

'Tread gently,' Our Doris shouted. 'Vigorous stamping is kicking up a right stink!'

The humans started making themselves comfortable in the Band chairs, as far away from the majority of corpses as they could. Wee Renee took out her cloth handkerchief and put it over her nose and mouth, just to cut out some of the smell. They did not have anything to say, they just looked sadly around them waiting in the darkness for the vampire vigilantes.

The only light was enough, a brief glimmer from the streetlights through the windows, and that was plenty.

When Carl and the vampire vigilantes arrived, they couldn't see much at all, not having the experience of being inside previously at the Battle, they couldn't make everything out. Only Ernie had been here on the night of the Battle, and that was briefly and unfortunately, for the other side.

Carl lit up his torch and shone it around the room. Various sets of eyes blinked at him at the furthest end of the room, on the stage.

'Keep your eyes off the floor, you don't want what to see what is about,' Liz said. Now, their eyes were getting used to the light, and they had the benefit of Carls torch, an awful lot was visible. Only the very corners of the room were in dark shadows, everything else became quite brightly lit. The torches lit up something else, many gleaming pieces of metal in amongst the corpses. Silver and gold.

'I tell you what,' Ernie said. 'I'm taking all these instruments back! They are not having any more for their Band!'

'Good prioritising,' Gary said sarcastically.

Pat thought that it was the same old Ernie deep down and smiled to herself. She would help him do that. Pat could see how that would make someone like him feel and she admitted to herself that these were often well-loved instruments and that none of the bloodsuckers should be able to have them. It wasn't a priority, but yes, it was important.

'Hello everyone, old friends and new. Right, what's happening then? Maurice asked.

'Not to teach our granny how to suck eggs or anything,' Wee Renee said. 'We have already got rid of one Master in Melden. So, we know what works. What we need to do is surround them in very small groups. Probably two is maximum. Trick Norman or trap him into a position he cannot get out of, with as few of his Lieutenants with him as we can manage. The fewer minions, the better. Once you take The Master the rest will fall. That's what we did with Anne.'

'Maybe we could seduce him,' Pat said. 'I know he has a thing for me and Rene, you could use us for bait and then surround him when he was melting the rubber buttons on my liberty bodice.' Pat said it all a little too happily.

'I'm sure there's another alternative to using you like a pair of sexy bait,' Ernie said. 'Besides that, I think he is enamoured with a vampire from Moorston named Penelope.'

'Yes, the world doesn't revolve around sex,' Terry said.

'Firstly Terry,' Pat said, 'it does. Secondly, if it were on a plate, Norman would take it, whether he is with Penelope or not. And I have met her, so I do know she is a bit more glamorous than me and Rene before you say anything. And thirdly, it was only an idea, and I will withdraw the offer of the pair of us, then!'

'Thanks for that,' Wee Renee said.

'No, we'll trap in some way,' Mark said. 'I saw him out last night for the first time in a while, so he has started venturing into the village again.'

'With the Band?' Sue asked.

'No. He was dealing with another snowmobile incident,' Mark said.

'Surely now with the numbers that we have, we should be able to charge through the Village just like he did with his Brass Band,' Gary said.

'Yes, how many has he got exactly? What would you say?' Andy asked.

'I would say because we've been getting rid of them … about 25 to 30 including his Lieutenants, but not including the vampire kids,' Adam advised them.

'Oh, I forgot about them,' Rick said. 'Is there more than those two that were on the donkey path?'

'Oh yeah, there is a lot more,' Adam said. 'There's quite a few up at the Primary School, and those lot aren't too bad considering. But there are some wild ones outside, I would say there are maybe three of them left. We got a few the other night. You don't even want to catch a glimpse of them. They have turned into spider creatures and have become deformed.' Liz put her hand over her mouth. She didn't want to see them, that was for definite.

'So, it's on the table that we can now join forces and walk through the village as one, without hiding and doing everything in secret. Work in such a way that we take this Village back without fear and boldly,' Ernie said, 'shall we vote on it?'

This was the Ernie of old, Tony thought. Lisa and Joe were quite astounded, and it proved again that these were vampires for good, acting quite humanely and civilly with their voting system. These vampires were very normal and likeable.

'To join and forge boldly ahead. Who's for it?' Ernie asked. Every hand shot up.

'Motion carried,' Ernie said happily.

Angela and Jackie followed Norman into his office. Penelope watched them shut the door, then went into the room next to it with Sarah. In there sat the man who had gone in just before them. His head was covered in gore, and he blinked at them through eyelashes that were matted with congealing blood.

'Hello ladies,' he said, seductively.

'This is Stephen,' Penelope said to Sarah. 'Just ignore him.'

They sat down in silence. Penelope was interested in what was going on. They could hear every word from the next room, which was precisely what Angela wanted.

8 Kin

'By the fact that Sarah is with you, I would imagine that a misfortune has befallen my sister Anne!' Norman said to the two young vampires before him.

'Yes, we avenged Our Master's death and thoroughly enjoyed it. I think Len would have to,' Angela said. 'Very long and very painful. And humiliating. But so much better than she deserved.'

Penelope and Sarah heard one of the snowmobiles approaching. It stopped outside, and it wasn't long before they heard the front door open.

Penelope put her head out so that whoever had been on the snowmobile would not enter The Master's office. She saw that it was Stuart and Marcel and beckoned them quickly inside the room. They entered, and Stuart addressed them immediately.

'What is happening?' Stuart asked.

'The vampires from Moorston have arrived. They have put The Master's sister to death and are talking to him in the other room,' Penelope told him. 'This is Sarah, she is under the Moorston vampire's protection.'

Stuart quietly sat down after being furnished with this information. It did not bother him one bit that these vampires had killed The Master's sister. All in all, when he had seen her, she had been a bad lot, he could tell. Good riddance to that one.

Stuart had seen Sarah on his visits to Melden with his Master and knew that she was Anne's former Lieutenant. How very interesting.

Marcel looked around the room, he raised his eyebrows at Sarah, who smiled back and then looked at Stephen

'You're a mucky pup,' Marcel said and decided to sit at the opposite side of the room to Stephen. Stephen did not know what to say to that. Then realised he must have a bit of food on his face after eating and wished he had washed his head in Vincent's mother's sink. He looked down at his hands, which were caked in bloody brown goo. *Yes, he probably had some on his face* he guessed. His hands were nearly dry, so he rubbed them together briskly. The dried blood dropped to the expensive carpet in a lumpy powder.

'Heathen,' Marcel said. Stephen didn't know what he should do next, so tried to make it better by rubbing his semi-clean hands on his face. This too resulted in more caked-on blood drifting to the floor.

'Eww,' Marcel said openly. Stephen thought he would give up. This Moorston vampire obviously didn't like him, whatever he did.

'And the rest of her creatures?' Norman asked.

'All gone. Children and wolves. Apart from Sarah of course, who has pledged herself to us,' Jackie advised him.

'Ah you have a new daughter, and I have a new daughter and son. It has turned out well for us, hasn't it?' Norman asked them with a slight hint of a smirk playing on his lips.

'Now we are here, we will take over the care of Penelope and Marcel. You don't have two worry about that,' Angela said. 'They are our kin.'

'You see,' Norman said, 'I do worry about that. I would like to keep Penelope and Marcel for my own. Most of my creatures are useless. I don't want any of them. It just happens that was what I had to work within this Village. But now I have two of Len's, I just think I'll keep them for my own. Take any of mine in return - I don't care. Take them all.'

In the other room, Stuart and Stephen looked at one another. Stuart was seething. He thought he had proved his use many times to the Master. Yes, maybe some of the others were less capable, but The Master had just tarred everyone with the same brush. What if Angela and Jackie picked him, as he got on so well with Penelope and Marcel. The sudden fear and anger opened up another avenue in Stuart's mind. An avenue that he had not considered before.

Stephen thought The Master was probably joking and he could have confirmed that if he had seen his face. He hasn't known The Master to have a great sense of humour, but he must have. Everyone had one. He probably cracked loads of jokes in private.

'We all have our different strengths and weaknesses, Norman,' Angela said. 'We're all of use. If you carry on like that, you will be starting to sound like your sister. Our Master Len never spoke about humans like that. He loved the human race and all it brings to us.'

'The humans are food and our vessels. They are no more than that,' Norman said. 'They have no feelings, they don't matter.'

'This was your sisters view too, wasn't it?' Angela said. 'To capture them, bleed them, make a bath out of them, inject them with God only knows what. Torture them, cut chunks from them. I've seen it all you see. All her dirty laboratory equipment in her basement, which I am told, by a certain person that you kept people in too.'

'I have been known to use my sisters' facilities, yes. I'm not ashamed of that,' Norman said.

'Well your brother didn't use those facilities, and he *would* have been ashamed. He did not know everything that was going on, or else he would have stopped it. But I get the idea that you knew Norman. And whatever she was putting into other people, she was putting more into herself. Do you know what was under her skin?' Angela asked.

'Bones, I should imagine, like all of our kind. She was still walking around upright. Her body hadn't turned to jelly,' Norman said, trying to patronise her.

'When I salted her flesh away, the morning light revealed her to be part crow and part wolf. Her legs under that long dress were curved and doglike with hairs that were grey like her wolves. Her head turned into a bird's head, her nose and upper teeth took the form of a black beak, and her arms underneath the skin had black feathers, which were revealed when the flesh blew away. In fact, under the skin, her whole body was covered with small black scales and feathers. That is the person that you were siding with,' Angela informed him.

In the other room, Penelope looked at Sarah for confirmation, who nodded once, her eyes downcast from the shame of her own Mistress. When Penelope went to catch Marcel's eye, he already had both hands over his mouth, his eyes huge, staring back at her. Stuart was pale, with his lips pressed together in a grey line. He listened to every nasty word. Stephen just looked very confused. He was sure he had misheard what Angela had said. That could never be right. Perhaps she was drunk. She didn't sound drunk.

'I don't believe you, that is not what is underneath a vampire skin,' Norman said.

'No. It's not, is it? I have seen under many vampire skins because of your sister, and none were like hers. But, oh I can assure you that it is true, and there were lots of witnesses to see it. In fact, over sixty people saw her like that. It was the only part of this whole experience we enjoyed, I'll give her that. At least we had a jolly good laugh at her expense. Don't you understand that the changes had to go on somewhere physically as well as what it did to her mind,' Angela said.

Norman was angry about the contemptuous way she spoke about his sister, but what she was saying was even more concerning

'I told her I didn't like all that stuff she was pumping into herself. I told her it wouldn't work. All that stuff on her table, preparing humans to be hybrids,' Norman said.

'So, you did know. You did see it all. And you just thought Anne should stop because it wouldn't work – not that it was wrong. But the ultimate joke was that she was the biggest hybrid Norman, but she's not here so she can enjoy the laughs. She had so much other animal in her that it slowly sent her crazy and you allowed her to run around in this world doing that to humans. And you let her kill our Master,' Angela said.

'You encouraged her, you egged her on,' Jackie said. 'You did it for your own profit.'

'I didn't egg her on to inject people, I didn't. Or herself. I just didn't try to stop her. That's different,' Norman said. 'I don't have to answer to you anyway.'

'I take it that you do not intend to deny the other parts then either?' Angela asked.

9 Useful

'What other parts? What are you trying to pin on me now?' Norman asked them angrily. He sighed as if he was now tired of them.

The two young vampires looked at each other for a few seconds and then both turned their heads to Norman.

'What I am referring too, is that you won't be denying what was in your sisters Diary,' Angela said.

'You read my sister's Diary?' Norman asked. 'That is very rude, to read someone's Diary, even I wouldn't do that!'

'Ooh, now he has a conscience I see!' Angela said, somewhat amused. 'Are you afraid of what we read? What we read about you?'

There was more noise at the front door. In walked Keith, Michael and Diane who had come up to The Grange to ask Norman if he would like the Band to set up, or what their orders were tonight. Again, Penelope popped her head out of the room and beckoned the three people inside. That room was getting quite full now. Keith and Michael looked over at Stephen. Keith sneered and sat far away from him, Michael looked at him in disgust.

He blinked at both of them. Short-term memory was apparently a problem for Stephen as he had forgotten once more what he had done earlier. He was wondering why they were like that with him. Stephen wondered why everyone was always *off* with him. No wonder he couldn't get a girlfriend if his vampire and his human brother couldn't manage to be civil to him. Penelope put her finger to her lips, in a *shushing* motion and they sat in silence waiting for this to be over.

'Did you read my sisters Diary or not? Or was it someone else who told you there were comments in there about me?' Norman asked.

'I did yes, and other people did too. We all came to the same conclusion,' Angela said. 'She should have hidden it a bit better if she didn't want it read out aloud when she was killed!' Norman looked furiously at her but did not speak.

'Yes, you were wrong earlier when you said that was the only part we enjoyed, Angela. We enjoyed that too, remember. Going through her personal stuff. Her underwear!' Jackie said, laughing.

'To be fair, you're right Jackie. Norman, what it said was that the two of you were together in this plan. She moved it forward a bit quicker than you were expecting but she moved it forward regardless. You wanted it all right and knew her plans for the future. You depended on her, in fact, to pull it off,' Angela said.

'What are these plans, you are talking about? What did she say in the Diary?' Norman asked.

'You know all about it Norman. That you and Anne would be King and Queen over this land. She said she was in love with you and that you loved her too. You encouraged that Norman. You did not put a stop to that. You knew how she felt and she was a psychopath. You used that to get her to do your bidding,' Angela spat.

'I didn't want her to kill my brother. Can I make that clear?' Norman said.

'You knew the way this was going. You realised he had to be out of the way for her to move forward with this plan. Why didn't you nip it in the bud? This idea of you two together, ruling the world. Just because she enjoyed torture more than you, it doesn't make you any better than her. She was crazy. From what I can see, for all intents and purposes, you are as sane as most vampires could be who. Who was the worst one? The one that chooses to be like this or the one that cannot help it?' Angela asked. Norman knew the answer was very plain there but didn't say it.

'What's your point?' Norman asked instead.

In the Civic Hall, the meeting had come to an end between the vampire vigilantes, the human vigilantes and the old Friarmere Band. They retrieved all the instruments remaining and music, picking their way slowly around the dead and out of the door.

They left footprints in the snow. Rotting flesh and faeces caked their shoes. They shuffled along, trying to clean them off.

Several of the party walked over to Maurice's house, where they piled the instruments up neatly in his back bedroom. Ernie was very contented after that.

Our Doris had brought over the soprano cornet, which she said was just her size and looked easy to play. Terry observed her over his eyebrows.

'It's not,' Terry said simply.

Haggis ran up Maurice's stairs after Our Doris, and so began the many shouts of *no weewee*. Haggis seemed particularly naughty in Maurice's house and seemed determined to give a little squirt over everything.

'You dirty little hound,' Our Doris shouted at him. 'Maurice, can you explain why he's being like this?'

'I used to have a Labrador, a choccy one,' Maurice said. 'He can probably still smell him and is trying to cancel him out.'

'Is he now?' Our Doris growled, still staring at Haggis. 'Pat take him outside, please. I'll get all this filth up if you have some disinfectant.' Maurice nodded and went off to fetch her some and a cloth.

After that, the four vampire vigilantes decided to get into position. Joe and his gang of men went out to burn out vampire nests. The rest of the group felt like they were quite safe if they quickly made their way back over to the mill. Adam watched from the roof, and he could see them get quite a long way down the donkey path and nearly home. Close to the Church, he could see the vampire children on the roof, and they watched him back. They did not come any closer. They seemed to be scared of other vampires for some reason, or maybe they just didn't want to be trapped again. Their freedom taken away, a future dependant on nightly hand-outs.

When the large group arrived back at the mill, Beryl was eagerly awaiting them for their safe arrival and all the news. The kettle was put on immediately, and they sat down to tell the little tale about tonight.

Bob was extremely descriptive about the state of the corpses in the Civic Hall. Sue pulled him aside after his first animated delivery of events and told him not to divulge any of that to the children in the mill.

It felt good to be able to go out in Friarmere in the night-time and return unharmed. They already felt free. Things were definitely changing.

'My point is,' Angela said, 'is that you are as guilty as her. You just used her to do what you didn't have the balls to do. Don't try and tell me you are innocent. You could have stepped in at any time. You must have known that she could not move forward with the crazy plan without getting rid of our Master. He would not have allowed it. Besides that, he wasn't included in the future at all. To say that you and her are going to Rule the Land means an absence of him. How was that going to happen Norman? There was only one way. You knew they didn't get on. You were either too weak to stand up to her, or you wanted her to carry on with her plans. If it was the former, you would have warned him so you could fight her together. Contain her somehow. Either way, it makes you guilty or a shit vampire.' Norman said nothing to this.

'And as for a Master? You talk about your children being useless? It is you that is useless. They have been doing what they liked while you have been up here, I have heard. I don't think that you will be trusted to have Penelope and Marcel if you can't look after the ones you already have got, do you?' Jackie added.

'I am having Penelope and Marcel. I am more in tune with them than any of my vampires. They are more useful to me than any of mine, especially Penelope. I like them here in this house. I trust them,' Norman said.

'Maybe that is because they were brought up properly, by someone like your brother, and not sired by you,' Jackie said.

'That does not make than yours either. If they are here they are rightfully mine, and I will be taking them and giving them the life that they are used to,' Norman said.

'The life they are used to? They aren't used to this shit. The misery here. We do not want to take this world from the humans. Just look how the three villages have become,' Angela said.

'There is nothing wrong with any of the three villages. I would've happily lived in any of them,' Norman said.

'Really Norman? There were hardly any humans left in Melden. How will that function as a village now?' Angela said.

'What do you mean?' Norman asked.

'Your sister either turned or murdered nearly everyone there. Wasted. For what? Baths of blood, that clearly had no effect only stain her arse. Oh, that was worth it,' Angela said.

Norman pressed his balled fists together. Apparently, it still irked him to have someone talk about his sister in a derogatory way. To Angela and Jackie, the more that he didn't attack Anne alongside them, or defend Len, the worse it got for him. That was more proof that he was as guilty as hell.

'As for Friarmere, I have been told that you are dragging humans through the streets on the back of your snowmobile for sport. That wild vampire children are living in bushes, in the trees and on the roofs, now deformed. Even your sister did not have that. You know turning children is forbidden but well ... ... rules mean nothing to the great Norman Morgan because he will soon Rule the World with his sister. She did what she liked, he does what he likes still. Birds of a feather,' Angela said.

'A crow in fact,' Jackie said.

'So, I ask you, is this how you want this country to become?' Angela asked.

Norman still did not reply. He did not think he should, and he could not deny the existence of the vampire children.

'I know you aren't a native of this country and maybe you do not care. Well, I am, and I do care. You say that none of the villages were bad to live in. The only one place that you are right about is Moorston, and that is the one place that you did not care enough about to save The Master there,' Angela said.

'What are you saying?' Norman shouted. 'What are you saying, you silly little girls?'

'I am saying that we are watching you, and if you don't clean up your act, you will go the same way as your sister. It won't be long before this snow melts, and life will get back to normal. How do you think you are going to go on then, with the rest of the country against you? You cannot go underground the way you are living here. You cannot integrate like us. You have been living in a false reality, trapped in the snow. Just think about that Norman,' Angela said.

'Don't threaten me, Angela. You are not at my equal!' Norman screamed at her, out of control.

'No, you're right. I am your better,' Angela said. 'Now that you have been given a reality check and a warning, these silly little girls are going to go back to a lot of people that love them and stand behind them freely. Enjoy the few stragglers you have, that you *don't* appreciate. We will see you soon.'

And with that, Angela and Jackie walked out of the door. As she passed through the hallway, Angela simply shouted *Sarah*, who got up and followed her Mistress out of the house. The rest of the vampires, the two Moorston ones and the Friarmere ones looked around at one another. They had been given a reality check too.

10 Squirrel

'Why didn't we kill him then?' Jackie asked Angela.

'Even though we were alone, there were other vampires in the adjacent room. I kept hearing more come in too. I bet they could hear everything. In fact, I counted on it. I wanted them all to hear the facts. He played into our hands when he said all of his own children were useless. That was unplanned and classic. What I didn't want them to hear was us killing them. We need to do this properly, Jackie.' Angela said.

'I do not want to give his children a heads up.' She continued. 'We need to get them all like we did with Anne's. If we had killed him, then they could have made their escape. He has far too many. They aren't weak either, and this village is bigger.'

'That's true. I heard the comings and goings in the other room. If we heard them, they could hear us. We might as well have been at Clapham Junction. Good job you didn't need it to be private. But you are right. Now he looks the baddie, and we looked like a pair of goodie two shoes. They won't run and a good job too,' Jackie said.

'Could you hear anything Sarah,' Angela asked her.

'Every single word. They are more worried about him calling them useless than you killing them all.' Sarah replied.

'Good because it would be a lot more difficult to find them here. They do not smell as strong as Anne's vampires because they do not have that part of them that is wolf. Norman's children have been turned a lot longer too and have roamed everywhere in this Village. There is no way that we could seek them out. Everywhere reeks of Norman's blood. This must be done very cleverly. At one point, when he has few vampires with him, we will strike against him, and then start on the others. Don't worry, I know what I'm doing,' Angela said.

'Well I'll be the first one to say it,' Michael said. 'That was a bit tense.'

'It was,' Diane said.

'It's just words, I'd have said a lot worse,' Keith said. 'In fact, those two bitches wouldn't have got out of my office. That's where he slipped up. Strike while the iron is hot and all that.'

'Oh, is that right Keith? You didn't hear all the conversation. It was certainly an education. You might have thought differently if you had heard all the facts' Stuart asked.

'What do you mean?' Keith asked.

'He said that all his vampires meant nothing compared to Penelope and Marcel,' Stuart said. 'No offence intended to you two.' Penelope and Marcel looked at him. Penelope nodded once at Stuart. She could see his point, she would be hurt if her Master had said that about her too.

'He just said it in the heat of the argument,' Keith said.

'Yeah, The Master thinks the world of us,' Stephen said confidently.

'He said it more than once, and it wasn't in anger every time, Keith,' Stuart said. Keith didn't say a word to this. 'Answer me this. What *does* happen when the snow goes away? To live like Len's vampires would be easy. What do we do? Does The Master have plans after this? It wasn't so easy for him before the snow came. If he has a clue about what we do after the thaw, he hasn't told me.'

'You don't know what you're talking about. You're talking a load of crap, and if you want to question The Master on that matter, I suggest *you* do it because I'm not. They have put him in a bad mood. I think I'll go and wait for him at the school. He's already ripped me a new one this week,' Keith grumbled. 'Who is coming a walk down with me?'

'We will,' Michael said. 'Me and Diane are having a bit of a date tonight, anyway. We won't bother asking about Band. It probably wouldn't go down well after that.'

'I'll wait here with these two,' Stuart said. Stephen looked around the room, got up and turned to Stuart.

'I'm not staying here,' Stephen said, 'it's boring.'

The four of them exited leaving Stuart, Marcel and Penelope in the room. After a short silence, Stuart cleared his throat.

'Stand watch, will you Marcel?' Stuart asked. Marcel had formed a good relationship with Stuart, who had ferried him back several times over to Moorston to visit Len's body. Marcel did as he asked.

'Tell me what you think about that? About what he said to them? I want you to be utterly frank about it,' Stuart asked Penelope. Marcel looked up the hall. The Master was nowhere to be seen, he still sat in his office, sulking.

'To be honest, as much as I think about Norman, as he is my boyfriend, I will always be for the Moorston vampires,' Penelope said.

'So, will I,' said Marcel.

'Now, so will I!' Stuart said. He looked at them both, trying to judge their reactions. This was very unexpected. 'I have not seen these diaries, and neither have you, but it seems to point to the fact that The Master has been overtly sly about all this. He has played a sister off against a brother to get what he wanted. His own sister and brother, unbelievably!'

'Very ruthless,' Marcel said, through gritted teeth.

'And yes, they are right, he is working in his sisters' image. Making the vampire children and the torture in her basement that he knew about but didn't stop. The difference is, she was a psychopath, due to all this stuff that apparently was running through her veins. I don't say much, but I do watch and take everything in,' Stuart said. 'I saw her. You could see a mile off that something wasn't right there.'

Marcel stepped forward to speak to them quietly.

'He doesn't realise how nice it was over there. How we looked after one another and our humans. We became friends and had such a wonderful time. It's miserable here. It's miserable in this house. I honestly would prefer to be back in Moorston alone with Len's body and all the ghosts than here. It's only Penelope I return for,' Marcel said very dramatically.

Marcel had stepped away from his watch, and The Master had come out of his office quietly. He heard what Marcel had to say and stood behind him. Penelope's eyes widened as she looked past him, and Marcel knew he had been rumbled.

'Do you have something to say to me?' Norman asked. Marcel's shoulders dropped. Then he turned to The Master to explain himself.

'It's just that it was very different over there. We had fun, and Len looked after us. Whether we were a human or a vampire, it didn't matter what use we were to him. That wasn't a priority to Len. We were just his. Think about Jackie's mother Sheila, over there in Moorston still, disabled and bedbound. But Len looked after her. He made sure that over all these years she had food and everything she needed. Medical supplies and care. He ensured she was very comfortable and safe at all times. What good was she to him - but she was one of his own, and he loved her just as much as someone who was a great fighter,' Marcel said openly.

'Why have you turned your back on us Master?' Stuart asked. 'You prefer the company of Penelope and Marcel. Why do you think that we aren't useful to you? Why can't you think about us like Len thought about this Sheila?'

The Master did not hear their questions. All that he had heard amongst all the words that had been spoken was that there was a defenceless Moorston vampire left alone. One that would strike at the heart of one of his accusers.

He had the chance to teach them a lesson. They would learn after this, not to threaten him. This Sheila would be of some use at last to one of them. She would be very useful to Norman – he didn't see it as a waste at all.

Penelope knew he wasn't listening, but she just could not work out what was really on his mind. Stuart knew he wasn't listening too. He thought it was because The Master considered him useless and not worth talking to. Stuart no longer was valid or was able to voice his opinion. In Stuart's eyes, he had officially become orphaned.

When Michael, Diane, Stephen and Keith got close to the School, Keith and Stephen decided to have a walk around the Village. It was getting quite late now, and there wouldn't be much time to pick up any food if that was what they were after.

When Michael and Diane entered the school, Christine was frantically trying to control the remaining vampire children. Her sequinned beret was askew, and one of her false eyelashes had come unstuck at the side.

'Have you seen Mrs White?' Christine asked. 'I'm not doing this every day. Do you know what, they ignore me and are a bunch of little brats? They can all run wild, for as much as I care. If she doesn't come back, I'm letting them out!'

'No don't do that,' Michael said. 'That will cause right chaos, besides that, it could be very serious and would be down to The Master to decide, not you. Don't think that you are going to start making decisions about that, hells teeth! Go and talk to him tomorrow and see what can be done. But don't you do anything before that. Don't let them out! You don't want to end up like Keith, do you?'

'All right, all right! I get the message, Michael!' Christine said, shocked at how adamant he was about it.

Michael walked off towards the School staff room where he entertained Diane and saw his vampire patients. He went in and shut the door behind him, leaning on the door once he was behind it. He sighed and then rubbed his eyes under his glasses. The last thing he needed was more vampire children out on the streets.

It was like he was trying to manage everything from the background and in secret. Trying to manage Mrs White, trying to manage Christine, trying to keep up this relationship and knowing that time was ticking away. It wouldn't be long now until he would have to try and get along with his old Band and return to the human world. It wasn't easy for him.

When he opened his eyes, he noticed that Diane was already waiting there. She must have come in before him. He sat next to her on the sofa, flopping back into the cushions. Immediately, she seemed quite amorous, which usually he loved, but there were matters to discuss before they got down to business.

'Wait Diane, what did you think of all that up there then?' Michael asked. He was hoping Diane would say it was terrible and she would prefer to take the side of Jackie and Angela, not that Michael had met them. He was pleased to hear that they seemed to talk sense. This was clearly why Wee Renee was working with them. Therefore, these level-headed vampires would soon be his bedfellows so to speak. What a thought?

He hoped that Diane would inform him that she would work against Norman and look forward to a different life. She could work with him as a partner. They could, as a team, bring this quickly to a head. Michael needed her as a confident, he was sick of doing all this secret squirrel stuff on his own. Most importantly he could save Diane from the inevitable cull if she was seen to be helpful. If the vampire Sarah, could be forgiven by Angela and Jackie, then anyone could!

'I think The Master should have taken a firm hand to those two whippersnappers,' Diane said. 'The Master is always in the right.'

Michael's shoulders slumped. Diane was going to be a problem.

11 Throng

Angela and Jackie arrived back at the mill at around three am in the morning. As it was crucial that some of the human contingent ought to know what had gone on between Norman and themselves, the two young vampires woke up a very sleepy Wee Renee, Pat and Our Doris.

They explained what had gone on at The Grange and that they were biding their time. That Norman had not really denied his involvement in Anne's plan, which was the same as him admitting it. There had been no expression of regret and the word sorry had not come into the conversation. He had also slipped up and had said some terrible things about his own children.

'Why couldn't you have got rid of the bugger while he was in your clutches?' Pat asked.

'I said that,' Jackie said.

'Yes, you should have done him there and then,' Our Doris agreed.

'No. Even though we had the opportunity, there were some of his children in the other room. Just think about what happened with Anne and Our Master – our very own example. A Master was killed in front of everybody else. This gave me the chance to take his place and carry on with his work. What did it change for Anne? Nothing. We need to prevent this from happening here. We need to make sure that we kill every single last one of his creatures.' Angela said.

'I get you. It doesn't matter what order they are killed in, as long as the others don't find out,' Wee Renee said, nodding.

Stuart had disappeared off somewhere. Norman was sulking and plotting in his room. Marcel was crying for Len again and the good old days in his room. Penelope was outside smoking when she saw Michael returning from his date.

He stood for a moment next to her, looking out at the last hour or so of darkness. Friarmere was silent and as pretty as a chocolate box.

'Well that set the cat amongst the pigeons,' Michael said.

'It certainly did,' Penelope said, lighting up another cigarette. That was good, as Michael wanted to quiz her about it all.

'Piss you off, did it?' Michael asked.

'Er no. Not really. Nor Marcel. We knew where our bread was buttered already,' Penelope said.

'You prefer the Moorston butter, I take it?' Michael asked.

'Yep, always will do. Tonight, the only feeling I felt was happiness. I was happy that they killed that cow that murdered my wonderful Master,' Penelope informed him.

'Ah, yes I know. That old bag from Melden,' Michael laughed.

'He really was the best of them, Michael,' Penelope said.

'Yes, he seems to have been very well loved, plus of course, if he could get humans to love him, he must have been a very decent bloke. I am sorry for you,' Michael said. They stood a little longer in silence before Penelope decided to speak again.

'*Someone* was pissed off tonight. Very pissed,' she whispered conspiratorially.

'Who?' Michael asked.

'It's not for me to say. I don't know if I can fully trust you,' Penelope said.

'Listen, Penelope, I've seen what has been coming for ages. I have connections with the other side, don't you worry. The side that the Moorstoners have taken up with. The Master's time is done,' Michael whispered.

'Right. I still won't tell you who it is. It is their secret to tell you when they wish to divulge it. That is only fair. But I will say for definite that a vampire has rejected a Master to take a Mistress. My Mistress. I think it is only the start. Norman is making too many silly mistakes,' Penelope said.

'Say no more friend. We are peas in a pod. Let's just keep each other posted on important matters,' Michael said touching his nose and went to bed.

Our Doris and Pat drifted off again quickly. However, Wee Renee stayed awake the rest of the night, trying to plan for Norman's destruction. She was trying to think of any way that she could help the Moorston vampires do this. It wouldn't be easy, but it could be done. They just had to use their experiences and be smarter than him. Easy.

She finally dropped off about half an hour before Beryl awoke and the others began to stir, so woke up again. Wee Renee watched Pat clump over to Beryl and whisper to her about the happenings in The Grange. Out of one eye, she watched Our Doris take out Haggis and Bambi on their leads. Wee Renee took a deep breath thinking about what would go on today. Finally, she decided it was no use trying to get back off to sleep, and she sat up. Only about half the people were awake in the mill. Today was going to have to be a matches under eyelids day. She stretched, stood up and walked over to help Beryl get the children's breakfast ready.

'After breakfast, we'll have a meeting. There are lots to discuss,' Wee Renee said.

Beryl made the porridge and cereal and when everyone else had finished, and the dishes were cleaned Wee Renee asked everyone, except the children, to gather around and sit down.

She told them all of the meeting the previous night with the vampire and human vigilantes in the Civic Hall, explaining to them that now the group would go en masse wherever they liked. They were all joined together now. Good vampires, vigilantes and occupants of the mill. In doing it this way, they should not have any fear about going about their business and being attacked. They were now the majority in the village. Not Norman's vampires. New confidence filled the mill.

Wee Renee then gave them the main details of the meeting between Angela, Jackie and Norman, saying that he showed disregard for his own vampires, for humans and didn't seem really shocked at what was found at his sisters. He also wasn't upset at the contents of her Diary. However, he was not aware of what her DNA testing had done and did seem horrified at that.

'Everyone must realise that *that* is the final nail in the coffin for him. His card is marked. Whenever we see him now, alone or with one or two other vampires we are to strike! Do you understand that?' Wee Renee asked.

Joe stepped forwards now.

'What I'm going to ask is two things. Bearing in mind what Wee Renee has said, who tonight would like to go out and become part of this throng? And who would like to stay here and look after the children on these premises? We can't all go out. We will have to split our efforts. Everyone raise your hands, who are interested in becoming part of the vigilante gang? Let's see what we have on that side first,' Joe said.

A lot of people put their hands up. They wanted to take their village back and thought that the quicker that they could help the quicker they would be back in their own homes and normality would be thankfully restored.

There were over one hundred people in that building and over eighty wanted to be part of the fight. That left twenty people to look after the children here. Joe considered that was enough, plus Haggis and Bambi, who had excellent hearing.

Joe began to split them up into four groups. He suggested that he and Darren took one group. Craig and Rick took another. Carl and Father Philip took another, and Wee Renee and Pat took the last group.

He suggested that they each had a couple of Moorston vampires with each group. If they could split the seven Moorston vampires, plus the four Friarmere vampire vigilantes, that would mean that each group could have at least two vampires with them.

In total it would give each group twenty-two members and two vampires. That should be enough to protect themselves against the whole horde of Norman's vampires.

Of course, even though Friarmere was the biggest Village, it was still a Village, and if there were four groups each containing vampires, they could alert one or two of the groups very quickly to come and help. Also, they had the added advantage that Sarah and Adam could climb on the roofs to see what was coming in many directions and so alert them against any impending danger. Everyone thought this was a brilliant idea

Each pair of leaders got to pick their groups. In the gentlemanly way of *ladies first*, Wee Renee and Pat got to pick their group first, before the males. Pat let Wee Renee decide as she knew she would pick a good mix.

Wee Renee chose Agnes, Paul and Rachel, Freddie and Our Doris, and started to just pick random villagers after that. She didn't want to select all the good ones. If her group didn't do any fighting, the rest would be at a disadvantage. As she got closer to the end of her picks, Miles and Lee put their hands up, asking to be in her group too. Which Wee Renee and Pat were flattered to agree to.

Brenda had opted to stay with Beryl, Louise and some of the others to help look after the children.

Most of the old Friarmere Band, Gary, Danny, Liz, Andy, Sue, Bob, Tony, the Moorston lot, Terry, Sally, Beverly, Kathy and Nigel split themselves amongst the other three groups. Joe did not want all the experienced fighters in one group either. Most of Friarmere Band wanted to be in either his or Wee Renee's group if they were honest.

Finally, it was sorted out reasonably with a mix of experienced and just willing people in all four groups.

The rest of the morning was put aside for everyone finding weapons and planning the best places to maybe corner Norman.

Anyone who couldn't find a weapon was going on a trip later to Joe's Hardware Store, where Gary would help them *'tool up.'* Wee Renee said she didn't want anyone going out less than 'Bad-ass!' Rick said he didn't want anyone going out without a Brass Neck either.

The group of vigilantes who had stayed in Friarmere, considered where they might be able to rush off to, in a pinch.

Twenty people could easily get into the Hardware Store or the corner shop, which was very close by. If two groups were close together, lots of people could hide there. There was also the Civic Hall, which would hold all of them, as long as they didn't mind the smell and could negotiate the rotting bodies inside. That might also hide their smell if they were being hunted.

Father Philip said maybe one group could squeeze tightly into the coffee shop if they wanted to. There was also St Dominic's Church. Father Philip said again that this would hold all of them, but he was sure that the vampire children were close by and although a few of them would be no match for the huge group, he still did not even want to put one life in danger. He suggested that they only went up there if absolutely necessary.

12 Offer

After lunch and still during their preparations, they had a very, very unexpected visitor.

At about one o'clock, there was a loud knock on the mill door, and a surprised Lauren was closest to it and opened it. In her mind, as it was light, there could be no danger of course.

When she saw who it was, a person that she had seen walking past the pub many times spying, she shouted to Joe. Immediately he ran over to find Michael Thompson standing very calmly and plainly with his hands in the air waiting for admittance, or for them to come out to him.

Michael could see through the gap in the door that there were lots of people inside, A lot of them he did not know. When Joe saw who it was, he shouted Wee Renee. Michael wondered how many people would have to be shouted until they spoke to him. Would he still be standing here with every set of eyes blinking at him at one point, each arriving one by one?

Wee Renee lifted her long thin nose in the air and looked down at him.

'What do you want Michael?' Wee Renee asked. Michael thought this wasn't the time to ease them in, so just came right out with it, in front of everybody.

'To help. To secretly join you. I have a lot to offer. Can we make a bargain?' Michael asked.

Wee Renee thought about it. She blinked her eyes slowly to sum it all up. Pros and cons. She didn't need long to consider it.

'Yes, let him in,' she said.

A few of them stepped aside allowing him to enter. The door was shut behind him. Michael stood quietly at the door. Lots of people looked over at him. Some people knew him personally, some people knew about him, other people had not heard of him at all. Wee Renee shouted over to the group.

'Can I have your attention, please? Michael wants to talk to us about helping. Who wants to be involved in this important discussion? If you do, please follow me. We will go to the first floor and talk it over if that is all right with you Father Philip?' Wee Renee asked.

Father Philip nodded his head. Wee Renee started to walk up the stairs. A few people began to step forward, following the initial party. They wanted to hear what Michael had to say. This would be priceless.

All Friarmere Band went up the steps. Every one of the human vigilantes, Our Doris, Beryl who had struck the former bargain with him, and Lee, Miles and Graham. Terry, Sally, Kathy and Nigel, who had encountered some of Michael's treachery in the Church the last time they had been to Friarmere, completed the negotiating party.

Michael stood near the window at the far end. He let everybody who wanted to troop in enter. When they were all there, and he could hear no more footsteps on the steel steps, he spoke.

'Ask me anything,' Michael said.

'What can you offer us?' Freddie asked.

'Information on Norman. Information on the current situation of him and his children. His whereabouts. If needs be, I could maybe bring him somewhere, so that you could capture him, I don't know. Surely that's enough for me to show you that I am with you. I don't see what else I could do,' Michael said.

'That's very generous if you can do it,' Wee Renee said.

'Oh, I can do it all right. I'm trusted by everyone. I'm also friends with Penelope, and from what I know she wishes to align herself with her former friends in Moorston, rather than Norman and so does Marcel. I won't give any more away, but there is another vampire that is not very happy about matters. A Friarmere one. He wishes to align himself with Penelope and Marcel,' Michael informed them.

'How do you know this?' Nigel asked.

'I spoke to Penelope just before it got light this morning. I have been privately consulting with her about other matters, the snowmobile incidents that you may or may not know about. She objected to that matter too, and we have worked together secretly to stop it. Then I brought it up about the discussions last night between the two vampires that came over from Moorston and Norman. She confided in me then. I told her that I have known what a long time was right ago and am really no longer working for Norman,' Michael said.

'I notice that you do not call him The Master anymore, but you call him Norman,' Our Doris asked. 'What's that all about?'

'I do not see him as my Master anymore, that's why. I am tired of him. He has not been attending to me and has forgotten to constantly drip feed me the infected wine. I feel that even though when I am close to him, I am compelled to do as he says, that it is slowly waning, and the old Michael is coming back. Now if I am on the other side of the room, it is far enough away for me to ignore him,' Michael said.

'You do know, you have an awful lot of explaining to do,' Pat said. 'This is not over just because you're going to help us now. We will be going through every action you've ever made. Especially against any of us.'

'What can I say. I haven't forgotten anything that I've done, and I'm sorry. But it was just in the moment and under his spell. You know how that feels, don't you Father?' Michael asked Father Philip, depending on his mercy.

'I do, and I only consumed one portion of his wine. I don't know how many you have had. But slowly, even without help, we can come back. *With help*, we can get back to a normal and useful existence very quickly,' Father Philip said.

'I can feel it,' Michael said. 'Are you still in agreement that you will spare me if I help you to do this?' Michael asked.

'I have already spoken to you about it Michael,' Beryl said. 'Everyone knows here about the agreement.'

Michael addressed Beryl particularly when he spoke again.

'Yes, we spoke about the formal agreement, but now I have more information, and I want to help more now you are all here. I come to strike a new bargain. Direct to the organ grinder and not to the monkey, so to speak,' Michael said, smiling.

'Thanks for calling me a monkey,' Beryl said raising her eyebrows at him. 'This monkey ended up saving your bacon that day.'

'You know what I mean. I asked you to intervene on my behalf, now I am asking myself. Without you having to intervene,' Michael said. 'I am big and hairy enough to ask for myself now.'

'As far as I'm concerned, I agree,' Wee Renee said.

'Let's face it, he is just a massive *grass.* I don't know whether I trust him,' Liz said.

'I don't think we ever will,' Andy said. 'Not fully anyway.'

'All that I can do is help you, and you can see if I've changed in my ways. You know I never gave you all up here, so that is proof straight away. Proof that I am on the level,' Michael said.

'That's true,' Terry said. 'We could have walked into a mill full of dead kids if you had told them where they were.'

'You didn't tell him that we were in Moorston either did you? After you had seen us go in the tunnel. Or else he would have told the Moorston vampires when we were there,' Sue said.

'No, I didn't,' Michael said. 'And that takes me to the point. Could I ask for a couple of favours?'

'You can ask. It doesn't mean you'll get!' Our Doris said haughtily.

'My brother Stephen is there any chance that he could be spared?' Michael asked.

'No chance,' Darren said.

'No. He killed Shaun. He's killed loads of people,' Danny said.

'He has definitely consumed human flesh. Sorry Michael,' Wee Renee said.

'Ah, ok. And for the first time in a long time I have a ladylove, but again she is a vampire. What about her?' Michael asked.

'Who is she?' Bob asked surprisingly.

'Diane from Band,' Michael said.

'Definitely not,' Carl said. 'She was right evil to Gary and me when we were imprisoned up at the school. I remember, and another thing I have been told by someone that she ate their next-door neighbour, so no. I think she's wrong 'un.'

Tony sniggered about the thought of Diane from Band and Michael getting it together. They were as different as chalk and cheese.

'Right, well as long as I'm safe that's all that matters. I knew it was a long shot asking for two of the vampires to be saved but if you don't ask you don't get. I'd better enjoy Diane while it lasts then,' Michael said. 'and then think about moving on.'

'Sounds like you are madly in love,' Our Doris said sarcastically.

'I have to take what I can get in these current conditions,' Michael said. 'The truth is, it's been good enough for me. It's a pity I didn't start this relationship off when she was still alive.'

'I don't think she would have given you a second glance when she was alive Michael. Let's be honest,' Liz said. Michael ignored that comment.

'Is her nose still split into two?' Wee Renee asked.

'Yes, it's not knitted together at all. It's still got the bulldog clips on it,' Michael admitted. They all burst out laughing including Michael, which was very strange. Beverly thought she had never been in such a surreal meeting in all her life.

'I'll get off then before they wake up,' Michael said. 'I'll be in contact don't worry and don't ever think I'm against you, I am just spying for you now against him, *right*?' Michael said, emphasising the last word

No-one replied to him, and he started to walk down the steel steps. He paused for a second, observing all the people on the ground floor of the mill. Gary came behind him.

'What's going on?' Gary asked.

'Who's that, the one in the penguin Christmas jumper?' Michael asked.

'I don't know her name,' Gary said. 'It's Mrs Shuttleworth's daughter-in-law. She's from Melden. Do you know her?' Gary asked.

'No but I'd like to,' Michael said.

'For your information, she's named Helen,' Beverly said to Michael.

'Oh Helen, that's a nice name,' Michael said, rubbing his chin. Our Doris looked shocked that Michael had already moved on in his head. He was lining the next one up.

Michael walked to the door of the mill. He turned back to the others before he opened it.

'I am off. Cheerio everyone!' He shouted and stepped out into the cold. As he walked along the path, he noticed how wet his feet were getting. The snow was deflating too. It was a thinner sheet on the ground now. He could hear the water running off into small rivers at the side. This all would be gone very soon. Everything.

13 Fly

As soon as Norman awoke, and it was dark enough to go outside, he took the keys to the snowmobile usually reserved for Keith. He stood beside it, looking down at the village of Friarmere. Norman really didn't feel like doing anything tonight, but this had to be done. It would probably stop a lot of messing around in the future. He was not his sister, and these silly girls had to realise that they were dealing with a strong, intelligent vampire.

He drove the snowmobile down to the School, parking it right in front of the main doors. Stephen was just setting off for the Village. He told The Master that he knew where Vincent was, so was going to the Village.

Norman found Keith in the school hall sitting miserably, while the children ran around him, screeching. Christine had said she had had enough tonight and had stormed out. If he didn't look after them, they could run amok, she didn't give a monkey's uncle. So, Keith reluctantly had found he was on duty. The Master had other ideas.

'I need you tonight Keith. You are on an errand with me,' Norman said.

'What about looking after these kids?' Keith asked. 'They'll get out.'

'Who's in the building?' Norman asked.

'Diane is about somewhere, but I think she's going out with Michael later. And Lynn will be on her way soon, I think. She usually turns up every night in the hope that Band is back on,' Keith replied.

'Diane!' The Master shouted, as loud as he could. Diane was in the staffroom with Michael, who he did not know was there. She came rushing out into the school hall. Michael followed slightly behind her wondering what all the fuss was about.

'Yes, Master?' Diane asked. Michael stood just outside the School hall listening to what was going on.

'I need you to look after the vampire children tonight or at least until Lynn arrives,' The Master said. 'I am going over to Moorston to set the cat amongst the pigeons.'

'Sounds interesting,' Diane said.

'I'm just going to put down a lame dog. The act alas, will not be interesting. I probably would have had more fun swatting a fly, but the resulting chaos will be fun. This act will guarantee that I get my message across to those two Moorston bitches, who are imagining themselves to be Mistresses,' Norman said.

Michael listened to this in the foyer. He didn't know what it meant, or who he was talking about, but it sounded important. He was sure that someone else would know who the lame dog was. He rolled the balls of his feet as he walked and disappeared back into the School staff room again.

Norman exited with Keith behind him. They immediately got onto the snowmobile, and The Master started it up. Diane rushed quickly to the school staff room.

'No date tonight Michael,' Diane said. 'I have to look after the vampire kids, and it's no use asking you to help me, as you are like catnip to them.' Michael gulped at the thought.

'No, I'll make myself scarce,' Michael said.

'Wait around if you like. You're safe in here. If Lynn turns up, we'll tell her The Master said she had to do it. Then we can enjoy the rest of the night,' Diane asked hopefully.

'No, you enjoy your babysitting duties. I might see you later if it's safe. Them lot in there are frothed up tonight. They will be taking nips out of me the first chance they get,' he said.

Michael waited until he could hear the snowmobile's engine distant in the centre of Friarmere, and then as fast as he could, he walked up to The Grange to tell his tale.

When he got there, he was out of breath again and quite hot. It had proved hard going up to The Grange, as now the thick snow was deep slush. Michael kept slipping on the slime underneath, and as the hill was so steep, he had ended up on his backside six times. Penelope was inside with Stuart and Marcel. They were having a mini conspirator meeting which Michael was not shocked about, after Penelope's comments earlier. Now he knew who the secret defector was.

'Listen something is afoot,' he said to Penelope.

'What do you mean?' Penelope asked.

'I'll just give you this message that The Master just told Keith. He said that there is a lame dog that has to be put down in Moorston and it will piss off the two Moorston Mistresses,' Michael said gasping.

Penelope immediately knew what this meant. Marcel, trying to help but failing, had given away that Sheila was there, alone and unprotected. The lame dog could be no-one else, and certainly, it would piss them off. Sheila was Penelope's vampire sister too, and although this was Marcel's fault, she had to fix it.

'It's Sheila, Jackie's disabled mother, Michael. We couldn't bring her, and she is there still. Marcel let it slip yesterday. Stuart, can you take me over to Moorston? Can we see if we can intercept them? Stop them from harming Sheila?' Penelope asked.

'Yes,' Stuart said. Marcel now sat with his head in his hands. He couldn't save Len, and now he had put Sheila to death with his big mouth.

'Marcel go and find Angela and Jackie,' Penelope said. 'Tell them what Norman is going to do.' Marcel perked up. Maybe he could save her.

'Do you know where they are? The Mistresses, I mean?' Marcel said to Michael.

'Why should I?' Michael said. 'I know where the humans are, but I'm not about to tell you. I have no idea if the Moorston vampires are there as well. I'll go and try and find them myself. You go and look everywhere else that I don't!'

Penelope got on the snowmobile, and Stuart started to drive off as fast as possible in the slimy slush, to rescue Jackie's mother.

Stephen didn't know why he hadn't thought of it before. Vincent must be in the Civic Hall. Probably having the time of his life in a feeding frenzy. He wished he'd have thought of feeding there again. They had the week after the Battle, lots of them. After that, it had become boring, and they started to hunt again for the sport of it. And the Civic Hall had just become forgotten.

When he opened the door, such a delicious smell hit him. These doors were really keeping it in. This was meat, well hung, sweet and so ready to come off the bone. His mouth watered.

He entered the Main Hall. Looking amongst the bodies initially, he couldn't see Vincent. He could be lying in a feeding stupor on the floor or hiding in case he was one of those vampire burners.

'Vincent! It's Stephen, Are you here mate?' Stephen shouted.

His voice echoed back. Vincent wasn't here, he could tell. He bent over and plucked a juicy arm off a young redheaded lady.

'Mmm … … good eating,' Stephen said out loud. He left the Civic Hall, the door now left wide open.

Keith and Norman looked down onto the wasteland that was Moorston village. They didn't know where to start. Marcel had not told him where Sheila was, and Norman thought it would be a dead giveaway if he had asked.

Even from here, they could smell the reek of rotting vampires and Anne's hybrids very strongly. Sheila would not be easy to find amongst all this, besides that vampires had been living here for several weeks and so the air was thick with their scent.

When they got into the Village, they drove past the central fighting area outside Moorston Church. Norman knew she would not be in the Bandroom, that had windows everywhere. No, it would be somewhere comfortable and dark.

He really did not know where to start, but if she was the only thing living here she was bound to give herself away at some point and they had all night. From what he had heard, she wouldn't be out hunting. He either had to see her through a window or hear her. That was the most likely.

The problem was compounded by the sheer amount of spirits that roamed throughout the village. They looked at Norman sadly. He did not show up to them as a bright light, and neither did his companion. The mournful spirits knew that no good would come from these two and they would not be showing them the way to where the laughter came from several times a night. Norman watched them too. Most of them he could see, there were just a few that were too faint to make out, either by choice or by design.

When they were doing their second lap around the Village, they started to hear another snowmobile engine. Norman angrily whirled his head towards Keith. He knew he owned the only other snowmobile. This was bound to be trouble on its way to the pair of them.

The vampire child was running across the roof, its friends were playing near the Church. He was after a little scrap of food. One of those things that hid under the bushes. He couldn't remember their real names, but they were usually near the river. They had fat grey hairy bodies and bristly pink tails. He thought they were named *lats*, but somehow that was wrong, he knew that. Lats was good enough for him, and it was good enough to call them too. He would catch one of those squeakers tonight.

All at once he caught a rich smell. Oh ... that smell was so wonderful. Where was it coming from? He skittered along the roofs, as the smell got stronger.

Finally, he found the source. A big building. This door had not been open before. The food was in there. Lots and lots of it. He thought he should fetch his friends. No – there might only be enough for him. He would see and bring them later after he had had his fill.

Michael quickly made his way to the mill. He did not come across a soul, living or dead, as he travelled down the tree-lined path. He was terrified that at some point a vampire child would come and get him, but he hoped that the sheer amount of people about tonight he would get a bit of a rescue. Michael was due some luck.

Marcel ran through the streets of Friarmere. The High Street was empty. Above him on the roof of the bank, Adam watched him. He did not know who Marcel was after. Adam knew exactly where all four groups were, but he wasn't about to tell Marcel, who had unknown objectives. It was only a couple of nights ago that he had seen him running around with The Master and the *fit vampire*.

Michael banged on the door of the mill. Once it was dark, they didn't open the door even for a human. Michael realised that they would think it was a trick. 'Hello! It's Michael!' he shouted. 'I need to speak to you urgently!' Beryl was inside along with Brenda and some of the others. Their eyes burned, glaring at each other. This was worrying. Were they under attack. And with hardly anyone here to help. Their breath quickened. What should they do?

'What do you want?' Brenda asked

'I need to find the two Moorston Mistresses,' Michael shouted.

'Why do you want them?' Beryl asked

'Because Norman has gone over to Moorston on the snowmobile to kill Jackie's mother. I didn't know what else to do, only come here,' Michael said desperately.

He heard lots of chatter behind the door that he could not decipher.

'They are out, and we don't know where they are. They are in four massive groups,' Beryl said. 'They didn't have a plan, just roaming. Honestly, I don't know what to tell you. I'm sorry.'

'Right,' Michael said. 'Well if they come back here before I find them, give them the message please.'

'I will,' Beryl said, and Michael turned on his heel and quickly began to retrace his steps back along the donkey path, still watching the trees and listening for any signs of the vampire kids.

In Moorston, Norman had decided to stop the snowmobile and wait outside the Bandroom. While he waited, he tried to imagine what was coming his way. He was sure that only one person could be driving it. It was probably Stuart on the front, but when it arrived, he was surprised to see that his girlfriend Penelope was on the back.

Stuart pulled up in front of the other snowmobile. Penelope got off the back and strode straight over.

'What are you doing over here?' Penelope asked. 'Don't make the situation any worse. There has to be a better solution than this.'

'Don't tell me what to do just because you share my bed. It is not for you to order me about, especially in front of two of my children,' Norman retorted.

'One,' said Stuart. 'I don't want to be aligned with you anymore.' He got off the snowmobile and stood beside Penelope. Norman was shocked, to say the least, and so was Keith. He could not believe Stuart's rudeness and idiocy. The Master would make him pay for this in the worst way. Keith could guarantee it.

'Oh, it's like that, is it?' The Master asked.

'It is,' Stuart said.

'Never mind. I'm not bothered whether you are with me or not,' Norman said.

'You made that abundantly clear last night. I am amazed that you have anyone following you know. Perhaps just the soft-brained,' Stuart commented.

Keith glared at him and curled his lip. He wouldn't let Stuart forget that comment. No chance.

'Of course,' Stuart said. 'What do you care? We are all useless according to you.'

'Shut up. Are you going to tell me where this bitch is?' Norman asked.

'Over my dead body,' Penelope said. 'She is another Moorston vampire like me, and I will not betray her,' Penelope said.

'Do not think because we are lovers that I will let you rule me,' Norman said.

'Let's pretend we never were then. Suits me,' Penelope said.

Norman went for Penelope. She was fast and just managed to get out of the way of his grasp. He was so angry and was acting a little erratically. Stuart was sure Norman was losing it. The Master was going to continue his attack, there was no doubt.

Stuart had brought a metal bar over from Friarmere, and he bent over and took this now from the side of the snowmobile. He stood in front of Penelope to protect her.

'Go back,' Stuart said. 'We aren't going to let you do this tonight.' Keith started to move now and walked slowly behind Penelope and Stuart. Penelope turned towards him, and Stuart faced Norman. Two against two. Stuart was the only one with a weapon, although Penelope did have her fingernails.

'You know you cannot fight me, Stuart. You haven't had one fight yet, have you? All in all, you are a bit of a wet lettuce really,' The Master said.

'Come on then. I'll show you just how wet I am,' Stuart said, and they began to fight.

Norman lunged forward and Stuart beat him back with the metal bar, with all his vampire strength. Penelope still stood with her back against Stuart facing Keith. He was only waiting for a lapse in her concentration before he struck.

Penelope wanted to help Stuart, but she knew that that would probably be the end for both of them. With her back to him, she could see nothing. Penelope planned to change that.

She moved backwards in the hope of getting to the side of Stuart and then being able to see the both of them. Penelope didn't really want to harm Norman, she did actually love him, but she was made a Moorston vampire, and nothing could change that.

It didn't take long before Norman managed to grab hold of Stuart. The Master's teeth were bared. He forcefully took the bar away from Stuart, throwing it away and out of use.

'Stupid child,' The Master hissed. With his great strength, it toppled end over end and shot through the window of the Bandroom.

'Just me and you now, let's see how that plays out,' The Master said.

With his supernatural speed, he unfairly sprung toward Stuart. Norman was right, he had not fought once. Penelope would not let Keith join in the fight but even one on one, she knew the way this would end up. Now Penelope had to find a way out for herself. When it got hairy, she decided she would make a run for it. It has been a mistake to not bring more to help.

The Master picked Stuart up easily with his two arms and brought him back down over the snowmobile. Keith watched him break his back, the sound was quite clear in the ghostly Moorston air. Norman leapt in the air and jumped on top of Stuart's broken body, right in the centre. With what looked like a small karate kick he split Stuart into two halves. It was quite awesome to see. Keith swung around to deal with Penelope, but she was gone.

Marcel who could not find Jackie or Angela anywhere. No-one whatsoever was on the streets, when Marcel tried to find help. No human or vampire was visible anywhere on Friarmere High Street.

Marcel had begun to run to Moorston himself. He would see what was going on there. Where Norman and Keith were – then he would decide how he could help Sheila. He felt that all this was firmly on his shoulders.

When he got to the top of the hill, he could see the lights of the two snowmobiles outside the Bandroom. From where he stood, with his keen vampire eyesight and knowledge of Moorston village, he could see two figures there. He should be able to see four. Norman, Keith, Penelope and Stuart but he could only see two. He could also not see a small old lady who was unable to stand. No, Sheila was not there.

Out of the two, he knew that neither of them was Penelope, as they did not have a red sweater on. One seemed to be talking to the other, and they pointed at the snowmobile and knocked something off either side of it.

It looked like one was getting on one snowmobile, and one was getting on the other. Marcel knew where Sheila stayed, and they were nowhere near her. They had been intercepted by the other snowmobile. Penelope was not there, which two of the three male vampires had survived?

Marcel ran back down into Friarmere. Soon they would be on their way back, but they had to go up and down. His path was all down bank. Plus, he would bet, that he could match the snowmobile in a race anyway, especially now it wouldn't exactly glide over what remained of the snow.

He was soon back in the centre of Friarmere. Marcel did not know what to do. He pulled at his hair and stamped his feet. Out of frustration, he screamed into the High Street.

'Angela, Jackie, where are you? I need to find you it's Marcel!'

At this point, Adam decided that this vampire looked desperate and in need of help. Now he knew exactly what he wanted, maybe he could help. He stood on the roof of the Bank. The bellowing echoed through the empty High Street, and even though they all hid in their various places and had heard a voice, they could not tell what was being said.

'She's in the Coffee Shop,' Adam said, making sure he caught Marcel's eye and pointed in a westwards direction. Marcel did not know where the Coffee Shop was, but he ran in the direction of Adam's finger.

'Angela!' Marcel shouted. 'Jackie!' Now that Marcel was much closer to them, they heard their names and rushed out. They both thundered out of the Coffee Shop entrance towards him.

'Now is the time to kill him,' Marcel said. 'He's on his way back from Moorston. He went over there to kill Sheila. Penelope and Stuart went over to stop him, but I think something has happened to them. Get ready. There's only one way they can come back on those snowmobiles.' Jackie was furious and immediately wanted to run over to her mother to check on her.

'Oh my God,' Jackie said. 'I bet she's dead. My poor old Mum couldn't defend herself. What a coward he is. Just like his sister. If he's not turning kids, he's killing the disabled.' Jackie immediately grabbed Angela, he eyes large and terrified. Her bottom lip began to tremble.

'No, listen Jackie. I looked over to Moorston. I ran up to the tops. They were nowhere near where she is. They were outside the Bandroom, Jackie. She's safe. Penelope got to them before they found your Mum. I am sure of it,' Marcel said.

Lynn had taken over the babysitting duties. Diane seemed desperate and was already at her wit's end. She had sympathy with Christine, who had borne the brunt for a whole day.

Lynn relished the chance of looking after the children. She missed her grandchildren, who were far away in Australia, luckily. Lynn was quite shocked but pleased that she still had a slight maternal feeling towards younglings. She thought all her human feelings had gone, but tonight had discovered this about herself. Maybe her humanity was coming back. That could be a good or a bad thing.

Michael was just on his way back up to the school from the mill, as he did not want to be missed for too long. He had decided that he was too tired to go back up to The Grange tonight. Michael would chance going into the staff room, kip on the sofa for a few hours. It did have a lock on the door after all. He only had to make it through the entrance hall, and he would be out of those kids clutches.

Michael would wait it out there. At some point, Diane should finish looking after them. They tended to fall asleep earlier than the adult vampires. Then they might squeeze in a little date, which was what he wanted to do. He felt good about himself today. Michael had earned a date and a few glasses of uninfected wine. After all, he had passed on the message to Penelope, then the message to the mill. That was two good deeds for the day.

Just as he was coming up to the School, Diane was coming out.

'Hello, where have you been?' Diane asked.

'Just keeping out of the way, you know. I've been on a lovely walk exploring. Can you feel the warmth, the difference in temperature? The weather's definitely changing,' Michael said.

'I can,' Diane said. 'Although what that'll mean to us, I don't know.'

'These tend to work themselves out. I wouldn't worry beautiful,' Michael said.

'Shall we have a walk down into the village?' Diane asked.

'I've just come from there, I'm knackered,' Michael commented.

'Well, I don't want to go back in the School. I've been stuck in there since you went, on my own with those kids. Boisterous isn't the word,' she said.

'Let's walk somewhere else then. Or go in a house. I think with all of what's going on, with the vigilantes and all that, I think we should keep well clear,' Michael said. 'We might find a king-size bed. Let's do it while we can.'

'There will be plenty of nights for that. No, I want to see what's going on with The Master. I'm going down anyway even if you don't. He should be coming over from Moorston soon. Killing some lame dog wouldn't take that long, would it? Moorston is not that far away.'

Why didn't she do as he said? He was trying to save her. Michael was trying to hide her from them.

'I don't think you should Diane,' Michael said.

'Well I am,' she said and just walked off down the road, leaving Michael behind her. He reluctantly began to follow.

'Wait up then, bossy boots,' Michael said. He supposed he would have to watch out for her. She was walking right into a hornet's nest.

14 Cankles

Christine was going nowhere near the School. She didn't want anyone else catching up with her and telling her that she had to go on babysitting duties again. She felt so strongly about it that she had decided that tonight she would be stopping at her own house up near The Grange so that when she woke in the morning, she would not immediately be asked to look after them. Christine had had enough of that job. She had done the right thing when she was alive – not having kids.

She had been roaming around the estate up near the tops but had decided to go into the Village to see what she could find to eat. Christine hadn't noticed any likely prospects earlier in those houses. It was a ghost town up there. Of course, it was near The Grange and her house, so they had taken most of the local food ages ago. All the remaining people must be lower down, nearer to their own food source in fact.

When she got closer to the village, but still above, she was shocked to see a horde of people and even vampires walking quite openly down the High Street in the centre of Friarmere, through a gap in the houses.

Christine had never seen the likes of it in all her days and certainly since she had become a vampire. They looked very dangerous. Not to mention it was very bold of them. Hadn't they learned where their place was on the food chain yet?

What did this mean? This wasn't looking good for her. It wasn't looking good for The Master either. She had better make her way up to The Grange to inform him of what was going on locally before everyone else got there. All this mob needed was a torch and pitchforks!

Adam and now, Sarah stood on the roofs of Friarmere High Street. They saw Christine on her way down. Then watched her turn back and start walking quickly up to The Grange.

Unfortunately for Christine, her sequinned beret twinkled quite brightly in the streetlights, as she tried to make her way up. Her plump body did not get away very quickly in the slushy snow, and that sequinned beret was like a flashing light bulb.

She had no idea that she had been spotted – the people were far away, so she wasn't trying to be discreet. Instead, she waved her hands around in panic, which made her even more visible.

Sarah did not know where she was going, but she could guess. It could only be one of two places. Also, the fact that she had spied them and could tell someone else meant that she was dangerous. She jumped down from the roof and immediately ran over to Angela and Jackie.

'There is a vampire that has just spotted us on the streets. She is going up to The Grange, I think,' Sarah said. 'I don't know exactly, but she is travelling in an uphill trajectory. You can't miss her, she's got a shiny hat on. '

'Thank you,' Angela said. Sarah turned away to get back on the roof but was stopped in her tracks by some of the humans. She told Our Doris and Pat initially. When she looked back, Angela and Jackie had disappeared up the street, off to find Christine.

Penelope knew Moorston well, she had been here a long time and knew every nook and cranny. She knew where to get so that Keith and Norman could not find her. It wasn't the nicest place, but she would hide there until they left.

It seemed a long time. Penelope kept hearing the snowmobile sounds as they weaved in and out through the streets of Moorston, looking for her. They wouldn't find her here. All that she hoped at this point was that Sheila didn't make a noise and give herself away after Stuart had sacrificed himself so bravely for her. She was the opposite end of Moorston to Sheila, but the snowmobiles never seemed to get that far. Plus, the noise of them both might block out Sheila's laughing, if she started.

After about thirty minutes, it sounded like together, the snowmobiles were going up the hill towards Friarmere. They were finding it hard going. The snowmobiles were only just getting through the snow. They made slow chugging noise, more like tractors than bikes. At this rate, if they had another good day of thaw, they would be totally useless tomorrow, and Sheila would be safe.

What this also meant that was it was another day closer to cars entering the villages and normality. Quite frankly Penelope couldn't wait for that moment.

She remained there another few minutes hoping that Marcel had warned Jackie and Angela. When she was confident that they were on their way back and hardly any more noise could be heard from the engines, she turned around continuing her way through her hiding place, the Standedge Tunnel. She would get to the other side roughly the same time as the snowmobiles. Only if she ran.

As her high-heeled shoes echoed through the tunnel, Sheila's laughs began.

When Sarah told the others about the vampire with the shiny hat on her way back up, several of them instantly knew who this was and were happy to help the other two vampires track her down.

'Did she have a fat arse?' Our Doris asked.

'Yes,' Sarah replied immediately.

'Tree trunk legs?' Sue asked.

'Cankles?' Tony asked.

'Yes. Well, I think so,' Sarah replied.

'That's Christine, that's her all right,' Pat said. 'She still feels she has an axe to grind with us because we pulled off her scalp.'

'How very enterprising,' said Helen Shuttleworth.

'Shall we block her from coming back down here if she decides to, she could double back? Then she can't get in on the fight,' Rick asked.

'That's a good idea,' Sarah said to Rick. '*Can you still see her*?' She shouted up to Adam.

'Yes, she is halfway up. I think she's turned into the estate. She must know that they are after her,' Adam shouted.

'You need to try and block her off some way so that she can't get to any known nests. We don't want her giving the game away to another group of vampires,' Sarah said.

Without another word, Terry, Wee Renee, Pat, Our Doris, Helen Shuttleworth, Rick, Agnes and Josh all began to move as quickly as they could towards the estate that Adam had said she was on her way to.

'She is on Wellmeadow!' Adam shouted after them.

There was only one way on or off Wellmeadow, as it was a long curve that ran alongside Church Road, with the entrance and exits near the top and bottom of it. The human party split into two. They could easily stand and make sure that Christine could not escape if she was on Wellmeadow. Sue watched them go off. She lived on that street.

'I hope she isn't after more of my sequined berets,' Sue said, her lips pulled into a tight white line.

'Trust you!' Tony said.

Christine was on her way up to the School, she had decided to check there first as The Master had said that he was going to be more hands-on and that usually meant that he was going to be at the School, addressing the others or forming a Band together. She would check here first instead of making her way right up to The Grange, to only come back down and find him at the School. She had no idea that she had been spotted. The quicker she found The Master, the quicker she could find something to eat, and she was starving.

When she was turning on the road to the School, she heard a shout from behind her. She couldn't quite hear what the words were, because she was rushing and not listening. Plus, the sequinned beret was pulled right over her ears, to fully cover the cling-filmed scalp underneath.

'Hey you, fat bitch!' Jackie shouted again. Christine turned around to see two young vampire girls. She thought they were a couple of teenagers and had never seen them before. Christine had no idea what she was dealing with.

No-one had advised her of the new Moorston Mistresses. Not that they were here and not that they were only teenagers.

'Can we have a word? Can you help us? We are lost and don't know what to do,' Angela asked, smiling sweetly at her. Now they were closer and facing her, she could hear them properly.

Christine wondered what they wanted with her. They were probably looking for The Master. *Probably two fresh ones*, she thought. They needed someone to show them the ropes. Either The Master, or an older lady that could take them in, and teach them a few things. She would volunteer, she decided. If Christine was looking after these two, she couldn't be asked to look after the vampire kids as well. What a godsend these two would be. She would fully embrace them into the fold.

Christine realised that they were very inexperienced. One even wore a little backpack. That would hamper her when she was fighting. Maybe she had not had a fight yet. Christine didn't know, but these girls looked as green as cabbage.

She walked towards the two of them, and sure enough, they moved up to her slowly, wide-eyed. They were clueless and scared, she could tell.

'You can come to me dears, it's safe. What are your names?' Christine asked.

'Abigail,' Angela said. Jackie giggled.

'That's nice, What yours?' Christine asked Jackie.

Jackie glanced over to Angela who had decided not to go under her real name, just in case this fat vampire had heard of them.

'Julie,' Jackie said.

'Well I am Chrissy,' she said. 'It's a good job you found me, Abigail and Julie. There is danger in the centre of the Village.'

'We don't know what to do,' Jackie said.

'Can you show us where The Master is please?' Angela asked.

'I'm one of The Master's Lieutenants. A very important lady. We'll go and check the School first,' Christine said kindly.

'Good idea,' Angela said. They got onto the School grounds and started to walk across the expanse of the School fields. Jackie ran just in front of Christine, grabbing both of her fat hands.

'Shall we play in the snow?' Jackie asked.

'I'm too old for that Julie,' Christine said to her. 'And I've been playing with some little vampires. So, I'm rather tired.'

She looked around to see where the other girl was. The brunette one. She was running towards the pair of them and looked like she was going to jump on her. *These are a right pair,* Christine thought. *They are like two little ones. I've walked out of looking after a lot of kids and come across two more. I'll dump these pair in the school, offload them, and they can play with that lot. I'm not going getting up to this lark*, Christine thought. *Kids of any age can look after themselves as far as I'm concerned.*

Angela was now on her back.

'No piggybacks!' Christine shouted.

Jackie glanced around Christine's head a little to look at Angela.

'Are you ready now Angela?' Jackie asked.

'Who?' Christine said, thinking that there must be a third one named Angela somewhere, but the thought had not finished running through her vampire head before the side of her neck got ripped out.

As Angela did this, Jackie yanked forward, pulling both the arms off Christine. Christine's insides quickly leaked out onto the ground of the school.

'That's one of Norman's family down,' Jackie said.

'Yes good. She was easy-pickings. We can't leave her here, she might give the game away,' Angela said.

'That's right,' Jackie said.

'What shall we do Jacks?' Angela asked.

'I know,' Jackie said. She ran over to the school, considering what a low roof it had. She looked at the wall with the plant pots at the side of it. 'Let's get all of it on the roof.'

It was hard getting Christine up on the roof as it was still quite a bit further than these two teenagers could reach and Christine was rather fat, but they didn't let that get in their way.

Christine came apart a few times after pulling her a little and ended up in five pieces. Angela managed to throw the two arms and head up there alone, the head bouncing and rolling quite a way. It's sequinned beret snagging on an air vent, revealing Christine's papier-mâché scalp.

The two girls had to drag up the top part of the torso and the bottom, which also included Christine's legs.

'She'll do there,' Angela said.

'There is a massive trail of black blood from where we killed her up to the roof. Bit of a giveaway really,' Jackie said.

'It can't be helped,' Angela said. 'All this will be over soon; besides that, it is at the side of the school. Anyone coming in and out of the Main Entrance won't be able to see.'

The two young vampires made their way out from the School and onto the road. They didn't know they had many humans waiting for them. Of course, they had seen no sign of Christine coming back out onto either end of Wellmeadow and onto Church Road, so had imagined that Angela and Jackie had in fact caught up with her at the school.

'Let's go back down before Norman gets here,' Angela said to the humans, without explanation. They walked back down to the village knowing only that Christine would be telling no tales.

'Did you kill her?' Sue asked when they arrived. 'That was one of my sequined hats that she had stolen.'

'Do you want it back? Because I can get it later if you want. She's on the roof of the School now,' Angela asked quite genuinely.

'No, you're all right on that one. You needn't bother,' Sue said. 'I'll buy another one in that colour.' Angela shrugged.

'Let's get into position,' Angela said.

15 Bait

'Okay, so it looks like it is Keith and Norman riding the two snowmobiles, on their way over from Moorston. That's what I think anyway,' Marcel said.

'I was snooping around the other day,' Wee Renee said. 'I have seen the way they go over to Moorston. They mainly use the roads and just pass up this side of the hill, where they blocked it off at the viaduct. Then they come through the centre of the Village, it was quite clear. We stay on the main road – somewhere between the viaduct and Church Road.'

'I see two problems with that plan of staying here, chucks,' Pat said. 'The first is that they are going to spot us from a mile off and the second is ... ...'

'How do we get them off the snowmobiles?' Gary interjected.

'Exactly,' Pat said.

'Aye, that is a problem,' Wee Renee said. 'I never thought of that. They can just scoot off when they are confronted.'

'It's obvious, isn't it' Terry offered. 'Someone has to lie down and be the bait. We will hide at the sides and spring out when they get off the snowmobiles to bite them! Simples!'

'Oh hell,' Sally said. 'Who'd want to do that?' Everyone looked at each other and then someone who felt that they have not played as much of a part as they should and had been a bit of a hindrance, offered themselves up.

'I will,' said Lauren volunteering.

'You aren't. Forget that,' said Rick.'

'Listen, think about it. It must be someone they probably haven't met in a fight. They might suspect that we will try and trick them because they have had the *heads up* that we are all back and have killed Anne. They haven't seen me with you lot, but *I know* he has seen me in the pub night after night so knows that I am from Friarmere. I've seen him looking through the windows, not as I let on. He might suspect I have been hiding all along and I've just wandered out for some reason, perhaps caught outside and locked out. I think I am the ideal person,' Lauren said.

No-one could argue with Laurens reasoning. Even Rick had to admit, she was the perfect candidate.

'What assurances are there against you getting bitten by him. Who can guarantee that?' Rick asked. 'You know how fast they are. I want her to have a weapon somewhere, and I'm checking that her brass neck is on safe, right.'

'Is everyone else happy with that. I am,' Lauren said.

They still could not hear the snowmobiles on their way back. Lauren laid a large scarf underneath her, so her face and the rest of her body were not touching the snow, which was fast becoming wet slush. It quickly soaked through but was better than nothing. Everyone else found places close by where they could hide in the shadows and rush out. Some of them had to go quite a way away as there were so many people wanting to join in with the battle and help. They situated themselves behind, in front and at the side of where Lauren lay, in the middle of the road.

Wee Renee told them, although they could not hear the snowmobiles yet, maybe the two vampires would see them from a distance against the bleakness of the snowy landscape. They were to get into position but could still talk until they heard them approach. Soon everyone was out of sight, and although Lauren could hear several voices, she felt very alone and scared. Every so often Rick would pipe up to check on her.

'Are you all right, Lauren?' Rick projected a loud whisper towards her.

'Yes,' Lauren answered simply. She wasn't.

Then a thought crossed her mind. What if the two vampires were talking and didn't see her. Lost in their conversation they might accidentally run over her. She hoped that someone else had thought of this too, and if the engines weren't slowing down, everyone would rush out and attack the vampires anyway.

As she lay there, she began to shiver. Whether this was because of the cold or fear, she did not know, but probably a mixture of both. She wondered why she had ever opened her mouth. Maybe afterwards everything would be okay, and she would feel brave and that all this was worth it. She could feel equal to the others for once, a hero. But for the moment she felt like a foolish young woman.

Adam and Sarah lay flat on the roofs right at either side of Lauren, above her. At her side Rick and Joe were taking the biggest chance, they were barely concealed in a low leafless clump of bushes, but they were the closest to Lauren and only about ten feet away. After a while, the chatter seemed to die down, and people just waited.

The gravity of the situation was upon them. For the Friarmere Band, they had needed to do this from the very beginning. It was the most important to them. But it was also the final Morgan on their list.

Kathy thought that maybe Wee Renee had got it wrong when they still didn't come. Perhaps there was another way up to The Grange on a snowmobile, and they would lose their chance tonight to corner Norman. Just as she was about to voice this, they heard the noise in the distance.

It had taken Norman and Keith a lot longer to get over here, because of the rapid thawing of the snow. The snowmobiles did not glide across it like they had before. They moved sluggishly on the wet patches, and there were even areas where there was no snow. Both had to weave around these, navigating an arduous path. There was no way that the vehicles could get up to full speed and they felt sluggish and heavy. It was still far more comfortable and quicker than walking, however.

Wee Renee had a quick, but essential thought just before the two snowmobiles got into the centre of Friarmere.

'Don't spill a lot of Normans blood,' she shouted. 'I need it.'

'Now you tell us,' Nigel shouted. 'Bloody hell.'

'You could have told us that one before,' Jackie shouted from a doorway, Angela beside her. 'We were planning to tear him limb from limb!'

'I was looking forward to biting his throat out. Wee Renee, you are a right killjoy,' Angela said.

'Sorry, everyone. That blood is spoken for,' Wee Renee reiterated.

Everyone drew back to their hiding places, and Lauren closed her eyes, hoping for the best. She hoped her blood would be classed as even more precious than his, but in the whole scheme of things she thought it probably wasn't.

She had wanted to lie facing away from them, but Our Doris had said that there was no point putting someone there who was obviously recognisable as a villager if they could not see their face.

Again, this was true. As she thought her eyes might give her away, she had arranged some of her long hair across them in case she twitched or blinked when they came to her. She did not know whether she was to pretend to be dead or alive or just passed out. She knew now she should have asked. At this late stage, she just lay and waited for the others to do their thing.

Luckily for Lauren, the two vampires noticed the body lying in the road when they were some way away. They slowed up their snowmobile's as they got closer, finally stopping about ten feet away from Lauren's body. Norman had not seen a fresh human body lying in the street like this since he had come to Friarmere. This was very interesting. Their engines were still on, and Norman decided he wouldn't be the one to see what the problem was, that was what he had minions for.

'Go to her,' Norman said to Keith who got off warily and walked over to Lauren's body. From where he was, he could tell that she was alive and warm but little else. He knew that The Master would want her and might even not give him any. The Master might even make her a replacement for Penelope.

'It's the barmaid from the Friarmere Arms,' Keith said.

'What is wrong with her?' Norman asked.

Keith thought that the best way of checking a human's status was by giving them a little nip. But as The Master was currently furious after his betrayal by Stuart and Penelope and also had not entirely got over Keith's disobedience, he had better try another way.

As his arm reached forward to touch her, it seemed to bring forth a lot of noise from around the sides of them, which was unusual. As he looked up, he saw that many people were coming out from bushes, bus shelters, doorways and from behind cars. They stepped over the dry-stone walls, came down from the roofs and out of empty shops. Like rats, they came out of every hole towards him.

Keith stood up and watched this, which was enough distraction for Lauren to start skittering away backwards from the two vampires.

Keith had a solid twenty people around the front of him, but the majority seemed to have gone to try to get around Norman. He was the one who was still sitting on his snowmobile, chugging loudly and could move off at any moment.

Keith's shoulders dropped, they were ridiculously outnumbered. There was no way even with the combined strength of himself and The Master that they could get out of this one. He just hoped that there was a local party of their own vampires, out on the hunt. After all, this was *their* Village, they should come and help them. Pushing through the crowd, Keith saw three unexpected assailants - Mark, Ernie and Maurice. His mouth dropped open. Well, they really had pulled the wool over his eyes. He felt a right mug.

'Oh fuck,' Keith said.

Norman watched all this as if in a daze. He could not believe this was happening. *How totally unexpected this was. When you are just coming home from a fun jaunt, you don't expect a whole army to come and trap you in your own village.*

Never mind he was still on this snowmobile, and before the others got to him, he would get away. He put it in full throttle and began to skate on the slushy snow underneath. Startled by his sudden attempt at escape, several people ran towards him especially Angela, Jackie and the Moorston vampires. He wasn't going to get away, but this snowmobile was dangerous with so many people around. Especially as they crowded in to stop him.

The vehicle still skidded this way and that, trying to find traction in the slush. They could smell it was getting hot, something was not able to cope with this slush and was burning out. Just as it finally got moving a hand was slapped on his wrist, which firmly held it. Norman turned to the right to see Angela's hand there, and another immensely firm grip came down on his other arm, as Jackie grabbed him. They both pulled backwards, and he was jerked off the snowmobile. It reared upwards on its last rev from Norman's hands, as he had been pulled back. The Master ended up on his rear in the snow. His female captors held his wrists fast. The snowmobile moved upwards and forwards, landing dramatically.

16 Slush

The crowd scattered out at the back as well as at the front. The snowmobile had sprung forward, rearing its front end up.

'Watch it!' Freddie shouted. Only one figure didn't move, and the great heavy machine landed directly on top of Keith. It went up the left side of his body with its last bit of momentum finally resting heavily on top of Keith's head. As the runners did their last few rotations, it shot minced bits of Keith backwards.

'Death by snowmobile,' Lee said and looked at Miles. Miles chuckled. As bad as it was, it was also something they didn't get to see every day.

Mrs Shuttleworth watched the events, but she seemed detached from events. It felt like she was watching some gory horror movie. She expected Christopher Lee to walk towards them at any minutes

'That was an easy one,' Our Doris said. 'We didn't even have to get our hands dirty.'

'He deserved that,' Father Philip said surprisingly.

The front of the snowmobile was smashed in slightly, and yet it still rested on Keith. From the side, Sarah suddenly saw a movement and knew he wasn't gone.

'He's not dead,' Sarah said running over and starting to kick at the perfect side of Keith, who occasionally jerked and shuddered. His hand clutched to find anything to help him pull himself away from this torture.

'Bollocks to that,' Agnes said. She ran around to the other side of the bike. On this side, Keith's arm was detached, and he could not grab her. Sarah's side was still very dangerous. Keith still did not manage to grab her even though she was only inches away. It seemed that he was in a world of pain and of course he was already blind, the machine had taken off most of his face and was still resting on it.

The snowmobile was a lot higher than usual as it was resting on Keith's body, but Agnes was about five feet eight, athletic and strong. She leant over the seat and revved the engine a few times while she pressed her body on top. With the weight of her body on top of the snowmobile, it seemed to snap a bit on some of Keith's skull as she revved. It proved quite resistant, so she kept pressing down, thrusting her weight down every so often.

Danny who was well over six feet, ran forward and added his weight to the snowmobile next to Agnes, who continued to rev the engine, and after another slight bit of resistance, there was a crack, the runners freed themselves and whipped Keith's head off into a frenzy. It sprayed the contents of Keith's skull thickly out at the back. Andy and Liz, who were trying to help Angela and Jackie contain Norman, got the brunt of it up in the back of their coats.

'Bloody hell Danny,' Andy said. 'Will you watch where you are spraying vampire clots!' Danny laughed, they were covered in tiny bits of vampire. Later Liz would find an ear in her hood.

Keith was most definitely gone now. Danny and Agnes pulled the snowmobile over to the other side of Keith onto the melting snow. He was flat all the way to the chest. The bones had disintegrated successfully after the height of the skull was not there to protect them. Keith only had about two inches of body left up at the top. The snowmobile had left a thin fillet from chest to scalp.

The residue of the vampire started to colour all the melting snow beneath it. It looked like a very unappetising slush puppy. The crowd cheered, and it rang through the streets of Friarmere.

'Shush, shush everyone. Immediately. Be quiet,' Wee Renee said. 'You don't know what that noise will bring.'

'She's right,' Freddie said. 'Remember, until we've got them all, we need to be secret.'

'Yeah, oh shit,' said Beverly.

Halfway up the bank to The Grange they were overheard, indeed. They were overheard by Diane and Michael, on their way down to see if The Master had returned.

'What the hell is that?' Diane asked Michael. He could hear it quite clearly too, but he didn't want the two of them interfering. With that many humans now hunting vampires, he knew it would only be a matter of time before they got discovered. Only disruption or death would befall Diane and Michael if they interfered.

'What? I didn't hear anything,' Michael said.

'It sounded as loud as a football match cheer,' Diane said. 'Don't tell me you didn't hear that Michael.' He didn't know what to say, so said the first thing that came into his head.

'I suffer from a lot of wax you know. And have been unable to use grommets since the invasion,' Michael said. It didn't sound convincing, but that didn't seem the priority in Diane's mind.

'Well clean out your ears another way. I'm telling you something is going on in the Village and we are going to see what it is,' Diane said. She grabbed his coat and started to run, pulling Michael along with her.

'If it's that wild hadn't we better keep out of it. Let's go home and get back up to The Grange, wait for The Master to come in. We can get him to help us investigate along with Marcel and Penelope,' Michael said.

'I want to know what we're dealing with, don't I?' Diane said. 'We will be discreet though, we just need to know what is going on down there Michael. The Master will need details. Who it is and how many, that's all.'

Michael did not have an answer for this. He did not want to give himself away as a spy, so would have to go along with it.

It was obviously the human contingent that was going to take back this Village. They would understand why he was with Diane luckily, he had discussed it with a few of them just that day, so he went along with it. He had no idea how tonight would pan out.

'Come on then Diane, let's have a look. But I don't want either of us in danger,' Michael said. 'Be careful!'

'We won't be in danger, come on, and I'm here to protect you, Michael. It would take a whole army to kill me, I'm a vampire, Diane said, 'don't forget that!'

That was just the problem, Diane, Michael thought. *There was an army.*

They continued to run down to the Village, Michael being pulled along by his coat, sliding every few steps in the slush. He could hear the water trickling loudly into the sewers. Odd bits of grey pavement poked through the white. This snow was on its way out.

After the shouting, Angela had looked at Sarah who instantly knew what she wanted and scrambled back onto the roof. Adam, who had remained on watch, looked even more thoroughly for any vampires after the unexpected outburst of cheering. This would bring one. They were always outside hunting, and this was the loudest noise Friarmere had heard for over a month.

The two vampires looked one way and another, no longer hiding flat on the roofs. Sarah was looking in the direction that Michael and Diane were coming in and saw them first.

'Mistress,' she said. There are two more on their way here from that direction!'

'I think we can manage two, don't you?' Pat said. 'Let them come all the way.'

Sally was armed with a garlic spray, and Kathy had a hairspray and candle lighter. They moved to greet the two new vampires, with Wee Renee and Pat. When they saw the two that were coming, a female vampire with bulldog clips on her nose and the human Michael Thompson been dragged behind, they relaxed. This was going to be a piece of cake.

'It's Michael and Diane,' Sally shouted back to the crowd who still couldn't see them.

'Good old Michael,' Terry said. 'Looks like he has delivered his girlfriend to us.'

'Unlikely I would say, Terry. We probably just scuppered his plans, and she is investigating the noise. We will see,' Our Doris said quietly.

17 Knitting

Angela and Jackie still had Norman in their arms. When he knew it was Diane in the distance, he shouted towards her.

'Run and get help and save yourself!' Norman hollered.

'I will help you, Master,' Diane said who, from where she stood around the corner of Ian's Butcher's Shop, could only see the small group of women approaching her at an angle, so had no fear.

'Fat lot of good she's going to do,' Pat said.

Wee Renee, Sally, Kathy and Pat fully stepped out from the corner towards the two new arrivals. They needed to be quick before she ran. Wee Renee, Pat and Sally grabbed Diane and Kathy held onto the human Michael, who was in effect, playing along with them. The three women pulled the vampire into the High Street.

Diane was completely around the corner now. She had seen all of them and what they were about to do to her own beloved Master. Unfortunately, she could not be released and sound the alarm, to save him, and herself from inevitable destruction.

'Come on love,' Pat said, 'join your boss.' Now Pat poked her along as she walked with her club hammer. Michael put his hands over his face. He had been told that they would not save Diane, but he never imagined that he would have to be there to watch it. This wasn't going to be his best day.

Diane and Michael passed the site of Keith's death first. *What the hell had happened there?* Michael thought. That was a bit of overkill, in his opinion. This was hardcore. Diane knew this was final.

'You are the last of the old Morgan Masters,' Angela said Norman. 'You should have learned respect and responsibility in your command that you enjoyed. You aligned yourself with the wrong one of your siblings. To plan to take over the world, to form human farms, these acts were bad enough. To plot against your brother Len was a big mistake. One that you are about to pay for, tonight. You live by the sword Norman, you die by the sword.'

Diane still could not take it all in. When she looked around at the sheer amount of people that surrounded her she was flabbergasted. The vampires from Moorston and from Friarmere, the vigilantes, people she had known from her Band previously. But she was not about to beg for her life. Not as that would have made any difference to the angry rabble around her. Suddenly Sarah jumped back down. Diane had seen her many times. *A Melden vampire!* Was the whole world against her Master?

'Go on. Do it. Kill me now. Don't mess around,' Diane said to Wee Renee.

'You'll have to wait your turn,' Wee Renee said to Diane, then to everyone she said, 'remember what I said about the blood. We need it.'

There were various weapons in the hands of the vigilantes and villagers. The nail gun, the old army Enfield, hammers, Ian's butchers knifes, Nigel's kebab knives, home-made spears from Hardware Store and Ricks chain. Also, Tony had picked up a circular saw blade to use as a Frisbee from the Hardware Store. Norman slowly regarded them. Amongst them, he didn't know who would be the first to start.

'Quick or slow,' said Our Doris out of the blue. Coining the phrase from one of the Moorston vampires, after they had been tracking Anne's hybrids.

'Quick of course,' Diane said. Michael still watched sadly from the back of the pack. He looked through the crowd. He seemed to be watching himself from above, a little like Mrs Shuttleworth. From the look on his face, apart from the cowardice, which showed there, Diane realised that he had had a part in this. She did not know how small or large. It was clear that watching this scene unfold was not such a shock to him. This tableau was inevitable. But she had had to drag him here. It was very confusing.

'I wasn't asking you, Miss Bull-Dog Clip 1962!' Our Doris said.

'It's such a pity that we have to save what is inside him,' Angela said. 'The fact is that I would like to paint this Village with his blood. Paying for his sins against humanity and my old Master.'

Freddie was the first to turn his gaze from the scene in front of him. Instead, he looked up the street towards the direction of Moorston.

'Eh, what's this,' Freddie said. Gary followed his gaze.

'Well, you Moorston lot, you are going to have *all* your family around you,' Gary said.

The whole crowd were relieved to see Penelope running towards them. She had run through the tunnel safely and successfully in her red stilettos. It had taken a little longer than expected. Railway sleepers and gravel were not bedfellows with High Heels, Penelope had discovered.

Surprised to see the huge posse in the street, she came to a standstill just behind the scene.

Mark appraised her. She really is *fit*, he thought. He wondered if she would still be about after all this. If she would be *single*.

'He killed Stuart, and they were hunting me,' Penelope told Angela, 'but he did not find Sheila at all.'

'Bit of a waste of time wasn't?' Angela said. 'All it did was put you into our hands. Tonight, we have successfully killed two of your own Lieutenants, and we have ripped apart another.'

Norman didn't have that many Lieutenants, and as the only other female one was in front of him, he realised that they must have meant Christine. Norman had a last-ditch attempt at trying to persuade his girlfriend to save him.

'Penelope we can rule this world. You and me, together. Save me, and we will go off into the night. I could give you everything. Persuade your old Moorston fellow vampires that your Master does not wish them any harm,' Norman said. 'You *know* me. You *love* me.'

'You are not my Master,' Penelope said amazed. 'I do not have a Master, I have a Mistress, and she holds you there. I loved you Norman as much as any vampire can love another, but then I started to have my doubts when the first humans came over and told me some facts about you,' Penelope said.

At this point, Mark thought that it could be a waste of time pursuing Penelope. After all, if she had been used to The Master as a boyfriend, then he would be quite a *step-down*.

'What are you on about?' Norman asked.

'How you acted in Friarmere, what you had done in the past. Then I came over here with those questions, and I realised that those facts were true. Put that along with the turning of the vampire children and I realised that you weren't what I thought you were. Me and Marcel want to be with our own kind. I'm sorry, but you cannot count on us,' Penelope finally said.

Norman screamed into the night.

Unexpectedly, Norman began to struggle violently against Jackie and Angela. They weren't perhaps concentrating as much as they should, and he managed to break free. He tried to run through the circle of people and unfortunately for Paul, Rachel and Mrs Shuttleworth, they were in his way.

They look shocked as he hurtled towards them. His face was monstrous, and the whites of his eyes were red. He tried to push Paul to the side of him, but Paul was not having it and grabbed his coat trying to secure him for Angela and Jackie.

With a snap of his arm, Norman punched him in his chest, ripping his heart out. The whole thing had taken no more than five seconds. His wife Rachel screamed, and he stopped her noise instantly by putting his hand in her mouth and ripping out her tongue. The Brass Neck's had been no use to these two Meldeners.

As he moved through those two, Mrs Shuttleworth was behind them, just by chance. She had brought her knitting needles as her weapons and had a lot of faith in them. She held them in front of her bravely and closed her eyes. Norman simply gave her a kind of karate kick in the face, which knocked her on her back. He took one jump and landed on her chest. Mrs Shuttleworth stuck one of the knitting needles in his leg, nice and deep. She continued to grind it in as his weight began to crush her. It made no difference whatsoever.

Angela and Jackie took hold of him again, yanking him off the old lady. Mrs Shuttleworth, Paul and Rachel had been enough of a hindrance for them to grab him. Agnes moved forward with her cutthroat razor towards him, making sure it glinted in the streetlight. She had not forgotten what to do. Agnes was still prepared to follow Wee Renee's request, but Norman did not know that. She smirked at him, as she waggled the razor in front of his face.

There was silence for a whole minute.

A short time for it to sink in Norman's brain that he was definitely on his way out.

A short time for Angela and Jackie to realise that they couldn't slacken their grip until this was over and a short time for everyone else to understand that this was not to be a battle without casualties on both sides.

The picture was almost beautiful. The figures might even be statues as they froze, waiting for the next move.

The only sound was the two snowmobiles that chugged along in the road beside them.

18 Wildlife

At the side of the road was a building that was used for a little Wildlife Museum. School children would come, particularly from the School that the vampires currently inhabited and have a lovely day out with their teachers. A usual day would consist of eating a packed lunch, learning about local wild animals and finally fishing for 'mini-beasts' in the pond.

On the outside of the building, it was fully furnished with dark wood panelling, very much like a Swiss Chalet. How apt, as it currently sat in all this snow. Angela pulled Norman briskly over to this building.

'Attach him to it,' Angela said. 'We need to have him still and in one place, for what we have planned today.'

Three taller vampires were instructed to hold him by the throat and lift him so that his feet were three feet up from the floor. Exactly what they were supposed to attach him to, they didn't know. This building was wooden and flat, with no hooks, brackets or anything else to dangle a vampire from.

Pat and Agnes dragged Diane along, and the whole crowd moved with them. Michael started to weave his way through the people until he got to the front. He didn't want to but needed to see what would happen next. Especially to Diane. She deserved that at least from him, even if he couldn't save her.

'Gary!' Jackie shouted. Gary stepped forward. 'Your nail gun - do you have it?'

'Yes,' Gary said. He knew what they were going to ask him to do, as he looked at the Wildlife Museum.

'Attach him tightly to this building with your gun. Around the edges. You can trap bits of skin, but not big holes. Okay?' Angela asked.

'Yes,' Gary said taking a deep breath. He would have to get very close to Norman to do this. And a cornered dog was very dangerous.

'Start at his head,' One of the Moorston vampires, Monica said who was holding his weight up high with a couple of the others. Gary immediately attached his two ears to the wood with his nail gun. Three nails in each ear. In some areas, he attached his clothes to the wood. In other areas, he attached Norman's skin.

He had just done the head and down one side of the body. It was already holding his weight. The nails had gone into the wood very nicely. He had to load up his gun with ammo however and was just about to do the other side when Norman glanced from side to side furtively, unable to move his head, but panicking. He reached forward and grabbed the nearest thing to him. A hostage. Something that would get him out of all this.

Pat had stood very close to Diane's Master so she could get a good long look at his downfall. They were the nearest, luckily for Pat, it was Diane he snatched around the throat. He drew the body before him, to see who he had managed to clutch hold of.

'This is your murderous boyfriends' fault. Look at him there, watching with them, the traitor. I know what he has done. Sold us up the river to secure his position in this group,' Norman said.

'No Master. It was I that forced him to come here when I heard this rabble cheering. He was dead against it,' Diane said.

Our Doris nudged Terry, who looked down at her. She gave a long slow wink, then mouthed the words *I told you so*. Our Doris enjoyed her moment being right about Michael.

'Yes, Michael's not as daft as he looks,' Freddie said. 'He's been against you for a while sonny.' This was indeed surprising news to Norman, who spat at him.

'I never suspected you for a moment. You are a very clever man. Looks obviously can be very deceiving.' The Master said.

'This is for you.' Norman squeezed Diane's neck with his one hand. Her hands reached out for help, grabbing at The Master's clothes, grabbing at Gary as he still punched the nail's as fast as he could, into Norman's clothes and small areas of his skin.

Gary methodically carried on pressing the trigger, trying to avoid the situation going on a few inches away from the situation. Each nail made everyone safer, including himself. Diane continued to thrash, but no-one came to her rescue.

The Master's eyes were locked with Michael's. This was the only way that he could have the slightest revenge against Michael's betrayal. With one hand still quivering in its strain, he squeezed and squeezed until Diane's head simply came off the top of her body.

The blood surged out of her neck, and her face looked so sad. The terror had gone, and now Diane looked depressed. Her body dropped down, and her head slowly rolled forward. The bulldog clips pinged off on the tarmac. The head came to rest in front of Rick, who looked behind him before giving it a backwards kick.

Undeterred by this interruption, Gary sighed but continued to put the nails into the edges of Norman, avoiding the free arm, he worked on his other leg low down. Norman could not bend to get him. Michael turned around, his eyes searching the crowd. They fell on Danny. Danny had a makeshift spear.

'Can I borrow this?' Michael asked quickly, taking it without any resistance. He seemed to be running on autopilot. Calmly and without fuss or anger, he moved forward and stuck it into Norman, through the heart.

'Just die. Stop it all and die,' Michael said plainly to his face.

The Friarmere audience gasped, they had not expected that. This act was not planned, and it was not what they wanted to do.

'Don't pull that out!' Wee Renee yelled at the top of her voice.

'I wasn't going to. He's not dead yet,' Michael said. The end of the makeshift stake was metal, a sharp hunting knife from the hardware store, but behind it was a heavy wooden broom-handle. Norman's heart was pierced with metal.

He stared down at Michael, taking his one free arm, recently used to kill Michael's lover, he grasped hold of the brown wooden handle. A single trickle of dark blood ran from his nose. He glowered at his former Lieutenant. But he could still get out of this.

Michael realised that he was going to try and remove the spear, so stepped back a couple of paces, before running with all his strength, his hands forward, pushing it further in, all his weight behind it.

The wood part of the spear finally inched its way home, easing into Norman's black heart. The second the wood made contact, The Master was dead. Just like that. The crowd in front of him gasped in disbelief.

'Michael! We have to save all his blood, you big banana,' Andy said. 'Why did you do that?'

'What good was that death?' Angela asked Michael, adding to Andy's comments. 'Rubbish! No torture! No humiliation! No reckoning and no justice!'

'He pissed me off too much when he did that to Diane. There was no need for it. It wasn't her fault that I was with you. She didn't know anything about me and you lot. I know she would have blabbed if I had told her. But it just wasn't bloody fair. So, it's happened now!' Michael said in explanation.

'Yes, but how do we avenge Our Master now?' Jackie asked. 'That wasn't enough.'

'By killing all the others in this village. It is still his bloodline,' Michael said. 'I'm sorry. I can't make it un-happen now. Stake me yourself if that's what you want to do, but in the heat of the moment, I needed to do that. Everything I've gone through. All the stuff with my brother and now Diane. I'm sorry, I'd had a belly full of him,' Michael turned to Wee Renee.

'Why don't you want me to pull it out. I thought we were trying to be discreet. If he's there pinned up all night it will be a dead giveaway,' Michael asked.

'Because it's plugging the hole,' Wee Renee answered. 'He is more important to us dead than alive, and I need what is in him.'

She stepped back and now really took in the sight of him for the first time. Nailed up to the wood of the building with a broom handle sticking right out of his heart. Pat and Our Doris joined her, looking up at the macabre sight.

'Well,' Our Doris said, 'We've done it!'

'Three down, none to go,' Pat said.

'Aye, three Masters gone. But lots of minions left,' Wee Renee said. 'Don't rest on your laurels, you two.'

Sarah and Adam stood on the roofs of Friarmere, still trying to see anyone who might discover this monumental moment by accident and totally give the game away. They didn't really know where everyone was, but they couldn't have wished for a better outcome. One Lieutenant with cankles, easily dealt with. Two Lieutenant's dealt with by Norman, one by accident, one by design. And finally, the Beast himself. Ready to be drained. It was as if someone was watching over them. Tonight had been pretty easy for all intents and purposes. Still, they could see no vampires on the prowl

'Right. Now the practicalities, let's sort that,' Wee Renee said. 'The most important thing is that the others don't find out about Norman and run-off out of our sight. What I can see obviously, is that we need to get rid of those snowmobiles. No-one else owns them, and not many of his lot drive them. They wouldn't be left unattended in Friarmere. Next, to hide Diane and Keith's bodies and to get rid of that awful bloody snow on the floor. After we've done with Norman, move him and hide him, so that no one else can find out and be completed alerted that we have them licked. Anything else?'

There wasn't a sound from any other person.

'First things first, Get the snowmobiles back,' Wee Renee pointed to a group of the men there, and they began to move. Andy was one of them. Lee and Miles too, with some other Moorston men.

They moved Norman's snowmobile off the top of Keith. Keith's snowmobile still sat happily switched on, waiting for its passenger. Now they could see the full extent of what the snowmobile had kicked up.

'Look at that. Keith made a right mess,' Our Doris said, pointing to the ground.

Michael seemed to be looking around the crowd. He pushed his glasses up his nose with his middle finger. He seemed to be surveying the people for someone. Finally, his eye settled on the person he was looking for. It was Mrs Shuttleworth's daughter-in-law Helen. He gave the briefest smile, straightened his tie and wandered over to speak to her, but she was, unfortunately, tending to her mother-in-law that had just been killed so brutally by Norman Morgan.

'Did you know her?' Michael asked, pushing the glasses further up his nose to look at the woman on the ground.

'Yes, she was my mother-in-law or ex-mother-in-law, I should say,' Helen answered.

'What do you mean by that?' Michael asked.

'No, you see, her son ran off with a woman from Halifax last year, so she was my ex-mother-in-law. She was a lovely lady though. We were still as close,' Helen Shuttleworth said, sadly.

'Ex-mother-in-law in more ways than one, now she's dead,' Michael commented, feeling very clever. Helen looked down at Mrs Shuttleworth sadly. Michael knew he had just blown it.

'Insensitive to the last,' Liz said, as she walked past him.

19 Tie-dye

As it happened, the death of Norman and the others had occurred at the east end of Friarmere. The nearest house to that site was Pat's house.

'Do you have a bucket at home?' Wee Renee asked Pat.

'Yes, I have. I've got one in my glory hole that'll do for that bugger,' Pat said.

'Will you get it for us love. We are going to need it for his juices,' Wee Renee said

Pat turned to make the short trip to her house immediately. All the way she laughed at the thought of Norman's juices in her bucket.

'Who can get those snowmobiles up to The Grange?' Wee Renee asked. 'I presume that they are like motorbikes, although I have no idea really.'

'I've ridden a motorbike before,' Gary said.

'I have too,' Nigel said.

'We can try. I suppose,' Gary said.

'I think Norman and Keith weren't having much success with them earlier. It needs more snow than there's left now,' Andy said.

'Stuart said it was hard going earlier,' Penelope commented.

'You'd better be quick then,' Sue said.

'I think a good idea would be to take some of the vampires with you, in case you meet some of Norman's gang on the way,' Wee Renee said. 'Or up at The Grange. If you just pop them outside the front of The Grange, the others will think that Norman has just left them there and is inside.'

'Does anyone want to come on the back of me then?' Gary asked.

'I will,' Joe said. 'I am sure I can make myself useful if they try to attack us.'

'Could I go on the back of you please Nigel?' Bob asked. His parents looked at each other shocked. 'It's just that I want to go on one that's all. It might be my only chance ever.' That was true, rides on snowmobiles were few and far between in Friarmere.

'Are you okay with that Nigel?' Tony asked.

It's fine by me,' Nigel said. 'Who else is coming?'

Mark and three of The Moorston vampires decided to accompany their humans up to The Grange and back again for protection. Gary and Nigel got on the snowmobiles and revved them a little. Getting the feel of them. Nigel's was slightly broken at the front. This had been the one that Norman was riding on before it had crashed on top of Keith.

When both men felt like their machines were operational, they moved forward slightly, now getting the feel of the bike on the slush.

'You can feel it's heavy going, can't you?' Gary asked Nigel.

'Oh yeah. We should get up there while we can. The snow is probably a bit thicker and colder up the hill. It's probably just in the centre of the Village where we have the most problems,' Nigel said.

'Good thinking,' Gary said. The two men slowly began to move off. Wee Renee moved onto the next problem.

'Right who can deal with Keith and Diane's bodies?' She asked.

Maurice and Ernie said they would organise that. They would just need a little help. The two vigilantes knew where to put them, and they would happily set them on fire. That would be the end of that.

All that was left now was the huge red and black mess that had melted into the snow. Wee Renee asked lots of people to run around on that area at every opportunity, while she did the other jobs.

Pat returned with a cream coloured bucket, which had brown stains inside. She passed it to Wee Renee who looked inside it and wrinkled her nose.

'Pat, you do know what this is for, don't you? Where the blood is going after?' Wee Renee asked.

'Yes,' Pat said.

'It is very heavily stained inside. What were you thinking? Don't you think it should be sterile? Have you been washing your 'taters in this?' Wee Renee asked.

'No,' Pat said.

'Whatever has stained this?' Wee Renee asked.

'You should know. It was you that stained that cream bucket,' Pat said. Wee Renee needed a short while to remember what she had done in a bucket at Pat's house, and suddenly, she had a light bulb moment.

'Oh yes, that tie-dying I did. I remember now. That's not a problem, it won't cause any infections. It's just you know, to hold the issue after it comes out of Norman,' Wee Renee said.

'Oh, I see. Norman's fluids,' Pat said.

'Does it have a lid?' Wee Renee asked Pat. 'So, the blood won't slosh everywhere when we are carrying it afterwards. There would be a trail to us then.'

'It's never had a lid. It didn't come with one. Don't you remember when you were tie-dyeing, we put a piece of foil on the top, so nothing would drop in it.'

'Oh aye, we did love. Foil might not cut the mustard this time,' Wee Renee said.

'I know what to use. It was right there then, sitting on the top of the bucket in my glory hole. I'll be back in two ticks,' Pat said and stomped off again the short distance to her house. While Wee Renee waited for the lid, she tried to sort out more problems.

'So, the next matter,' Wee Renee announced to the crowd, 'is we need to keep everything as normal as possible until we catch them all. That means primarily pretending that Norman is still alive.' She turned to Penelope and Marcel. 'Do you think you can stay at The Grange until that happens. Just say that he is not up to going out or is visiting another area or something.'

'Yes, I don't see why not,' Penelope said. 'The only people that usually come up are either dead or here anyway. Like Michael.' Penelope stopped to think about everyone she had seen.

'Sometimes Stephen comes, and on occasion an older lady. I don't think either of these are dead yet. But it was mainly Keith, Stuart, Christine, Diane and Michael that come,' Penelope confirmed.

'Aye, that older one will probably be Lynn, I bet. Are you okay with all these arrangements, Marcel? Wee Renee asked him.

'Anything for you darling,' Marcel said and beamed at Wee Renee.

'And Michael, you have to go up with these two as well,' Wee Renee said addressing him.

'Really? Never mind. I don't suppose it'll be for long now,' Michael said. 'I was hoping to never clap eyes on that place again.' Michael mock shivered.

'You have to act like your life depended on it. Remember, you three must pretend you are going to win an Oscar for this performance. Everything has to appear normal,' Wee Renee said. 'After all, if they find out their Master has really gone, they'll run away,' she raised her eyebrows at them in shock and surprise.

'What are we going to do about the others?' Michael asked.

'Yes, we got lucky tonight,' Angela said.

'And there are too many to hunt like we did in Melden plus their smell is everywhere. We would never find them,' Jackie commented, a little desperately.

'I can't think about what to do now, but I will, I promise you,' Wee Renee said.' I have got to do this now and a lot of my time tomorrow will be taken up with sorting all that out. I have to do it tomorrow, after all, I don't know how fast his blood will clot, and become unusable,' Wee Renee said matter-of-factly.

'Before I do that though, I will sleep on it. I have a bit of a plan bubbling, and it involves you, Michael. Can you come over to the mill tomorrow, very stealthily again, don't get seen? I will either see you myself or will have left a message with some of the others,' Wee Renee said.

'Oh yes,' Michael said, 'We're really getting there, now aren't we?'

'Now,' Wee Renee took a deep breath, she wasn't looking forward to this part, 'after I have drained the beast. We will need to get him down off there obviously and get rid of what is left, can anyone do that?'

'I'll do that. I've seen him dispose of other people. His flock won't find it. I know exactly where he dumps his remains,' Michael said.

'I bet you do,' Our Doris said. 'I can't imagine what that place is like.'

'Probably worse than the black hole of Calcutta,' Pat commented behind them, holding a makeshift lid for the bucket.

'What the hell is that?' Wee Renee asked Pat.

'The black hole of Calcutta?' Pat asked in reply.

'No *that* in your hands,' Wee Renee gestured.

'My plastic colander,' she said. 'It fits perfectly on the top of that bucket. That's where I keep it, and I've wrapped some foil around it, so it will keep the blood fresh. We'll just jam it on in there when it's full,' Pat said. 'It won't spill anywhere. Jobs a good 'un,' she sniffed.

'Time will tell about that. I'd better get on with the job,' Wee Renee said. They walked over to where Norman's lifeless carcass was suspended. Pat was sick of holding the foil-covered colander, so placed it upside-down on top of her head, like a soldier's helmet. As she already was wearing her fur covered Russian hat, it looked like quite an elaborate Easter Bonnet.

'Okay, don't get the wrong idea about this, but we don't want any of his clothes absorbing the blood.' Wee Renee said, considering the best way to do it. 'When I take that spear out, the blood will start to flow down. Hmmm … … besides that, I am going to make an incision in each foot after a short time and see what I can get out of his legs.' That was a good start for Wee Renee. This part was unplanned. She had to make decisions on her feet now. She smiled at the rest of the people watching. 'Yes, that's what we'll do!'

'Remember Rene, I've only got that one bucket,' Pat said, 'he might fill it several times over!'

'We'll just have to leave the rest out then. Dump it. Let's suck it and see,' Wee Renee said.

'Next problem, who's got something I can cut cloth with?' Wee Renee asked.

'I do,' Agnes said. She took her backpack off her back and fiddled around in there, finally retrieving a very sharp pair of scissors, out of the bottom, which she gave to Wee Renee.

'We need to cut his clothes off directly down from that spear,' Wee Renee said. 'No clothes on at least that half of him. Totally naked. The clothes will absorb too much blood.' She reached up but being quite small her hands barely reached his collar.

'I'll do it,' Pat said licking her lips.

'I thought you might,' Wee Renee commented.

'I'll be honest about it. I'm champing at the bit to look. He's a right sexy pig, and I'd love to see what he's got in his underpants. I bet if you lot were honest there are a lot of you here who want a butchers too,' Pat said. No-one else said anything. 'I mean with them looks, and how he acted, I hope he can back himself up.' She elbowed her way right next to him 'Let the dog see the rabbit!'

Wee Renee was very rarely surprised at Pat, but tonight she was. She gave a little chuckle.

'Oh Pat, you are one,' Wee Renee said.

'I'll tell you what, I'll help, and you can give the pieces of cloth to me,' Our Doris said, winking at Pat.

'I thought so,' Pat said. 'You know he'd have had all three of us if he'd have had his way. If he were alive now, he'd be enjoying this. Kinky bugger. Are you ready? This is going to be a humdinger.'

'The one in the tunnel wasn't,' Liz commented from the side of the women.

'Oh yes, the lair of the white worm. Not looking forward to this quite as much now,' Pat said.

Penelope remained speechless at the back. They had forgotten that she had had carnal knowledge of Norman Morgan and she wanted to keep it that way.

Wee Renee and Pat started to cut away Norman's clothes, below where the spear was right down to the foot. They cut off the bottom half of his burgundy shirt. Which heralded a cry from Pat.

'Hey, what was he up to?' She looked under his shirt the other side, which was still intact.

'What's wrong?' Agnes asked.

'It's his nipples!' Pat said.

'Are they barbed?' Terry asked strangely.

'No Terry. He hasn't got any!' Pat exclaimed.

'Maybe he absorbed them?' Liz asked.

'Why would he do that?' Lauren asked.

'Extra protein, maybe,' Liz mused.

'Wait – he must never have had any. I have them, and my Mum does,' Jackie said.

'Perhaps it's the strain? Norman's, I mean. Anne had them. We saw them,' Freddie said.

'We so did. Long, grey puppies,' Rick said, dry swallowing.

'So, did Len. I could vouch for him,' Marcel said dreamily.

'Is there any of Norman's vampires still here?' Lee asked. 'We could ask them if they drop off after transformation?'

Everyone looked around. Mark was up at The Grange still. Ernie and Maurice were off with Keith's body. The only one left was Adam on the roof.

'Young Adam?' Our Doris shouted.

'Yes!' Adam asked.

'Funny question but … … Do you still possess nipples because Norman doesn't?' Tony asked. Adam quickly felt his chest checking that they hadn't just dropped off.

'Affirmative. Nipples still in place,' Adam replied.

'Right, listen you lot. We are going to be here all night if we are talking about how weird all of him is. What if his *frank and beans* are unusual? How long are we going to chew that one over?' Wee Renee asked.

The whole crowd laughed, and Wee Renee didn't get it.

'Come on Rene, bless you,' Pat said, wiping her tears of laughter on the arm of her coat. 'Let's get it done.'

Pat cut down the side of his trousers, one side of his jacket. Finally ending in Our Doris taking off his one sock and shoe.

'If we fill a bucket out of this I won't do the other side,' Wee Renee said.

'It's quite exciting really,' Jennifer said crossing her arms and watching the goings-on.

Wee Renee wanted the spear taken out gently in case there was a sudden spurt of fluid from the wound. Miles and Lee agreed to do this, and they stood either side of the spear, their hands alternately placed on the broom handle, waiting for Wee Renee to give the go-ahead.

She positioned the bucket underneath his left side directly onto the foot, which was on the naked side of him.

'Take it away lads,' she said. They took the spear out bit by bit in millimetres. At first, it was wedged into the wood outside at the back, and they thought that it would come free with a jerk. As soon as the tip of the spear wiggled free of the last few splinters, they just began to gently remove it out of Norman's soft parts.

There had been a hole made at the back of him, so the first few drips came from behind Norman. They made a loud dripping noise into the bucket. It sounded heavy like mercury.

Our Doris who was the smallest of them was closest to the bucket. She looked down, then back up at them.

'Well he's still juicy,' Our Doris said. 'At least we don't have to worry about that.'

Lee and Miles continued to inch the spear out of Norman's chest. Wee Renee had a thought in the back of her mind that if the stake was removed from his heart, it could revive Norman and she really hoped that this was just over thinking it. She hadn't voiced it to anyone else, but that was the only worry that she had.

Luckily as the spear finally came out, he was quite clearly still dead. The insides of Norman were thick and blackish red. In the liquid there were thicker bits, tissue maybe, and for one second Carl thought a load of worms would extrude out of the hole. But no, the tar-like substance ran lazily down from Norman's wound. Gravity brought it splashing into the bucket below him. A clot occasionally snaked down, which gave a very satisfying sound when it dropped into the bucket.

'We don't want to be here all night. He's not a fast runner. Agnes, can I borrow your cutthroat razor?' Wee Renee asked.

'Of course,' Agnes said, passing it to her.

Wee Renee bent over and grasped Norman by the ankle. She took the cutthroat razor and drew a think cut across the heel of his foot underneath on the sole. Now they could hear the bucket filling up far quicker. But after a minute that too began to slow.

'It's probably stuck in his arms. Nothings pumping now is it?' Our Doris said.

'We'll sort that if we have to. As long as the buckets full, I'm not bothered.' Wee Renee said. After about five minutes the drips stopped, and the bucket was only half full.

'I'm going to use the razor on this foot now,' Wee Renee said. 'Can you get him ready?' She said to Our Doris. Wee Renee moved the bucket over to the other leg. Our Doris took off his sock and shoe again, and Wee Renee drew the cutthroat razor deeply across his heel again. This gave a decent stream into the bucket

'It's getting nice and deep now,' Our Doris said. The flow stopped again.

'Yes, I think that'll be enough. I've only got a few to do after all,' Wee Renee said.

Sue and Michael moved the bucket, which seemed very heavy now. Norman's blood was like lead. Pat took the foil covered colander off her head.

'Shall I put the lid on?' Pat asked Wee Renee.

'Yes, love. We don't want it going all dry, they will have to eat it rather than drink it!' Wee Renee said.

'Like black pudding!' Pat said.

'Have you seen Norman now?' Angela commented. They all took a good look. On the naked side of Norman, the skin had shrunk completely around the bones. It was thinned and papery. Norman had been shrink-wrapped in his skin. With no visible flesh or muscles, it was like the only contents of him previously had been bones and blood.

'Very weird,' Rick said, 'but certainly not as weird as his sister.'

'It's something to be pleased about,' Maurice said who was going to supervise two of the people from Moorston, as they took Diane's body and head over to their corpse burning place. 'I'm happy about what's inside him at least I know that there is no crow or wolf in me.'

'There is that,' Ernie said, nodding.

There seemed to be a lot of action on the roofs suddenly. The rest of the crowd knew something was going on in the Village and surged forward a little like a herd of lemmings going towards a cliff.

'What's going on?' Jackie shouted up. 'Have we been spotted?'

'No,' shouted Sarah, as she ran along the roofs. 'It's some vampire kids!'

'Oh god,' Michael said, 'they are vile.'

'Don't we know it,' Father Philip said who particularly rushed to take up his arms, determined to get in on this war after his night in St Dominic's. Several of the villagers got ready to help the two roof vampires with their prey.

The first vampire child stayed on the roof, Sarah chased it and luckily managed to get above it. She was a lot stronger than the poor creature. This girl had not seen Sarah but was watching the crowd surging in the street beneath her, as her head now naturally hung downwards.

All that lovely warm food in the street, just waiting to be eaten. She was so hungry, and they looked so tempting. The small child, previously named Molly in her human life, drooled. She had not seen as many humans together since she had been made a monster. Molly had thought they were all gone, but no, this meant survival for her and her kind. They could live on these for years. Molly just had to get one to move away from the others.

All her attention was on the food, which meant she didn't see her killer. Sarah grabbed the thin, spindly child and brought her downwards onto the edge of a satellite dish. The edge was quite broad but seared through the tiny monster, acting like a giant scythe to split the child into two.

The crowd had seen Sarah's action, but could not see what had happened to it, as the satellite was beyond their view on the roof. Now, with nothing holding it together, the front half of the creature began to slither down the pitched roof, the angle too great to keep her on it. The shocked crowd beneath the house enjoyed the confirmation of Sarah's kill.

First the head with its useless neck, then the upper torso, appeared bit by bit over the guttering. Finally, the whole top section of the old Molly tumbled end over end and landed in a laurel bush below. The bottom half had started to slide too but was held by the bracket from the satellite dish.

There was just one now, the one that Adam was chasing. Adam was slowly catching this one up, and this boy, knowing he had been spotted had decided to run downwards and take his chance through the gardens of the houses of Friarmere. Sarah ran along catching up on the other side of the street. She could see the creature quite clearly, even though he was often inside the snowy bushes. The foliage rustled wherever he was.

The hideous child was panicking and not being careful whatsoever. Most of the people who were fighting in Friarmere had not seen a vampire child, and this one sprang out suddenly, jumping ten feet into the middle of the road right in front of them. With a streetlight on either side of the child, they got the best view they ever could have.

It squealed into the night when it finally saw how many attackers it had. That made it even more determined to carry on with its task, he was still going to try and run and hide. He began to skitter quickly, centrally, right in the middle of the street. It was evident to one person where it was trying to go, the clump of bushes near St Dominic's Church.

It was Father Philip who knew precisely where it was going. He ran forward, determined to get him before he escaped. Father Philip had been given an axe from Joe's Hardware Store. In his other hand, Father Philip had a trusty fireside poker out of one of the fireside companion sets in Joe shop.

He never wanted to do anything so much as this. Father Philip was going to face his demons once more, and this time be the victor. This would change the way he felt about himself, he realised. If he could just manage to pull it off. Adam shouted after him to be careful and ran down the house himself, trying to get to the child.

Adam thought Father Philip was weak and would be overcome, but The Priest knew somehow that this time he would win. He would destroy this evil and make it safe for his parishioners.

As Father Philip got about four feet away from the creature, who continued to bound four-legged through the slushy snow, he made his move. He jumped forward, axe and poker downwards, to kill the beast. It seemed to anticipate this move and flipped it's head up, on the wretched wasted neck. The creature latched on to Father Philip's arm with its teeth, snatching at the limb and pulling it under itself to eat

Now the vampire could only taste Father Philip's coat, but he would work through that, he knew he could.

Unfortunately, Father Philip couldn't do anything as he was mid-flight. Now one arm was underneath the creature, the axe-wielding one. With an almighty noise, Father Philip crash-landed on top of the beast. The vampire child folded under the weight. The teeth still held on to the arm, but now the head folded underneath the creatures four limbs.

The poker hit home. It went straight through the chest of the beast, spearing the head, which happened to now be situated under the chest and through Father Philips own arm, into the tarmac beneath.

It took a while for everyone to realise what had happened, especially when Father Philip, who was obviously still alive, didn't get up. He tried as hard as he could to contain the screams. But this also meant he couldn't tell them what had happened.

The horde of people moved quickly, including Adam and Sarah. So many hands helped the Father. Picking him up, gently removing the weapon out of his arm and dragging the child away from the scene. They checked it for a bite but could see straight away that the vampire had not been successful. Sue wrapped Father Philip's arm in a scarf, tightly. They would see to that in the mill.

Wee Renee, Pat, Our Doris, the Moorston vampires and a few of the other humans had waited at the side of Norman's corpse, rather than follow this new terror. When the others returned and told them about what the threat was, they were relieved that it was over and that it had not been a spying vampire of Normans that would give them away.

'Come on, we need to hurry now. Some of you, do some more running around on that mess of Keith,' Wee Renee said. 'And Maurice, make sure you burn all the vampires in the Park.'

20 Dog Poo

Stephen was sitting in the foyer of the Primary School. Not long ago, he thought he had heard Norman and Keith go back up to The Grange on their snowmobiles. He didn't feel like going up and socialising with them. Suddenly he felt low and tired, but it was nowhere near his bedtime.

Lynn had been sitting in the hall looking after the children. She felt wretched, something was wrong. She saw the back of Stephen's head in the foyer, so went in to speak to him.

'Is your brother in the staffroom Stephen, I need him?' Lynn asked.

'No there's only us here, and the kids of course,' Stephen replied.

'I have been waiting to see him. I don't feel very well,' Lynn said.

'Neither do I,' said Stephen. 'Maybe we've eaten something.'

'I haven't eaten since yesterday,' Lynn said. 'Maybe that's it. Perhaps I'm hungry, or … … I know, did you eat the same person I did? Maybe they were infected with something,' Lynn asked.

'What person? I didn't eat any person,' Stephen said, trying unsuccessfully to pretend he hadn't recently eaten Vincent's Mother, who he was now feeling guilty about.

'The person that is still half over your face,' Lynn said. 'Who was that Stephen?' He didn't want to tell Lynn but thought that it could be the root of the problem so had to admit it.

'You know yesterday, I was looking for Vincent,' Stephen said.

'Yes,' Lynn said. She wondered where this was going.

'Well, I didn't find him. But I ate his mother,' Stephen said.

'Fair enough, waste not want not,' Lynn said surprisingly. 'I haven't eaten any of her, so it can't be that.'

'Have you been in the Civic Hall feeding? I have,' Stephen asked.

'The Civic Hall? Unless there is someone new in there, you shouldn't be feeding on them. That meat will be bad, Stephen. No wonder you are ill,' Lynn said, concerned.

'It wasn't bad actually. It was sweet, so there,' Stephen said.

'Let's just rule that out then, for diagnosis purposes, Lynn said.

'Well yes, if you don't feel good either, it can't be food. It must be a bug. I just feel weird and tingly and kind of nervous, really off. Like there is going to be an earthquake or a thunderstorm or something. Like something is happening, I don't know, and I feel a bit sick.' Stephen said.

'That's exactly how I feel. It started a little earlier tonight. We need to go and talk to The Master about this, and we need to ask some of the others. See if they feel the same. Maybe The Master had an infection and it's a slow acting one. If it's a common ailment, I suppose we must have all got it off him,' Lynn said.

'I'll speak to my brother when he gets here. See if he knows anything about it or can help us. If he can't help, there might be someone else who could do it. I don't know who though,' Stephen said.

'Mark knows lots of stuff. You know, about blood and things. Perhaps he will know something about it or have a cure for us. He might suggest that we should have to drink something or have someone else's blood to dilute ours. I don't know,' Lynn said. 'We need to sort this out, I don't want to be like this forever.'

'No, neither do I,' Stephen said.

Gary, Bob. Nigel, Joe and the vampires with them were on their way back down to the centre of the Village. They had delivered the snowmobiles without being observed at all. Nigel had decided to park the damaged one, with its front inside the folded down gazebo that was still about after the Bonfire Party. They parked the other one behind it. Hopefully, no one would notice something was smashed in.

They took the keys with them too. They didn't want anyone other than the hero party, getting on them and managing to get over the tops to Melden or Moorston and escaping on the last lap of this adventure.

Wee Renee and Pat were on their way to Maurice's house. They held the bucket of blood between them, walking either side of it, each having one hand on the handle, carrying it between them. Maurice stepped in front, to let them in. Ernie, Adam and Mark were doing the cremations in the Park. Maurice was going to go back out later when they had delivered this bucket. He could help deal with the remainder of the arrangements. Ernie was going to go to try and get back in the house before Lynn arrived home.

Wee Renee said she wanted to store the blood in Maurice's house. She did not want to trust anyone else on this mission. The snow was extremely slippy now, and Court Street was on an incline. If she slipped and dropped it all, she could admonish herself liberally, but she would never forgive herself if someone else had slipped and she could have done it successfully.

Maurice let them in, and Wee Renee decided the best place would be under his kitchen table. The two of them walked very carefully holding the bucket steady and placed it ready for the next day. Then Wee Renee had left instructions that when she returned they would go back to the mill, so she probably wouldn't see him again tonight.

'Rest easy tonight and get the others to rest too. Tomorrow's a very big day for you lot. A rebirth,' Wee Renee said.

Craig, Josh and Ben carried the two vampire children through the darkness in the Park. They were after a sign of where the incineration pile would be, but it was very well hidden. After about twenty minutes, they finally found the area near the river.

Ernie's vampire bonfire was already lit, so they threw the pieces on bit by bit. The creatures made colourful sparks as the burned. It was quite beautiful really.

'Mesmerising but grizzly,' Craig said.

'You're not wrong. Those kids though, are freaky pieces of shit,' Josh said. Their faces glowed orange in the fire from the creatures and their clothing. Like Wee Renee on a different night, they could smell toast and mushrooms.

Pat and Wee Renee were on their way back to the site of the massacre, but the others were moving things along nicely themselves.

'We need to get all them nails out,' Danny said. 'He'll probably just drop down in a pile for us then.'

'No, he looks proper weird,' Michael said. 'I don't want him going up with me like that. He freaks me out.'

'What do you mean?' Freddie asked.

'Well, he's like a really thin Popeye with those big arms still inflated,' Michael said. 'Not to mention, I bet there is some weight in them babies.'

'Oh, I see what you mean,' Tony said. 'Like a badly stuffed Guy Fawkes.'

'Or a Charlie big arms,' Terry said.

'What's one of them Dad?' Sally asked.

'I don't know, I just made it up,' Terry said, smiling at her.

'So, we want to get rid of those arms,' Michael said. 'There's no point in them being there.'

'All right,' Our Doris said. 'You don't have to keep harping on about it. We get it.'

'We'll have to drain them off,' Freddie said, rubbing his chin.

'We haven't got a bucket to put the blood in,' Our Doris said. 'It will go everywhere. We're trying to keep this area clean, so they don't honk him.'

'There must be something we can use,' Michael said.

'I've got this empty backpack,' Kathy said. 'I'm not going to use it, and it's waterproof inside and out. We could fill it and then we'll get rid of it.'

'Are you sure?' Lisa asked. 'It'll ruin it. Did you see how black his blood was? It was like tar.'

'I know,' Kathy said. 'I can always buy a new one. This need is greater. Just use my backpack, honestly.'

'I'll get rid of it,' Michael said. 'I'll chuck it in the river or something. Don't worry about that.'

'Are we going to do it then? I'm getting no younger, standing here,' Freddie asked them all. The group still looked at Norman on the wood panelling. Agnes sighed.

'Look, we've all got knives and everything. How many people does it need to decide to cut him open? And why is it always *me* and *my* stuff?' Agnes asked. Stepping forward and selecting one of the wrists, she went to cut it while holding the backpack underneath. *Sod this*, she thought, *why am I doing it all?*

'Our Doris, will you come and hold this bag?' Agnes asked. Our Doris obliged, opening the backpack wide six inches underneath the wrist.

'Go for it, our kid,' Our Doris said. Agnes cut him deep. She felt the razor drag on his flesh and pressed deeper. To ensure quicker emptying, Agnes bent the wrist back on itself, so that hand would empty as well as the arm. Within two minutes that one was done, and she went around the other side. Kathy's backpack was now half full of Norman's dirty blood.

'Oh yes. He looks far more balanced now,' Terry said.

'And that's important isn't it?' Freddie said. 'He's half-naked, has deep open gashes in the soles of his feet and both wrists. Has nail holes all over him and a massive spear hole through the middle of him. Don't forget all his skin has shrunk back to his bones, but as long as his body is balanced, we're happy,' Freddie said laughing.

'Don't forget he has no nipples,' Our Doris said. 'But that's balanced too. They are absent on both sides.'

'We need to get him off now so I can take him away,' Michael said. 'But he is nailed to that.'

'I'll pull them out, I can do that. Although I don't see why it's always me,' Darren said. The others let him do it, without bringing up the fact that he had done nothing for the whole night. He started at the top and began to pull out the nails with the back end of this claw hammer, which was one of his weapons that remained pristine and unused in a flashy tool belt he had procured from Joe's shop.

Some of them took a lot of effort, they did not want to come out. And Gary had put a lot in.

He carried on working, Lee and Miles supported Norman underneath as more and more nails came out, but there was a significant decrease in his weight now after the drainage. When Norman finally fell, and they had the full weight of him held in their arms, they realised that maybe he was the same weight as a young child.

'Well, there he is,' Our Doris said. 'Feast your eyes on the last of the Morgans.'

'How are you going to get him up to The Grange?' Angela asked.

'Well,' Michael said. 'I was hoping we could split him up into pieces. Carry him up between me Marcel and Penelope. We could take him under our arms.'

'Nice,' Andy said.

'What about this blood, Michael?' Kathy asked.

'Hide it somewhere, it will only be a few hours. Where is there?' Michael asked. He looked around quickly. Outside the Wildlife Museum was a black waste bin, with a picture of a dog on it. Michael walked up and looked inside.

'Put it in there. No-one's going to use that before I have got to it. I'll come back down tomorrow for it.' Michael said.

'The only place you can think of is an empty dog poo bin?' Kathy asked.

'Why are you bothered. You said you didn't want the bag back. It's as safe as houses in there. Who's going fishing in there – nobody,' Michael said.

'Fair enough,' Kathy said and dropped it in.

At this point, Wee Renee and Pat returned. She was glad to see that Norman was no longer suspended on the side of the museum. The only sign left was a few holes in the wood, which were indistinguishable unless you knew what you were looking for. The only place that drew her eye was the rich big red one that had been behind Norman's heart.

Wee Renee noticed that there were a few drops of blood on the floor, so the others kicked the snow over them.

'Some of you lot, throw as many snowballs as you can right at that target,' Wee Renee said, pointing to the red spear hole. 'Nice wet snow, so it washes it away.'

Few minutes of fun was spent doing this until you really couldn't tell that the blood had ever been there.

Several of the Moorston people had removed Mrs Shuttleworth, Paul and Rachel. They had taken them to just outside the mill and put a tarpaulin over them, securing it with a few broken pallets. The site looked entirely clear again.

'I'm sure they'll never know,' Wee Renee said happily.

'No,' said Angela. 'We have done well. I know it has happened here, but I just smell the gas of the snowmobiles and for some reason a faint whiff of toast and mushrooms. But even that is quickly fading.'

Penelope, Marcel and Michael split up Norman's torso. Penelope and Marcel twisted him at the waist until he came apart. Penelope took his legs, and Marcel took his upper half. Michael took the head, which he put triumphantly under his arm. It was quite surprising how small he had become once his blood had been removed.

'Cheerio then. I'll see you in the morning. We could probably finish this tomorrow if we use our nuts,' Michael said, gesturing to the head under his arm.

'Good one,' Jackie said laughing.

'I want it done tomorrow, and it will be. I have got a bit of a plan. It's not quite come together yet, but I will sleep on it and it will be fully fleshed by then,' Wee Renee said.

Norman's pall-bearers made their way slowly up to the empty echoing Grange. The largest party went back to the mill. Adam joined Maurice in his house to stare at his fate underneath Maurice's kitchen table. Ernie was long in bed before Lynn had got home.

When the horde of people arrived back at the mill, Beryl, while thrilled that they had killed The Master, was very sorry to see Mrs Shuttleworth, Paul and Rachel go. Privately they each had feared that their losses would be far greater on the night they killed The Master.

'Poor Maude,' Beryl said, wiping her nose.

'Who's Maude? Bob asked.

'Mrs Shuttleworth,' Freddie said. Apart from her daughter-in-law, only Freddie, Jennifer, Beryl and Terry, who attended to her dental treatment, had bothered to ask her name. How sad, as she had been such a brave old lady.

'God Bless Maude,' Wee Renee said, closing her eyes.

'I will say a few words in the morning,' Father Philip said, his face very white. 'For those who would like to celebrate, all their lives.'

Haggis, Basil and Bambi were pleased to see everyone arrive back. After the initial euphoria, and disappointment, the group told everyone of Father Phillips bravery with the vampire child. Wee Renee hoped that they would tomorrow or at least the next day get him into a real hospital as his arm was severely damaged with the poker and he wouldn't be able to fight any more. As it was, Terry dressed it as best as he could and was able to give him strong painkillers and antibiotics. Luckily for the right-handed Father Philip, it was his left.

Wee Renee felt extremely peaceful as she started to prepare for bed. There were no more old Masters left. The end was nigh. The future was looking far sunnier now. The new Masters were different.

The seven female vampires stood outside as the humans went to bed. They would wait there until just before morning when they would crawl back into their second-floor cave and wait for the continuation of their mission the following night. They remained without speaking, looking into the night, listening to the drips of the melting snow.

21 Earplugs

Adam had had an idea when he was on the roof looking at the vampire children. A way he could help the cause. Then everything else had happened, and he had forgotten to mention it to Wee Renee. She was long gone now. Probably fast asleep. Now he couldn't talk about it to her before implementing it. It had to be tonight. He kind of only had one chance if Wee Renee's plan worked. Adam brought it up to Maurice, to ask his advice on the matter.

'What do you think? Is it a good idea? Do you think it is best that we do it now or should I just leave it and ask her tomorrow?' Adam asked.

'It is a good idea, and I think it's better done tonight. The loss of Mrs White will probably start to seem very fishy if they put it together with the missing Master, Keith and Diane. They will start to close ranks. Wee Renee will be very pleased if you could pull it off. It will be a nice surprise for her and lesson her load in the bargain. Let's have a wander up to Marks farm and see if we can manage this,' Maurice said.

Mark was fumbling around at his Farm attending to his human donors when there was a knock on the door. In the dark, he knew it was probably a friend and went to the glass. He saw Maurice's and Adam's smiling faces, who both began waving at him. He opened the door.

'We've got a good idea,' Adam said.

'No, *you've* got a good idea,' Maurice said, 'and you are taking all the risks. Let's tell Mark all about it.'

Mark invited them into the kitchen of the farmhouse, then Adam told him of the plan.

'It's quite a lot of waste for me,' Mark said. 'but it's a great idea. And I have no doubt it will work'

Mark filled a whole crate full of milk bottles with blood. While he did that, Maurice rooted around in the cupboards underneath the farmers sink. He came back with various preparations that would do the job. Mark and Adam examined the haul and picked which were best.

'Let's make a cocktail,' Mark said. They mixed some rat poison, some household cleaning products including a scouring cleanser, and ketchup to hide the taste. It started to fizz.

'What do you think it will do, Mark?' Adam asked.

'You know our constitution isn't strong, and the only thing we can consume is blood,' Mark said.

'And Monster Snacks,' Adam offered. Mark laughed.

'I think it will either make them very ill, or they will die. With no other person to run to, to ask for help and no Doctor on the premises shall we say, they would probably drink more to try and make themselves feel better. I don't know really. I'm guessing. I tell you what though I don't feel very good myself,' Mark said.

'Neither do we Mark,' Maurice and Adam said.

'I know what that is though, for definite. I felt it at the moment he died,' Mark said gravely.

'What are we going to do about that?' Maurice asked.

'I have no idea,' Mark said.

'Do you not feel like doing this tonight? We can leave it,' Adam said.

'I don't, but we'll manage. Let's face it – this could be how I feel forever. I will either have to get used to it or find a fix somehow,' Mark said. 'Now let's put an equal amount of the poisonous cocktail into each of the bottles of blood,'

They all helped to speed along the process, using three teaspoons, after which Mark sealed them with a foil top.

'Are you ready?' Mark asked.

'Yes, just a minute though. I have to be sure,' Adam took off one of the foil tops and sniffed the content of the bottle.

'Spicy! I can't smell it at all,' Adam said.

'The walking along will gently mix it in too,' Mark said. 'Don't worry. It'll be fully absorbed into the blood and totally undetectable.'

'Let's face it, they won't think twice about checking. They'll be too hungry by now. Beggars can't be choosers!' Adam said. The three of them walked over to the school. The journey was wordless, they all felt quite queasy.

Maurice and Mark stood at the gates while Adam walked up with the crate. He went into the School Hall and quietly took out each bottle of blood and laid them along one side of the hall on the floor.

The children were right there at the back of the hall watching him. Hungry but waiting for him to leave. They would not be captured. This one had looked after them before, he must be looking after them now Mrs White had gone. They suspected nothing. Adam left the Primary School. It was the last act he did as a vampire. The children ran for bottles of blood and greedily drunk them down.

When Maurice and Mark had stood outside the School, they realised that Ernie was in exactly the wrong place that he should be. Yes, he needed to have come back to his house that night, so Lynn would think everything was normal and he had done that successfully. Now it was close to daylight, he had to be over at Maurice's with Adam to receive the procedure.

'Oh no,' Adam said. 'We've messed it all up!' When they told him.

Mark shook his head, he thought he could make his way into Ernie's house and get him. It was one hour before dawn. Probably Lynn had already gone to sleep for the day, and he could retrieve Ernie, get him over to Maurice's house and get back to the Farm before daylight. When Lynn awoke tonight, it would all be over.

If she awoke during the extraction, they had the option to kill her right there and then, but they did not really want to do that. In time it would become inevitable that it would happen, hopefully by someone else's hands.

If Ernie had changed his mind, then they would leave it at that, but the last time they spoke to him he was champing at the bit.

The vampire's stood outside Ernie's house under the streetlight, Mark trying to pluck up the courage.

In the School, all the blood had been consumed. As the last drops were being lapped up, the first signs that something wasn't right began. Two of them clutched their stomach's. One burped. The other started to stiffen and spasm. Another child clutched their stomach. They all began to scream. There was no-one in the School to hear them. No-one to help.

Mark crept in. There was silence in the lower level of the house. The kitchen, the hall, the living room all were dark and empty. They were both upstairs in bed. Luckily for Mark, not as he knew it, Ernie had had a snoring problem in life, and Lynn slept with earplugs in.

Tonight, was no exception, the earplugs were in, and she was turned away from the door. Mark silently moved into the bedroom. Lynn was the closest to the door, and Ernie was the furthest away. Typical.

Mark crept around the bottom of the bed, all the time looking at Lynn. He could not see that she had earplugs in and imagined he would see her eyes slowly open at any time to watch his progress.

He did not know how to wake Ernie without him jumping up and yelling, thus giving the game away. So, he decided to be a fly. Mark picked up a tissue from the side of the bed and kept tickling Ernie's nose. Ernie kept wrinkling his nose, twitching it, then he scratched it. Mark did it again, and Ernie opened his eyes to swat away the annoying fly.

Mark's face was looking back at him about twelve inches away. He put his finger up to his lips, then beckoned Ernie. Mark quickly left the room and Ernie followed him. He had fallen asleep and wondered what Mark wanted. Ernie was still very drowsy, and his brain wasn't functioning at all. When they got onto the landing, Ernie shut the door behind them.

'Are you coming?' Mark whispered.

'Coming where?' Ernie asked in a regular voice. He was still half asleep.

'Shush Lynn will hear you,' Mark said.

'Lynn wouldn't hear a Brass Band coming in the room even if they were playing triple forte. She's got some heavy-duty earplugs jammed in there, because of my snoring,' Ernie said.

'I'm glad about that,' Mark said. 'Listen do you want to be human or not because you three are getting it done today don't forget.'

'Oh yes,' Ernie said.

'You'll never get another chance because the blood might dry up. So, if you want to back out now, that'll be it,' Mark said.

'I don't want to back out at all. Let me pull some clothes on, and I'll be right down,' Ernie said.

'I'll wait outside,' Mark said. 'Adam and Maurice are with me. Hurry up, we haven't got that long before light.'

'Right you are,' Ernie said. Mark went downstairs and went outside. Within two minutes Ernie joined them.

'Oh no, I have forgotten something. I've not brushed my teeth,' Ernie said.

'Do you still do that?' Adam asked.

'Of course, I do,' Ernie said. 'It's a bit of a nuisance, now they are well, more fang-like, isn't it? I've got to keep them clean for when I've got the real stuff pumping around again,' Ernie said, laughing.

'Well, I'll be up the dentists once I've turned back for sure. I didn't do lots of things I *had* to do before when I was human. One of them was that,' Adam said.

'What else haven't you done?' Ernie asked.

'Washed my neck,' Adam replied.

Mark left them at the junction of Church Road and off they went to Maurice's house. Maurice thought that they might have quite a strenuous day that day and after today, maybe they would be keeping a different body clock. From tonight they probably needed to be awake the opposite of what they had gotten used to.

'I think we should have a little kip now,' Maurice said. 'I'll leave the door unlatched. Carl will probably come over with Wee Renee, and whoever else is planning to help. Let's try and get some rest. It's going to be quite an exciting day.'

When Wee Renee awoke a few hours later, the rest of the mill was sleeping peacefully. Haggis looked up at her as she got up to go outside, but he wasn't desperate enough to go out in the cold for a toilet, so closed his eyes again.

She had an idea that the Wee Faerie was going to come. Wee Renee felt like he was waiting outside, waiting for them to have a private chat. She might be wrong, but the least she could do was check. Wee Renee trusted her instincts. They never let her down.

She got outside to find it was a mild, damp day. The wet, sloppy snow was falling in clumps off the trees. Everything was wet. There was a soft drizzle, which was helping to thaw the snow. Wee Renee's coat and hair were soon coated in a tiny mist of moisture droplets.

'Hello! Are you there my wee friend?' Wee Renee asked. At first, she thought she was mistaken. Then from nothing, the voice in her head came loud and clear with the intermittent blinking twinkle of the little fellow close by.

'You have done it, Wee Renee. You have completed your mission,' The Wee Faerie said.

'Not quite,' Wee Renee replied with a little laugh. 'Got to kill a few more bloodsuckers, until I can say that.'

'For me, for the greater purpose, you have already changed the future, and that is what we desired, is it not?' He asked.

'I suppose it is really. I still have two main jobs to do, dear Faerie. What about tonight? Do you have any information for me?' Wee Renee asked.

'It will be easy compared to what you have faced before,' he replied. 'You will overpower them. Use fire. It will cleanse the site and eliminate any evidence. You need to know no more.'

'That's a relief. And strangely, I always planned to use fire, but you probably knew that, didn't you? Can you tell me anything about the procedure I must perform on the vampires today? To transform them back to us?' She asked.

'It will be painful, but it will be successful. They will want to back out halfway through, in fear of further pain that they are suffering, that is all. But that is when they are closest to the end. Transformation of any kind, which is unnatural, *remember from death to life is unnatural*, is painful. Do not let them stop you in your mission. They will become more terrible than ever. They will thank you for it after. You will need help to do it. Many hands. The vampires will be desperate, and they still will be monsters until the very end, so be careful,' Wee Faerie said. 'His bloodline will try and defend itself of course. It has not survived this long to be so easily bested.'

'Oh dear, that doesn't sound very good, but I will take plenty of help. And I'll do it one at a time. Nice and calm. Then at least I only have one monster to fight, if the worst happens,' Wee Renee said.

'You know what to do. I have great faith in your work. That is why this won't be the last of my visits. It is the start of a new calendar year tomorrow for you. A whole new start,' said the Faerie.

'Oh yes, it's 31st December today, New Year's Eve. Perhaps we should have a party to celebrate,' she said.

'Maybe you will,' The Faerie said. Then said no more.

Wee Renee remained outside a little longer. She felt at one with nature and very content. The drizzle continued to fall. Making her long white hair frizz up. When it started to get too wet, she made her way in.

After Joe and Beryl had awakened and pulled themselves together, Wee Renee spoke of her plan for a New Year's Eve Party.

'Do you think we can pull it off in such a short time?' she asked.

'Definitely,' Joe said.

'We'll make a list right after breakfast. Don't you worry. Me and Joe will sort this one,' Beryl said.

After everyone had had breakfast Wee Renee told a few of others in her group what she had to do today.

'Any vampire who would like to be turned back can be if he has not consumed human blood. I have been led to believe that three of them - Adam, Ernie and Maurice have not done that and want to be human again. The cure is supposedly very painful but not difficult to do. They must do consume the blood of their own Master. You probably got that bit after my zealous draining of the beast last night,' Wee Renee advised them.

Bob wrinkled his nose. Rather Adam than him. That stuff looked like death in a bucket.

'It says in my book that they must consume two flagons, taken out of a metal container. I will take it that a flagon is about the size of a large mug. I'm after one of them now. That is the only way they can be saved. Would anyone like to come with me?' Wee Renee asked.

'I would like to be there for Adam,' Bob said. 'It sounds like he probably has a bit of a raw deal coming up.'

'Of course, he will need a friendly face,' Wee Renee said to Bob kindly.

'Then we will come too,' Sue said.

'Yes, we will help support Adam,' Tony said.

'I'll be coming with you Rene,' Pat said.

'That's good,' Wee Renee said. 'I was banking on that, love.'

'I'd like to stand for Maurice,' Freddie said.

'I'll come with you too then. I don't want you doing that alone,' Brenda said.

'Thanks Bren,' Freddie said.

'Will anyone come and support Ernie?' Wee Renee asked. 'Obviously, he can't count on Lynn in this instance, and I don't think he has anyone really close to him here.'

'We'll see to Ernie,' Gary and Danny said. 'We always got on with him at Band, and he has been working on our side for a while. He deserves that.'

'That's it. We're sorted, I think,' Wee Renee said.

'I'd like to come over too. I have known this lot for a while now, and I'll meet them for the first time as humans later hopefully. I'd really like to do that,' Carl said. 'And besides that, if they are under the weather, it's about time that I took my turn in making the tea.'

Wee Renee gave him a big smile and nodded, then looked at her watch. 'I just knew you would Carl. You are one of their gang too, I know.'

'I'm not going to come in to help, but I know of something that can help you,' Lauren said, tentatively.

'Oh, aye love. What?' Wee Renee said.

'You say flagon or a mug made of metal. What about a metal beer Tankard? There is a brass one in the pub. I could get that for you,' Lauren offered.

'That's marvellous Lauren, Thank you so much. A brass one too. It couldn't get any better, could it? All boxes are ticked now!' Wee Renee said.

'We'll come over with you, give you the Tankard and then I'll come back with her here if that's all right. Unless you really need us in the room' Rick said.

'No mate. You've never been in Maurice's living room, have you Rick? It's lovely and cosy, but you can't swing a cat in there,' Carl said. Basil's ears pricked up. He sidled off to play with the children.

'It is getting on now, 11 o'clock. I'd like to go over soon. I've had a plan about how to use Michael though. A good one. So, could you give him the message?' Wee Renee asked Joe.

'Yes, certainly,' Joe said.

'It's a simple one, you won't forget,' Wee Renee said. 'First, tell him to inform Marcel and Penelope to meet us at Friarmere Bandroom as soon as it is dark. Tell him his orders are to round up all the players in the Band and form them up to play one last time. March them to the old Bandroom. Parade around the village, retrieving all beasts from any nests that they hide in. Tell him if they resist, that they are under orders and that their Master waits for them there. Tell as many lies as he can to get every vampire there.'

Liz and Andy beamed at one another.

'He won't have a problem with that,' Liz said sarcastically.

'This is going to be brilliant,' Andy said.

'I know,' Wee Renee replied.

22 Preparation

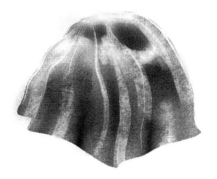

Wee Renee and her small group of medical helpers trekked down the donkey path towards Friarmere. She half imagined that Michael would be on his way over, and they would meet each other but it didn't happen. She hoped he would get the message she would like it to be done and dusted tonight so that they were ready to face the New Year, fresh.

Up at The Grange, Michael had only just awoken. It took a long while to remember the happenings of last night, he was exhausted, and then a big smile spread across his face.

Penelope and Marcel were in The Master's room. Or should he say the old Master's room? He probably wouldn't hear a peep out of them all day.

Yes, yesterday was a funny and unusual day. Today could be even more entertaining. He was just so relieved that he had got through the events. After all, he had lived with a group of monsters now for several weeks and had survived. And then, to top it off, he was lucky enough to ingratiate himself to what had formerly been his enemies, and it looked like he was going to survive this phase too.

Perhaps he should have gone into the Diplomatic Services. He could have served his beloved England, like a James Bond. Michael concluded that even though life had been shit recently. *Actually, life had always been shit*, Michael thought. There must be someone, somewhere, watching over him.

He thought about what he could eat as his stomach complained. Michael was sure that there was nothing here for him. He had three choices. To forage around people's houses to try and get some food. To eat the non-existent food from the shops. Or to go over to the mill and see if he could invite himself to a meal.

Well he was with them now, wasn't he? And he was going to do more with them. Wee Renee said she had an inkling of a plan, which he had to find out about as it was. Yes, he would go over there quickly and see what he could eat, while he listened to their plans for him.

The first stop was the Friarmere Arms. Lauren opened the pub up, and the familiar smells wrapped up the gang in the past. The regular homely past that they pined for.

'Any chance of a quick half?' Freddie asked, rubbing his hands together.

'As long as it *is* quick. We've got a job to do,' Wee Renee said crossly.

Lauren took up her place. Everyone had a drink, even Wee Renee who took a sweet sherry for medicinal purposes. They were all in and out within ten minutes. Pat had the Brass Tankard under her armpit. They waved Lauren and Rick goodbye and set off up Court Street.

When the group got to Maurice's house, Carl said he would go in first. He knocked and waited, but there was no reply. He went to knock again but his fist pushed on the door first, and it opened.

Maurice had been having a lovely dream. Sweet Rosie was there, her petticoats spread out on the grass again, making daisy chains, He thought he heard a shout on the fields, something distracting the peace that he felt when he was with her.

The next thing he felt something on his arm shaking him. His eyes shot open to see Carl's face.

'Were you having a nice dream?' Carl asked. 'You had a right sloppy smile on your face.'

'I was actually,' said Maurice, 'but I'm glad to see you here now.'

Adam had fallen asleep, lying on the floor, the games controller still in his hand. The television had turned itself off. Ernie sat up in one of the armchairs, a white cloth handkerchief over his face. Maurice had been on the sofa. The other people trooped in behind Carl.

'I'll put the kettle on,' Maurice said.

'I'll do that,' Pat informed him. 'Wee Renee is going to go through everything with you. Wake them pair up.' Pat went into the kitchen, and after the sounds of a few banging cups and clattering of cupboards, accompanied by grumbling from Pat, they started to hear the kettle begin to boil.

'Can you wake them all for me, Wee Renee?' Maurice asked. 'It takes me a while to come around when it's daylight. Maurice started to pull himself together on the sofa blinking his eyes even more.

Bob went over to Adam and started to jiggle his game playing arm around with his hand. He crouched down beside him and kept just saying *'Mate … mate … mate.'* Bob wasn't having much success. 'These vampires really go into a deep sleep, don't they? I might just have to let a bomb off to wake him. Oh, I know, what to do...'

'No farting,' Tony said. He remembered how Adam and Bob were. Bob sighed, that was his fun out of the window, so he continued to say *'Mate'* until Adam began to stir.

Sue decided to try and wake up Ernie. She didn't know whether they woke up a bit vicious, so she had picked up Maurice's stick from the corner and was gently poking Ernie in the arm.

'Ernie Love, … Ernie … Ernie,' Sue continued. She must have said it about ten times and still nothing. Sue looked at the rest of them, shrugging. 'What shall we do now?'

'Leave it to me,' Maurice said, who was a little more awake. He got up stiffly, struggling out of his hollow on the sofa. Maurice took the handkerchief off Ernie's face yelled 'Ernie!' loudly in his face. Still, Ernie did not budge.

'Is he actually dead?' Danny asked.

'For all intents and purposes, he is,' Gary said laughing.

'Ernie!' Maurice shouted, and everyone saw one eyelid flutter. 'Ernie!' Maurice tried again and this time they saw him swallow and his eyes were moving around beneath the eyelids, then they opened. Ernie was awake now.

'Hello, gang. What's going on?' Ernie asked.

'Everyone is here. It's going to happen now. Are you alright?' Carl asked.

Yes, I'm ready for it,' Ernie replied.

'Right are you all listening?' Wee Renee asked. Everyone said yes apart from Pat who was still in the kitchen.

'I believe this isn't a nice process. It's got to run through your system, changing your blood back to normal. It's got to restart your heart. It's got to heal everything that has become dilapidated and not used for a while. You know, like your lungs. Now understand this before you start, once I start I'm not going to stop. You will probably ask for it to stop because of the pain but that is what everyone says, and that is when it is working, do you understand. The pain means you are being brought back alive. And it is brief,' Wee Renee said.

'When you say, everyone says it painful ... who are you referring to please Wee Renee?' Adam asked.

'The person who wrote the ancient tomes described many experiences. I don't know anyone's names in particular. Maybe you will or won't agree with them after. You tell me,' Wee Renee said with a smile.

The three vampires nodded after. They all felt like backing out, but they really wanted to be human again. If this is what it had to take, at least they were *all* doing it today. They were all in the same boat.

At that point, Pat came in and asked if there were any more mugs as she could only find four in the cupboards. Maurice thought for a moment and then spoke to her.

'I think I've got ten altogether,' Maurice informed her. 'They could be on the draining board, or in another cupboard.'

'Right you are,' Pat said

'Do you still want us to go through with it? Bear in mind that no matter how much pain you have, I will not stop,' Wee Renee said. 'If I stop then it will have very grave consequences. You don't even want to know. But it is worse than you think.' She looked at them individually. They all made gestures to Wee Renee that they did want to continue.

'There is going to have to be a bit of a process going on here. Me, Carl and Pat are going to do the actual turning of you each. Then each vampire has a couple of carers, as I don't know what you will be like once you are human again. Adam has got Bob, Sue and Tony. You have got Freddie and Brenda, Maurice. And Gary and Danny are standing for you, Ernie.'

'Thank you very much. I don't expect or deserve it,' Ernie said.

'Don't be daft and you're welcome,' Gary said. Danny smiled back at him.

'Can we rally around as well, to support ourselves as we go through it,' Maurice asked.

'I see where you are coming from there, but the problem is I don't want you to back out when the first one goes through the process. The next two might think it looks too bad to go through and will stay as vampires. That's just the luck of the draw with who goes first. They could be the worst turning by far, then the others would never put themselves through it. What I would like is that I do it one at a time, maybe on this sofa. Afterwards, the people who are with that person can take them out of the way to one of Maurice's bedrooms and help them recuperate, get them drinks or whatever they need and then I will do the next etcetera.'

'Good thinking,' Brenda said.

'I'm hoping to have it all done within an hour,' Wee Renee said.

The three vampires liked the thought of it all happening today, even within the hour. But they thought it must be horrible if they couldn't even watch the others go through it.

'Won't it be wonderful. In an hour you could be the same as us and walk right out into the daylight and plan your life again. Just hold on to that thought. In a short hour, which is nothing in our or your lifetime, you will be back, so let's not think about what you may have to go through during that hour. When you are going through it, it will seem a lot longer I can assure you. It will be worth it and such a short time in reality.'

'You're not exactly selling it, Wee Renee,' Freddie said.

Pat clumped in with the cups of tea.

'Listen, Rene, I have heard everything you have said, and you are putting the right fear of God into the three of them. Surely it is not going to be that bad!' Pat exclaimed.

'You are right, Pat. No-one knows for sure, and I would say that the three of these will all have different experiences of the turn, due to their age and how long they have been turned. It may be the person that relayed their turning to the author of the book, was a real Jesse with pain. I don't know, but what I am saying is that it is a warning to them, so it could well happen. I mean when you think of the actual medical process I think it might do a little bit more than just tickle,' Wee Renee said.

'Who wants to go first?' Carl asked.

'I will,' Maurice said. 'I have been changed the longest, so it should be worse for me. I can have a longer recuperation time can't I, than the others. Especially if we must fight tonight. If it does work on the criteria you mentioned, if I am the worst, you will have had a bit of experience when you are turning these lot. And if it doesn't work I'm happy to sacrifice myself,' Maurice said sadly.

'Right Maurice, you're first. That's decided,' Wee Renee said.

'I want Adam second,' Bob said.

'Is that alright with you Adam? Don't let him push you into something like this,' Sue said, then she turned to Bob. 'You may be my son, but this is not down to you.'

'No, I'll go second,' Adam said, 'that's fine.'

'Looks like I'll be having the dregs in third place. If there's enough for me,' Ernie said.

'Don't be silly. From what I know just two mugs of the preparation will be enough, and we have plenty more than that. Plus, there are reserve stocks too,' Wee Renee nodded.

'What preparation?' Ernie said. 'What have you got to do with it? Or have done with it?'

'Nothing. I thought it sounded better than The Master's blood, that's all. I don't have to put anything in it. I just have to serve it in a Brass flagon, which Lauren kindly found for us in the pub,' Wee Renee advised him.

'Fair enough,' Ernie said.

'If everyone gets out of the way now,' Pat said,' we'll get on with it. We still must be all away before dark, you know. There is more stuff for us to do tonight.'

Adam, Sue, Tony, Bob, Ernie, Gary and Danny walked out of the room and upstairs to the main bedroom. They got themselves comfortable, sat all around Maurice's double bed.

'Get the blood please Pat,' Wee Renee asked. Pat squatted down, at the side of Maurice's kitchen table and picked up the bucket of blood with her arms around it

'Argghh it's bloody cold,' Pat said. 'I can feel it through my cardigan sleeves!'

'Well let's face it, it wasn't warm when it was inside him,' Wee Renee said. Pat put the bucket down and laughed loudly, throwing her head back.

'That's a good one Rene,' Pat said loudly, banging Wee Renee on her shoulder with her palm.

'What does it feel like?' Wee Renee asked, looked down at the foil-wrapped colander on top of the bucket, the blood wasn't visible anywhere.

'Just cold,' Pat said.

'I meant, has it firmed up,' Wee Renee told her. She leant over and picked the bucket up by its handle, she gently moved the bucket left and right, feeling the sloshing inside.

'It's still liquid. That's good,' Wee Renee said.

'What shall we do?' Freddie and Brenda asked.

'Just sit in the armchairs for the moment. I'm going to get him to drink this and then you can lie down Maurice, while it happens,' Wee Renee said.

Maurice watched all the goings on. He felt a bit like he was in a daze. Was this really happening now? Would it work?

'You need to take two portions of this from the Brass Tankard, and you need to take them quickly because as soon as that first one hits your belly, you aren't going to want to take the second lot, but you need the second. Do you understand?' Maurice nodded. 'If you don't, Pat is going to hold you down, and we will all hold your mouth open while you swallow it. You have agreed to this, and it will run its course. Right, Maurice?' Wee Renee asked him, putting her long nose in the air.

'That's fine I'll go with it then,' Maurice said.

'Pat, can you pass me a Tankard full of the preparation?' Wee Renee asked. Pat went to pop the Brass Tankard into the bucket but then had a sudden thought.

'Do you have any marigolds?' Pat asked Maurice.

'I have no marigolds, but I do have some heavy-duty black rubber gloves in there,' Maurice said helpfully.

'Where are they?' Pat asked. 'I don't want to get any on me. You never know if I've got a tiny cut on my hand or something, it doesn't bear thinking about.'

'They are under the sink,' he said. There was silence as they heard Pats two feet, going from carpet to linoleum, opening the sink cupboard rummaging around and then after banging around in there. There was the sound of the cupboard door slamming, and they heard her clumping back to them.

'Can I have a word, something's bothering me Rene,' Pat asked. Wee Renee frowned and followed Pat back into the kitchen.

'What happens if he only takes one mug?' Pat asked, trying to keep quiet but the occupants of the other room could hear everything she said.

'What?' Wee Renee asked.

'You keep harping on about them having to take the full course if they start. What would happen if Maurice took only one mug?' Pat asked.

'He would become a Monster. Far worse than Anne or Norman. An unfettered vampire with no restraint. He would kill us all,' Wee Renee said.

'And the hits just keep on comin',' Pat said. She walked back into the living room. From the looks on everyone's faces, she knew they had heard every word. She decided to not address this.

'I got them Maurice. They are black, just as well considering,' Pat said as she pinged them both on her hands. 'Nice,' she sniffed.

Pat picked up the Brass Tankard and dipped it into the blood. It made a thick glugging sound as it filled. She pulled it up, and the outside of the Tankard was now black, coated with the viscous liquid that used to run through Norman Morgan's veins for hundreds of years. Thick drops plopped back into the bucket.

'Here you are,' Pat said she passed it to Maurice who wrinkled his nose.

'Just do it. Don't think about it,' Freddie said, from the chair. He moved to the edge of his seat watching Maurice, who looked with fear at the Tankard in front of him and suddenly, he threw it back down his throat as fast as he could. Half remaining in his mouth, he held out his arm with the Tankard and Pat took it and quickly filled it again.

He swallowed the remainder of the first Tankards contents quickly, as he watched Pat fill it with the filth. The second that the Tankard was ready, and Pat's hand began to reach out towards him, he snatched it off her. She hadn't had time to let the drops finished dripping, and he drunk it straight back even though his body did not want to accept it.

With this mouthful, he focused on the two drops of blood that were now on his carpet. Maurice stared at that, concentrating. Forcing his throat to swallow. He finally did and then lay down on the sofa. The pain radiated from his stomach and went outwards, and he had a sudden urge to vomit but didn't.

Then he felt like his lungs were being squeezed as The Master's blood ran into him, returning him to his human self. Without notice, he had a huge spasm, his front arched high into the air in a crablike pose. Maurice yelled out.

The others upstairs heard his cries. The next thing they heard was Wee Renee shouting *'Hold him down, Pat. Hold him down for god's sake!'* Ernie dry swallowed. He wished he had gone first. There was some mumbling from Freddie, and they could not make out the words and Brenda was doing a few quiet screams. They heard something fall over. *'Nothing important is broken, don't worry,'* Carl said loudly downstairs.

Maurice was still arched; every muscle was rigid. His hands slightly quivered us the blood began to pump in through his heart. He had kicked over the coffee table, containing most of his cups. Brenda was trying to move everything out the way.

While all this was still going on, Pat held Maurice down by the shoulders. He looked up at her but did not really see her. She looked down at him, his face upside down. Pat didn't know how much of this Maurice could take. His cheeks puffed out, the skin becoming lighter like two pale skin balls at the side of his mouth.

'Er... I think he's going into shock,' Pat said.

'Shh Pat. He is in a limbo between hell and earth,' Wee Renee said. As she said it, every muscle that was tense, relaxed and he kind of deflated onto the sofa, his eyelids closed. The humans in the room looked at each other

'Is it done?' Freddie asked. Wee Renee shrugged her shoulders. She moved carefully towards Maurice, knelt down and laid her head on his chest. After about five seconds, she got up again without saying a word.

'What's going on?' Brenda asked, her brows knitted together.

'His heart is beating,' Wee Renee said quietly,' but he seems to be either asleep or unconscious.'

'Hell yes! He's breathing, I saw his chest move,' Carl exclaimed.

'You bloody did it Rene,' Pat said.

'Aye, but it wasn't me, it was the books. It was hard to trust their instructions but thank heavens they were right. I did have my concerns,' Wee Renee admitted.

'Now you tell me,' Maurice said. He opened his eyes and gave them a weak smile.

'How do you feel?' Freddie asked.

'Exhausted and hungry,' Maurice said, 'and unbelievably the pain in my leg is already coming back. How long did it take? It seemed like forever.' Carl looked at his watch.

'Seven minutes. Was it bad?' Carl asked.

'Let's put it this way,' Maurice said. 'Probably better to not let the others see the reality of it. That was genius, keeping them upstairs. If they knew, they would be backing out by now.'

'Oh no. That bad, was it?' Freddie said. 'Come on let's get the next one down before they change their mind. We weren't in a soundproof box. They will know it was no laughing matter. Brenda, shout Adam and his lot down please.'

They started to try and get Maurice gently up off the sofa. They would be putting him in the spare bedroom while the others waited in his main bedroom. Brenda shouted *Adam, love!* Sue, Tony, Bob and Adam appeared at the top of the stairs.

'Come down now, it's your turn,' Brenda said. When Adam walked into the living room, he could see instantly that Maurice was human. Even though he had heard all the commotion going on, and had been extremely worried, he was just so glad now that it worked.

Adam didn't care now about the next few minutes. He was nearly human.

Freddie and Brenda helped Maurice up, and they all slowly started to walk to the bottom of the stairs.

'Don't worry lad, you'll do fine,' Maurice said.

Adam took his place sitting on the sofa. He looked down at the watch Maurice had given him to check the time. He wondered where the big hand would be when he was looking at it for the first time with human eyes.

'Come on then, do it quickly before I back out,' Adam said, but he had no intention of doing that. He was just sick of waiting. Sue and Tony sat in the chairs, Bob stood in front of the fireplace, his anxious young face watching every move.

'You'll be all right,' Wee Renee said. 'Two Tankards drunk quick. The second will be hard as you will have started changing. Pat will force you if you don't take the second. It has to be completed once the first one has been consumed.'

'I understand,' Adam said.

Pat filled the Tankard for the third time tonight and passed it to Adam.

'As quick as you can, do it, Adam. Imagine it's a big Coke,' Bob said.

'Fast,' Carl said, his eyes wide. Adam threw down the first one, and Pat took the Tankard off him and filled it again. She gave the dripping Tankard back to him. Now there was more blood on Maurice's carpet. Adam took the second one down. He looked like he was going to be sick, then he lay down.

Adam squeezed his eyes and lips shut. An unnatural groan came from him, and he said the word *'no.'* He gritted his teeth and shot quickly in the same convulsion as Maurice had. But he went at it so hard, that he looked like he was suspended in the middle by a massive cord.

'Oh no. I can't watch,' Sue said and put her hands over her face.

'Maurice did that,' Carl said. 'From what we can see, its normal for them to do it.'

'Not as high as that though,' Pat said.

'No that's true. Adam is more supple – younger you know. That's probably why,' Wee Renee said.

Adam was bent nearly in two. He could have reached around and easily grabbed his own ankles on the sofa, his body was contorted that hard. He did not scream. Adam gritted his teeth, lips open. His eyes were wide and shaking like two jellies. Pat stood close by, ready to hold him by pressing down or to be of any assistance. This was a silent affair, and they just waited for it to take effect.

The others sat upstairs and could not hear anything this time. They did know whether this was a bad or good sign.

Adam did the sudden relaxation that Maurice had done, but fell with his knees underneath him, uncomfortably. Sue got up and pulled his legs straight.

'What happens now?' Tony asked.

'Maurice was awake within about a minute. Just wait,' Wee Renee said. She put a hand on his chest and could feel his heart beating. 'He's going to be fine.'

Adam coughed and opened his eyes gently. He looked around at them.

'Oh, shit that was mental,' he said.

'Are you a real boy again, or are you still a Pinocchio?' Bob asked.

'I'm a real boy,' Adam said.

'Six minutes,' Carl said. 'That's all for that one.'

'How do you feel about standing up?' Pat asked. 'Or do you need more time to pull yourself together?'

'I feel great,' Adam replied.

'Right let's get you upstairs and get Ernie done,' Wee Renee said. Bob, Sue and Tony went to help Adam upstairs to the spare room. Up there, Maurice lay on the bed and did not look very well. Adam sat beside him on the bed, next to his knees.

'Are you alright, Maurice?' Adam asked.

'I'm as alright as I ever was when I was alive,' Maurice informed him. 'This is me. This is what I was like Adam. I've got a dicky leg and loads of things wrong with me. Close-up I'm not able to see without my glasses, and now without them, I can't see bugger all! I don't know, what was I thinking when I wanted to be human again.' Adam laughed.

'Right Ernie,' Carl shouted from the bottom of the stairs.

'I think I might want to back out,' Ernie said.

'No, you don't,' Gary said. 'You are going through with it because the alternative is that tonight everyone is hunting down all the vampire's and staking them dead. So really, this is your only chance of survival,' Gary said.

'After everything I've done?' Ernie said.

'Yes,' Danny told him. 'Get downstairs, take the cure. Be a big boy, Ernie.'

Ernie, with a drooping head, made his way down the stairs and went into the living room. The three faces looked back at him. Pat with her black rubber gloves on, glistening wet, covered in Norman's blood. Wee Renee with a big smile on her face and Carl sitting in the chair looking quite exhausted.

'Take a seat,' Wee Renee said. There was a massive heavy sound outside, and Carl got up quickly, looking out of the window. 'What is it?' Wee Renee asked.

'All the snow is falling off the roofs in massive sheets,' Carl said.

'It's not Lynn then?' Ernie asked.

'It's still light Ernie, you fool. The cavalry will not be coming after you yet,' Pat said.

'Come on Ernie. No-one will know anything about it or try to interfere,' Carl said.

'Fine I believe you,' Ernie said.

'Now you've got to choke two Tankards worth of this down, and we're going to make sure you drink two of them, do you understand?' Wee Renee said.

'Yes,' Ernie said warily.

'Don't worry Ernie,' Carl said. 'The average time it's been taking with the other two, is six or seven minutes. That's all you've got to get through. The next six or seven minutes, all right mate.'

'I can do that,' Ernie said. Pat dipped the Tankard into the blood. There was very little of the brass showing through now. Ernie thought it looked like melted chocolate in the half-light. He would try and imagine it was that he decided.

'Listen,' Ernie said. 'Before I do this, I have to say straight off I owe you one. I owe you all one. Do you understand?'

'Yeah we get that,' Carl said.

'Don't thank us too quickly,' Pat said, passing him the Brass Tankard. Ernie flared his nostrils looking at the contents.

'Don't look at it,' Wee Renee said.

'It's bloody thick!' Ernie said.

'Yeah it's good stuff, that is,' Pat said. Ernie put his lips to the Tankard and was about to say, should I take a sip first, to see how bad it is, but Carl could see what was on his mind.

'Take it quick,' Carl said. 'Straight down. Don't think.'

Ernie glanced over the Tankard at Carl, and then his mouth opened, tipping the contents straight in. Pat grabbed the Tankard off him, glugged a full portion into the Tankard. The bucket's blood level went down another inch, for the final time and she passed it back to him.

'Ah, I don't think I want another,' Ernie said. 'There's something wrong with it. It hurts. It's not right, that blood. I think it's poisoned.'

'You get that down, right now. Do as you agreed Ernie. I'll not accept it!' Pat shouted. Wee Renee and Pat were terrified of him not taking the second portion. They did not know the window of time they had between portions one and two. The others had worked, but the longer he waited, the more chance Ernie had of turning into a Monster.

Luckily, the fear of an angry Pat still put the willies up Ernie, and he did as she told him. Ernie drank the second portion then lay on the sofa. He began to shake. There seemed to be a kind of growling deep inside his stomach.

Ernie clenched his fists together as the growling continued. Gary and Danny stood over him watching to make sure that he didn't get violent with the women. Somehow, Carl, Pat and Wee Renee knew that this was going to be the worst.

A trickle of blood started to run out of Ernie's nose, and momentarily Wee Renee thought that he might be the one that did not do the crablike spasm. But before she knew it, Ernie went up, not as far as Adam, but farther than Maurice. There was a crack. Ernie screamed.

His toes were pointed outwards, and his whole body vibrated. There seemed to be static electricity in the room, and all their hair started to lift.

'Hold on, everyone!' Wee Renee said in a quivering voice.

Ernie looked to be having the worst symptoms of turning. His hands were clenched into fists pushed down on Maurice's sofa, supporting his crablike weight. Then one leg kick got kicked upwards, so he was only balanced on the other, in his arched position. His head was bent underneath him. Wee Renee remembered Adam.

'Straighten his neck. Once he relaxes, he could break his neck. He'll be human and brittle like us,' Wee Renee said. Carl and Pat realised she was right and had to act fast before it happened. They forcibly pulled his head against the spasm, so that when he collapsed, it would come the right way, and not underneath him. It took a lot of effort from the two of them to tilt his neck.

Ernie was like that for a good ten minutes, and they thought he was never going to drop. Carl felt like his head was going to somehow bend totally backwards, and press against his back, a bit like one of the vampire kids. For those ten minutes, Carl just wished repeatedly that the second Tankard had worked, and he wasn't waiting right next to a Monster's head.

Ernie relaxed suddenly with a sound, which was quite like a pleasurable long *'Ahhhhhh'*.

'Oh hell, that was a close one, I think,' Carl said. Wee Renee put her hand on his chest. Her shoulders visibly relaxed in relief.

'He's done it,' she said closing her eyes in relief. 'We've done it. We've done all three. She blinked and looked at them all. When they looked back at Ernie, spookily he was already looking at them.

'What was that like?' Gary asked Ernie.

'What do you bloody think it was like?' Ernie asked while undoing his tie and shirt collar. Gary shrugged in reply. 'Surprisingly worse than dying, that's what it was like! But I'm back now, and I'm ready for Band!'

23 Thaw

Michael was just setting off from the Mill. He had been given a very decent lunch of beef casserole with dumplings and was content. He enjoyed his time now with humans. This was where he had belonged all the time, who had he been kidding?

He wasn't rushing. It was far better to either be at the mill or be outside. Michael had left it as late as he could. There was no reason to spend time at The Grange anymore, especially as the people who might see him there, were all very fast asleep for a few hours.

He was looking forward to tonight. Michael had been given an important role. This plan couldn't work without him. And Michael loved that power. He would do everything they asked of him. Michael realised, however that he could work with either side. That was a gift that only this situation had revealed. But he really did need a long break from a vampire life. For now, anyway.

Lee, Kathy, Beryl, Sally, Miles and Our Doris, with Haggis on his lead, stood outside of the mill. There were huge patches of grass now visible through the snow. Everything was wet, and all the snow was slush. Our Doris wandered around, and Haggis was trying to jump on the piles of snow but kept disappearing right through to the bottom there was nothing to hold him up there. There were westie shaped holes everywhere. Haggis was having a whale of a time.

'It's just water now,' Our Doris said. 'One touch, and it tumbles like Jenga.'

Soon they saw a smaller party on their way back from the turning of the vampires. Carl, Sue, Bob and Tony had remained with the three new humans. The others had returned. Their trousers wet up to their knees.

'How did it go?' Beryl asked.

'We did it!' Wee Renee said ecstatically. 'All of them are back in the land of the living. I couldn't be happier, Our Doris.'

'*You* did it,' Pat said. 'We would've had no idea what to do. Never in a million years would we have ever even tried that. Especially using a Brass Tankard. Who would have thought that Brass in the Blood was the key?'

'Yes. Brass in Norman's blood to be precise. Well whatever,' Wee Renee said, 'it's done, and we have three more humans in Friarmere than we had yesterday.'

'I want a full low down,' Sally said. 'Was it like a miracle?'

'It was really,' Pat said. 'Bum clenching for a while, but then each had their own miracle.'

'Have you seen how much it is thawing?' Lee asked.

'The High Street is nearly clear,' Gary said. 'It's just the two obstructions on either end now. We walked up to the bus blocking the viaduct end before we came here. There are large patches of red bus showing through the snow. The corners have all melted away, and it won't be long before that's free.'

'You know, we could always wait until the proper authorities come if it won't be long. Let the experts take over' Sally said.

'That's not happening,' Wee Renee said. 'We can't trust them to hunt each and every one. They don't know how to trick them or trap them, and once that barrier is down, if they are not hunted straight away, they can escape out into the night and be anywhere. No, it's got to be us and more important than ever with this thaw, it's got to be tonight.'

Lynn was awake well before light. She was surprised that Ernie was not beside her, but occasionally it had happened before. Very rarely had he risen before her but it was not unheard of.

Lynn wondered why he was up. What was stopping him from sleeping? Ernie slept like a log, dead or alive. But now this insomnia had set in. That was a clear sign that something was on his mind. He was up to mischief. It probably was making the insomnia worse as he knew he was lying to her. Something he certainly did not do when he was alive. No, Lynn had had enough. When she got downstairs, she was getting to the bottom of this. She would mention Mrs White and Vincent. Watch his expressions. Ernie had never been a good liar.

She got dressed and made her way downstairs. Ernie was not in the house at all. As she could see that it was still light outside, he couldn't be out, tinkering in the shed or cleaning the car in the garage. How would he get out to either of those? It was too early for him to go out somewhere else, he would be burnt to a crisp. Which meant he must have gone out when it was still dark, hours ago. Maybe there had been a problem at the Blood Farm, but surely, he would have left a note. It was very rude not to do that. Ernie would know that she would worry. Lynn thought she would make her way up there and find out as soon as it was dark.

Michael had returned to The Grange after his lunch at the mill. It was a very happy and jolly atmosphere there, and he felt the quiet and moroseness of this place even more so after he had returned.

Now he had his instructions, and they were easy enough to do. They wouldn't suspect a thing. Just before darkness, he would make his way down to the School.

He left a note for Marcel and Penelope to inform them of what they should do, which was to turn up at Friarmere Bandroom as soon as it was dark, before leaving just after 2 o'clock. Michael wanted to make sure he was down at the School before it was dark so that he did not miss anyone.

When Michael had arrived there, wading through the slush, he had discovered all the dead vampire children in the main School Hall. That was unexpected. He hadn't been warned about that. He thought about the job that was paramount last night - always ensure that no vampire found out that anything was wrong.

This was a dead giveaway. He dragged each and every one into the room where Carl and Gary had been kept. No-one entered this room because the door was unlocked on the other side. It had Kate's dusty carcass still next to the door. It had only been used anyway to keep humans in there.

He pulled each small child in there quickly. They were so light he could do two at a time. He didn't like to touch their cold bird-like bones, even now they were dead. The only thing that kept him going was thinking that finally, he had had the last laugh over those little terrors.

Just as he shut the door to the classroom, he heard the first arrivals in the entrance hall. The vampires were starting to arrive at the School, waiting for their instructions. Michael's instructions.

24 Ritual

Everyone was getting ready to go into the village. Tonight, was quite clearly, *the night*. A few of the ladies were staying behind to look after the children, who would also be enjoying a late night tonight.

When the others came back, and the word was quite definitely *when,* there would be a New Year's Eve Party.

This served several purposes. It was a celebration that all was over, and normality was back. It was New Year's Eve anyway, so should be celebrated, and it also served to keep everyone who was remaining in the mill, busy. They needed a distraction tonight from whatever was going on in the Village, something they couldn't help with or witness. Anything could be happening. Anyone could perish. And they would know nothing until the survivors returned.

When the vampires awoke, they immediately sent for Wee Renee, Pat and Our Doris. Monica, one of the Moorston vampires came down the metal stairs and asked if they could have a private talk upstairs with the whole party of undead on the second floor.

'What does Angela want?' Wee Renee asked Monica as they walked to the stairs. 'You know we are all going out.'

'You will soon find out. It won't take long,' Monica said.

'Maybe my slip is showing,' Our Doris said glibly.

When the three ladies got to the second floor, all the Moorston vampires, plus Sarah stood majestically waiting for them. Pat gulped.

'Oh God, what's going on?' Pat asked.

'Nothing's going on. We just wish to impart you with some information. Just you three. We don't want to panic everyone else. Call it a *gift*,' Angela said.

'It's definitely not a gift,' Jackie said to her shocked.

'Knowledge is power. Power is a gift. Do you agree, Wee Renee?' Angela said.

'Aye, tentatively I'll agree. As soon as you said the words *panic everyone* though I'm sitting on the fence until I know a bit more. This sounds bad.' Wee Renee said slowly.

'It is,' Sarah said.

'Go on then. Get it over with,' Our Doris said.

'You three, we have to tell you, that we are not the only supernaturals that are in this area,' Jackie said gravely. The three women laughed loudly.

'Oh, is that it?' Pat asked. 'You had me going there, chucks. Bloody hell, that's old news to us,' Pat said.

'What do you know?' Angela asked.

'Since we've been doing this, we've seen ghosts, and things in the trees on the tops of the hills. Yeah, we know. It's a weird area we all have chosen to live in,' Our Doris said.

'And there's Rene's fairy,' Pat said. One of the Moorston vampires laughed.

'I can confirm he's real. He has visited me many times. He exists. Just because you haven't seen one, it doesn't mean the wee blessings aren't about,' Wee Renee said, a little sternly.

'Oh right, a real Faerie. I thought you were going on about something else,' the Moorston vampire said, still laughing a little. Pat caught up with the joke and winked at her.

'Wait until you hear about Rene's tinsel triangle,' Pat said and guffawed.

'Aye, can we get back to the matter in hand. We have to get off soon,' Wee Renee said.

'Is that what you've seen then?' Angela asked.

'Oh, there were those *monkeyluss* as well,' Pat said.

'Yeah about sixty of them,' Our Doris confirmed.

'What?' Jackie asked.

'They mean homunculus. I saw some on our journey over here. I drew one,' Wee Renee said.

'Ah, we didn't know about them,' Sarah said.

'Is that all you have seen?' Angela asked.

'Aye ... ... 'Wee Renee said carefully. 'But I am led to believe, by my Wee friend the Faerie that there might be more matters to deal with as they come up, or come here, I might add.'

'They are already here,' Monica said.

'What are?' Our Doris asked, who knew the least about all these matters.

'Beings that even we do not want to tackle,' Angela said.

'Shit!' Our Doris said.

'Listen, do we really want to know all this when we are just about to go out for a massive fight. We think that it will be all over tonight – and you are making out is has just begun!' Pat said.

'This is our gift,' Angela said.

'Well Happy New Year and all that,' Our Doris said. 'But you can keep your gift to yourself.'

'No, we need to hear it. Tell me alone, if the others do not wish to be encumbered,' Wee Renee said.

'I'll stay with you Rene,' Pat said. Our Doris sighed.

'Go on. Give us the Grimm Fairy Tale,' Our Doris said.

'Last year in the summer Monica was on the Moors in the night. She likes to run, for fitness. Don't you Monica?' Angela asked.

'I do. I used to run when I was alive. Marathons. I feel so free now, running at top speed, leaping the moors. It's wonderful. Anyway. One night I saw it,' Monica said.

'What?' Wee Renee asked.

'I don't know. It was a glowing a bit, and it didn't see me because I was sprinting. But I saw it as a leapt over a hill, and its back was towards me. So, I crouched down, so it didn't see me. And I watched it,' Monica said, her eyes wide.

'What was it doing?' Our Doris asked.

'Hunting,' Monica said. 'And it caught its prey too.'

'Hunting what?' Wee Renee asked.

'Pheasant?'' Pat offered.

'No. Other supernatural creatures,' Monica said. By the tone in her voice, this seemed a bad thing.

'Wait a minute then. Is this glow-beast doing *our* job for us? It's a goodie then?' Our Doris asked.

'Oh no,' Monica replied gravely, and all the vampires shook their heads.

'Listen. I have been plotting rare occurrence's, missing people etc., for ages in the Melden triangle. I realised a while ago if Anne and Norman had moved here recently and Len had been here ages, and he didn't take human's, that it couldn't have been you lot. I knew something was on the prowl,' Wee Renee said.

'That is true. But this entity takes humans and supernaturals for evil purposes,' Angela said.

'By entity, do you mean ghost? Is it invisible or made of smoke or summat?' Pat asked.

'No. The entity is physical. You could touch them.' Monica said. 'After that night, I saw it again. Several times. But I was aware of it, so was careful. It never touched animals. But I saw it kill some rare creatures, drain a ghost and one time I came too late as it was already feeding on a human. Not as I could have done anything, anyway.' Monica was quite clearly sad about this.

'Len forbade her to run any longer and said we would deal with this. He asked Anne and Norman when they came in the Autumn, before the snow, if they could all band together to try and rid the Moors of this predator. But they weren't interested,' Angela said.

'No surprise there,' Pat said and sniffed loudly.

'Any more information on this critter?' Wee Renee asked.

'Not on their whereabouts, no. But well, from what it left behind, I am talking about its victims now, I think they are taking certain er … parts of them. Particular pieces,' Monica said.

'Nice. Why?' Our Doris asked.

'We don't really know. The Master thought they were maybe for some kind of ritual,' Jackie said.

'Great, more good news. They are probably going to summon something worse. Like a devil or a man with a goat's head!' Pat said.

'They don't have to summon them. They are already on the moors,' Sarah said. 'Even I've seen one of those. They are common things.' Our Doris laughed loudly.

'This just keeps getting worse. You've got to laugh, haven't you,' Our Doris said.

'Aye, you have. But I don't think it's a devil. I'm thinking an Evil Black Dragon,' Wee Renee said.

'Don't go there Rene. Please, I don't want to think about that tonight,' Pat said.

'Thank you, Angela,' Wee Renee said.

'Thanks a bunch,' Our Doris added. 'Next time you want to give a gift, I'll have Youth Dew, Ladies.'

The three women returned silently to the ground floor.

25 Witches

When the first tendrils of darkness came drifting down, Lynn put on her coat and boots. She looked outside from the safety of a mirror at an angle. It seemed very wet out there, not snowy and cold. That meant everything would be muddy up at the farm. Drat! She decided to wear wellingtons today instead of warm snow-boots.

As soon as it was dark, Lynn started to make her way up to Mark's blood farm. It was hard going up bank, but she was determined, ploughing through the slush in her wellies. With all things considered she made great time and was there within ten minutes of darkness falling.

She could see Mark pottering about. However, there was no sign of Ernie. Until she saw her husband, she really did not want to knock on the door, because Mark didn't know that she knew where this was. Why would Lynn be up here? It wasn't somewhere Lynn would see by chance. Mark could work that out - realise that she had been following them. If he thought she suspected him of hiding something, he would be cautious in what he said or did.

About half an hour after she had got there, Mark left the building. There was still no sign of another person up there, living or dead. Only Mark and his donor's. He locked the door behind him, and without even noticing that she was there, he started to walk down to the Village. He strolled down the footpath in the opposite direction to Lynn. She noted that he did not have any crates of blood, which was unusual. Lynn wondered where he was going. With the added fact that Ernie was missing, she thought that she might just learn something new if she followed him.

Stephen had spent the day in the Civic Hall. He was guarding his food. Last night, when he had arrived for another snack, both doors, outer and inner were wide open. Someone had been here in the last few hours. A careless vampire who had left the larder open. When Stephen arrived, there were already seven rats feasting on the remains.

After finding them all and destroying them, he thought he should hang around here in case the culprit arrived. Stupid vampire – he would have a lot of explaining to do when Stephen caught him. All that meat was nearly ruined.

Stephen made his way straight up to the School once it got dark. He was pleased to see Michael about, as he wanted to discuss the matter of feeling so ill.

Eating again hadn't made him feel better. But also, it hadn't made him feel worse. So, it wasn't the Civic Hall meat.

'Michael, has anyone come to you about feeling ill?' Stephen asked.

'No – who are you on about in particular,' Michael asked. This was a weird question from his brother.

'Anyone. Lynn? ... ... I don't know. Just yesterday, we started to feel really ill. I don't feel any better today,' Stephen said.

'You've probably been eating summat infected. The lot of you,' Michael said as if this was a final diagnosis.

'No. We haven't. Definitely, me and Lynn haven't eaten the same people,' Stephen advised him.

'What about Mark's bottled blood. Have you had a bottle of that from him? You know his stuff doesn't come with a sell-by date. I bet it's that,' Michael said.

'I've not had any off him for a few days,' Stephen said. 'Since the night I last saw Vincent!'

'Maybe it's viral. Listen, Stephen, in a way, this is the ideal time for this to happen. There is a meeting tonight, and we will all be together. Everyone. We'll put it out to the gang. The more facts I have, the better my diagnosis will be,' Michael said. 'And even more exciting, I have been told to form up Band too!'

Lynn followed Mark at a great distance. She could see him from a mile off, he was the only person about. Mark seemed happy enough, walking along to wherever we was off to, occasionally whistling.

When Lynn came out into the Village off the footpath, she decided to quicken her pace so that she would not lose him amongst the streets. He never looked behind himself once.

'Hmmm!' Lynn said when she saw him going into a house, which she knew was Maurice's house. She might have known.

Maurice had acted unusually since he had been turned and so had Ernie. Mark was another one. The three of them must have been working together. That was probably where Ernie was, not up at the blood farm. This was probably where he had been a lot.

Lynn boldly walked up to the door and was just about to bang on it when she smelled something quite unusual. There were humans here. Humans and vampires. There must be if Ernie, Mark and Maurice were in there. *What the hell was going on?*

Lynn wasn't about to let that stop her anyway. If her husband was in there, she wanted him out, and he'd have to have some good answers for why he was in there too. And *where* he had been all day. Lynn knocked loudly on the door.

The only vampire in that house was Mark. He had entered to discover that his three former vampire vigilante friends were now human vigilantes, and were happily eating chips, egg and beans that Maurice had made. Adam was only just starting his story about their three transformations when they heard a knock at the door.

'It must be our lot,' Sue said, 'although I didn't think they were calling for us.'

'I haven't even finished my tea,' Ernie said. 'And this isn't even touching the sides. I'm starving!'

Sue smiled and began to walk to the door. A split second before she opened it, Mark smelled who was there.

'Don't!' Mark said. 'It's not our lot,' Mark looked at Ernie, 'It's Lynn!' Ernie dropped his knife down onto his plate with a clatter.

'No,' he said, 'she'll bloody kill me!'

'You should have thought of that,' Carl said.

'Come on, there is enough of us here to tackle Lynn. Do you think she's on her own?' Adam asked Mark.

'Yes, I think she is,' Mark replied confidently.

'Come on let's get it over with Maurice,' said Mark, and swung the door open.

'Lynn,' he said, 'how nice to see you and how unusual to see you *here*!'

'What's going on Mark?' Lynn asked. 'Where is your blood crate? And where is my husband?' Ernie sank lower in his seat, as he heard their conversation.

'Please Lynn, calm down. Besides that, you may not want him back!' Mark commented with a little laugh.

'What have you been up to?' Lynn asked. 'What have you got him into? And Maurice? I'm ashamed of you. You know Ernie is easily manipulated!'

'I am not!' Ernie shouted from his chair. Lynn tried to look through the door at various angles to see her husband, as she could not enter - she had never been invited. She was unsuccessful as he was effectively round three corners and out of sight.

'Tell him to come here!' Lynn ordered Mark, furiously. Ernie got up and shrugged his shoulders, resigned to his fate.

'Come on,' Tony said. 'We'll go with you.' They walked to the front door. As many people as possible huddled in Maurice's doorway, looking out at Lynn. She saw Tony, Maurice, Carl, Adam and Ernie.

'Oh, so you're in with them too, are you Adam?' Lynn asked. 'Another of The Masters rejects!'

'Yes, that's right,' Adam said.

'And you! I thought you were dead,' she said to Carl. 'Don't tell me you know these lot of losers, as well?'

'Yeah they saved my life, including your husband,' Carl said.

'Get out here at once,' Lynn said to Ernie. 'I'm not washing my dirty linen in public. Us two will have this out at home!'

The group surged forward outside onto the doorstep, she stepped back down the path and towards the front gate. As they came towards her, out of the ex-vampire's lair, she could smell each one of them finally. Lynn knew that Carl was human, and so was Tony, but when she smelled that Adam, Maurice and her own Ernie were too, she was horrified.

'You're human again, what has happened? How have you done this?' Lynn asked. 'Is this you, with your Blood Farm and your pipes and stuff?' Is that what you were doing, planning to turn people back?' Lynn wagged her finger at Mark, angrily.

'It's not my doing?' Mark said. 'I wish it was, though Lynn, so there.'

'You can't do this to everyone,' she said. 'We're happy how we are! Did you use witchcraft? Is that it?'

'Eh? What witches?' Ernie asked, confused.

'No. We aren't doing it to everyone,' Tony said. 'And rest assured we're not going to do it to you!'

'You just wait until The Master hears about this,' Lynn said. 'You just wait. All your Band will be turned back into vampires. He will see to that, don't you worry Ernie, and then I'm gunning for you. All of you, you sneaky lot,' Lynn said and ran loudly up Lee Street away from them, in her wellingtons.

The small collection of people stood in Maurice's front yard looking up the street.

'That was quite comical really,' Ernie said.

'Especially the sound the wellie's made when she was trying to be hard and running off,' Adam said.

'Yeah,' Carl said, 'you can't exactly make a grand exit when you are wearing loud wellies.'

'I always said those wellie's, made her sound like she was parting with the wind, but she never listened. Come on. I'm finishing my chips and beans,' Ernie said and wandered back inside. 'I'm even more hungry now. It's nervous energy!'

'But what are we going to do about Lynn?' Maurice asked.

'Even if she finds someone to tell,' Bob said, coming out from Maurice's kitchen with a chocolate biscuit. 'What's she going to say - that some vampires have been turned back to human? So, what – who's going to believe that anyway? She isn't telling them that The Master is dead and that is the thing that we need to keep secret. Lynn can do what she likes. Say what she likes. But I think we should shift before she can get a posse to come back here.'

Lynn ran through the streets of Friarmere. She would run up to The Grange first, and the quickest way was back up the footpath past Mark's Blood Farm onto the top road and straight to The Grange.

As she did this, Lynn thought about how she would probably have to kill one of those humans to recoup the strength that she was using to do this run. *The Master would reward her greatly, that was without question*, she thought. When she got to The Grange, she ran straight inside the large doors.

'Hello!' Lynn shouted. 'Hello! Master! Penelope! Marcel! Anyone! Quickly, help!'

Her voice echoed back to her. She went to the first room – no-one. She went to The Master's office – no-one. She ran upstairs not really knowing which room The Master slept in. Lynn thundered through several of them and found them empty. She rushed outside, discovering the snowmobiles. Lynn concluded they mustn't be in Moorston. There was only one place he could be. The Master must have gone to the Primary School.

26 Pile

Michael waited for as many of them as he could. From what he could remember, all the vampires that usually met up there were present. He knew that others joined them as they processed. Michael asked Stephen where all the other nests were. Stephen told him. He never had an inkling what his brother was up to.

'Everyone, The Master has instructed me to form up Band, and we are to progress to the Bandroom where he is waiting for us,' Michael said.

Stephen was excited. They hadn't played together for a few days, and it looked like something might be going on. Something different in the Bandroom. The Master must have had some new ideas when he had been alone in The Grange for a few days. Maybe they were going to start rehearsals again. Plus, he was interested to find out how everyone felt since yesterday.

'What if we don't do Band? Some of us don't you might be interested to hear,' One of the ladies asked. 'I can't play a Brass instrument. What do we do? Why does The Master need us at the Bandroom?'

'You are to march at the back. It is a meeting for Band and everyone else. And as it's very important, I will play the bass drum, just this once. You'll have a good time,' Michael assured her.

'Have we got to bring the vampire kids?' Stephen asked. 'I haven't seen them. Who's looking after them?'

'Er … … They are already there, as is Mrs White. She has been preparing the place for us,' Michael said.

'Ah, I was wondering where she was,' Stephen said. 'And Vincent?'

'Yes, he is,' Michael said.

'You could have told me,' Stephen said.

'I didn't know myself until tonight. I can guarantee you'll be where he is now, very soon,' Michael said, truthfully. 'Now let's go outside and get into line. When we start, give it some welly. Let everyone here we are coming for them, and we are on our way!'

They lined up, and when everyone had taken up their instruments, they started to play. Michael played the piece quite quickly. He set the beat so they would march promptly to the Bandroom.

Michael was following instructions to weave around the Village, passing any nests he knew. These vampires would come out to be with them, or they could send someone to call, thus picking up every straggler who had decided to make their own nest.

This they did, and everyone joined them, without being called for. Soon they were all behind Michael, either playing or in the grand procession.

Sarah watched them from the roofs of Friarmere. She was the only one that could get up there now. She followed along as they picked the people up. Sarah didn't think Michael was doing too bad really, for a former spy. Michael led them merrily, and they all marched to their doom with a smile on their faces. Soon they would be at the Bandroom and this all would be over. Really over.

All the party from Maurice's house arrived at the Bandroom to find the others waiting for them. They told them excitedly about their encounter with Lynn and that she had gone to alert The Master.

'She won't be having much luck, will she,' Freddie said.

'Even if she finds one of the others, all she can say is that some vampires are now humans again, not that The Master is dead. We aren't bothered. It will be fine,' Bob said.

Sue had the Bandroom keys and opened up. She put the lights on as if The Master and the other vampires were in there. Joe, Rick, Craig, Darren and Father Philip were under instruction to do a particular thing at a particular time. They were stationed in the trees, one roughly on each corner with their apparatus. All the vampires had to be inside before they did it.

Lynn got to the Primary School. She rushed in and shouted again. Her voice echoed back at her. Immediately this felt like The Grange. She was sure that it was empty. She entered the Headmaster's office, which was empty. Michael was not in the School staff-room attending to any patients, and she could find none of her kind, including the vampire children.

She decided to check every classroom. Lynn knew now that something wasn't right and on top of all this, she had felt ill since yesterday. Now with all this Ernie business too, it seemed like everything was wrong. Lynn was panicking as much as a vampire could. She had nearly checked all the classrooms when she decided to go to the darkroom, as they called it. When she opened the door, immediately she saw the pile of vampire children's bodies and knew there was a lot more going on, than what was happening to Ernie.

Lynn ran straight into the classroom, past the pile of kids, through the dusty remains of The Master's favourite Lieutenant, and out the other side, out of the exterior classroom door. Where was everyone? There were certainly no other dead vampires up here, only Kate and the vampire kids. They must be somewhere. Where was Stephen too? He was always hanging around.

Lynn stood at the classroom door looking out over Friarmere. She felt desperate. She didn't know where to go now. Where was The Master?

Then just on the hint of a wind, she heard the Band playing quite a distance away, but she knew in which direction. Lynn started to run again, her wellies making a farting noise, as pockets of air squelched through the arches of her feet and the gap between her footwear. What a night to be wearing wellies. She should have been wearing running spikes. She ran as fast as she could towards the Band, help and her Master.

Penelope and Marcel arrived to greet their Mistresses. They were to have an important role tonight too. These two Moorston vampires were the only two apart from Michael that the vampires would trust. They were to go inside the Bandroom as a pair of regular faces along with Michael.

'Once everyone's in there, give us at least five minutes to do what we need to do outside, then all three of you, make an excuse and come outside. We won't start until you do,' Gary said.

They went inside and shut the door behind them. The three stooges, Our Doris called them after they had all gone inside, Freddie nudged her.

'You'll get in trouble for saying that, Our Doris,' he whispered.

The rest of the heroes could hear the Band playing. At first, it was only Michael, his drum beating like a lone heartbeat through the Village. Which was ironic as his was the only heart beating there. There was barely any snow now on the trees, and the ground was muddy and sodden with water. Over eighty humans and good vampires waited in silence.

27 Crunching

As the drum got very loud, the humans retreated into the trees. They were fortunate that the Bandroom was surrounded heavily by trees, bushes and other vegetation.

Angela had assured them that this place stunk of humanity. Wee Renee just hoped that the vampires would think it was an ancient stink and not a recent one. The humans could only smell how wet and damp everything was. Wet soil, wet weeds, wet gravel.

Michael brought the Band down the path behind him. As he played in front of them, his eyes darted this way and that. Michael hoped that he could not see one of the others and happily was not able to. Even knowing that they were there, he could not see a hint of them, which was an achievement. Then he had a split second of panic. *What if they weren't here?* How was he going to explain everything when The Master failed to turn up? No, he took a deep breath, as he missed a beat of his drum. *Calm down Michael*, he thought. One thing he could say about Wee Renee and any of her plans was that she was dependable.

Considering the number of humans that he knew lived in the mill, and last night's posse, there must be quite a lot of people around in the trees and bushes for this last push. Michael still could not find a single one of them. To be fair there were many places to hide – he knew that better than anyone. He had stood outside this Bandroom many nights in the Autumn with The Master. Adding to that, the outside of this place was so dark. Sue had deliberately not turned on the outside lights. But the inside lights were on, and that automatically meant that everyone's eyes were drawn to that place. Like a beacon shining out in the black ink of the evening.

The Band finished up their piece outside the Bandroom with a flourish and started to take off their instruments. The vampires walked up the couple of steps to the portacabin and flung open the door to find Penelope and Marcel waiting for them, a brief smile of greeting on their faces.

'What have we got to do?' One female asked.

'Just take a seat, The Master will be here very soon,' Penelope said. Penelope sat at the front near the conductors stand with Marcel. The rest of them filed in, taking a seat where they could. Stephen looked around the room.

'Where are the kids?' Stephen asked.

'What?' Marcel asked.

'The vampire kids are supposed to be here with Mrs White,' Stephen said.

'I think Mrs White and The Master took them outside for a play, they can play in the fields here, supervised. You know, it's a change for them Stephen,' Michael said from behind the group of vampires. He winked at Marcel and Penelope.

Michael had taken a seat on the timpani chair and was fiddling with the pedals. No! Someone was missing. He didn't know who to tell. Not everyone was here. The person who played these most of the time was missing. *Where was Lynn?* No! Michael had failed in his mission. He stared at Penelope hoping to attract her attention, but she was looking at the ceiling, waiting for the right moment. She just had to give them a couple of minutes to prepare.

There was an awkward silence. Penelope felt it getting uncomfortable, but it was Stephen again who saved the day.

'It looks good, doesn't it?' Stephen roared.

'What's does?' Penelope said.

'That trophy that we won mid-October. The last one, the old Friarmere Band, won. Behind you,' Stephen gestured. 'The massive shining star.'

Penelope turned around to look in detail at the gold angular trophy.

'Oh yes, it's a Bobby Dazzler, that is,' Penelope said. Stephen grinned at her.

'Well, we're not giving it back to them. Instead, it'll get engraved, and we'll keep it. We can do things like that, can't we?' Stephen said as he laughed.

'Oh yes,' Marcel said. 'We can do anything really.'

Outside Joe's vigilantes had waited for the procession to file in and then they began to creep forward, one at each corner. Each had a large canister of petrol which they started to glug around the edges of the portacabin in a clockwise direction, so they joined up at the edges.

'Can you hear something?' One of the young male vampires asked. 'Like gravel crunching?'

Penelope had heard it too. She looked at Michael again for an answer and nudged Marcel.

'I don't hear anything. Anyway, haven't you just been told that the kids are outside. Moron,' Marcel said.

'I tell you what. What about us having that CD on. You know the one you lot recorded. I love that,' Michael said with a slow nod at Penelope and Marcel.

'I'll put it on,' Stephen offered. There was an old CD player behind the desk, which also had a radio. Ernie had bought it many years ago. The Band still had about 250 copies of their CD for sale, so there was always one to play whenever they required it.

Stephen put it on, and Penelope talked loudly all the time he was fiddling with it, trying to cover the noise outside. Soon the Band were listening to a rousing version of *Knight Templar,* and it would drown out any sounds. Stephen sat down.

'Let's just wait for The Master and listen to this, shall we,' Marcel said eyeing up the male vampire who had asked the question as if he was a child to be entertained.

The sound of the Band CD began to boom out of the portacabin walls. Joe wondered correctly if it was to cover their noise.

As the people outside concentrated on what seemed now the deafening gravel crunches and the sound of marching music coming from the Bandroom, they were not aware of the person that was running down the path towards them.

Luckily the outside lights were still off, and they were all dressed in dark clothes. The ones at the sides of the Bandroom heard the approach first and rushed around the corner. They just stood at the back of the Bandroom, blinking at each other. The others who had just begun to come out of the trees heard it too now and retreated as fast as they could.

Lynn ran down the path. It had been a combination of the farting sound of the wellies, and the gravel that had given her away. When she found The Master, she would get him to investigate what the hell was going on

Sarah had seen Lynn running through the village but could not get in front of her. She was behind her now, keeping up with Lynn's pace. At the same time, trying to be as discreet as possible as the trees.

Lynn ran towards the Bandroom. She could hear the CD. The CD that she had played on herself and could tell that the Bandroom was full. She had found them at last. They sounded like they were having a good time, what a shame that she was going to burst their bubble.

Inside, Penelope, Marcel and Michael were unaware of what was going on outside. Penelope stood up.

'We are going to try and find The Master. He is taking a little longer than we thought. Perhaps he doesn't know that you have all arrived. Michael, I wish you to come along with us. As an extra set of eyes,' Penelope said.

'Do you want me to come?' Stephen asked.

'That won't be necessary,' Penelope said.

'Eh, I've just thought, you said Vincent was here too. And where's Keith?' Stephen asked. The three conspirators pretended that they hadn't heard him.

Michael got up and wandered towards the door, trying to appear casual. This was about to go down. The three of them opened the door, strolling outside. Everyone was happy inside, listening to music and waiting for The Master - doing as they had been instructed.

Wee Renee and all the others thought that everything was happening a little too fast. The door had opened, and the three people they were saving were coming out, but Lynn was less than one hundred feet away from the Bandroom in her farting wellies and would be in there directly, giving the game away.

Michael, Penelope and Marcel once at the bottom of the stairs, immediately turned right to go towards the bushes, to wait with the others. Marcel was at the rear of the small group, about to shut the door.

The people at the back, the ones that could have ignited the petrol and sorted it instantly, did not see that Penelope, Marcel and Michael were out, as they were hiding from Lynn. Also, they did not hear it, because of the CD player. They were not about to set fire to the Bandroom until instructed.

Wee Renee did not know whether to step out and intercept Lynn, thus giving the game away or not. She couldn't reach her from where she was in the bushes.

Beyond the Bandroom, further away, the Moorston vampires could not help either. They had been told to keep well back until the very last minute, as Moorston vampire was not a smell that was natural at Friarmere Bandroom. They had no idea what was going on.

The only person that could maybe get to Lynn was Sarah, who now jumped down from the trees and was pelting behind. Lynn was so intent on her mission, looking at the front, that she was not looking back.

'Good girl,' Wee Renee whispered.

Beryl tried not to look worried about the war tonight. She had to keep it together for the children in the mill. Tonight would see the end of it. Beryl hoped that they would have a lovely New Year's Eve party. God knows if anyone deserved it, they did after all this.

She hoped it wouldn't take all forever. Until she saw the mob return safe, it would be a very long night. Until then, she had to act as happy as she could, so that the kids were not screaming inside like she was.

Just before Sarah caught up with her, Lynn shouted *'Help! Help!'* The door was still open, Marcel still had not shut it. Lynn pushed past him when she saw she saw that The Master was not with them, she began to spill the beans to the vampires inside. The three conspirators rushed quickly to the safety of the bushes. They didn't know what was happening, or what to do.

'Everyone! The kids are dead, stacked up at the School. Some of us have been turned back into humans. Where is The Master?' Lynn screeched. Most of the vampires thought that Lynn had gone stark raving mad. *Turning us back into humans!* Rubbish. Only Stephen believed everything from anyone.

'Outside somewhere, er …. with Mrs White and … and the kids,' Stephen said.

'Don't hang around you fools. It's a trap. We're all in one place. Everyone is here apart from The Master and a couple of others! Get out, get out!' Lynn hollered.

This was true. The monsters began to move.

Lynn ran back outside and Stephen being seated close to door also got out. Two more vampires managed to get out too before Sarah pushed past them and went into the Bandroom.

Sarah went into the room and shut the door behind her.

'No you don't,' she said.

28 War

Wee Renee, Pat, Gary and all the others surged forward outside. The friendly vampires were still way off the perimeter and didn't know what was going on inside. Someone had to tell them. Penelope ran inside to help immediately.

'Lauren, run to Angela's lot. Tell them what's happening. Bring them now,' Pat said to Lauren, who was slim, young and a fast runner.

Still, the Brass Band music played on. Lauren ran back to where the Moorston vigilantes stood, who saw her coming and ran out to meet her. She quickly told them what had happened. They ran around to the door.

The Moorston vampires surged into the Bandroom to help Sarah. She and Penelope were alone with over twenty enemy vampires. Although when they entered, to be fair, it seemed like there was more arguing that fighting.

Marcel stayed outside to help the others with the four Friarmere vampires that were preparing to kill them. Apart from Mark, he was the only vampire to help to deal with at least two very formidable Friarmere vampires.

As soon as the original vigilantes realised it was now happening, Joe shot out from the corner of the Bandroom. He picked up his chainsaw, locating the switch at the back and approached one of the young vampires around the corner knowing that now, the noise would not to be a problem. This model had a light for guiding the blade fitted, and this was exactly what Joe needed this dark and cloudy night.

Surprise was the key here, and when he was close enough, he pressed the button. His battery-powered chainsaw roared into life, cutting the vampire in a diagonal line from his shoulder to just above its heart. As he withdrew the chainsaw, it cut deeper through to the other side. The people at the front saw it chunk through each rib at the front, before Joe pulled it upwards at the same angle.

The young male seemed to freeze and look down at the cut. The vampire had never even realised it was happening. Now he felt very strange. Joe tilted the chainsaw and made the exact cut at the other side of the vampire, creating a nice V directly below the clavicle. The vampire dropped. That was one.

Inside the Bandroom, Angela had already ripped out a vampire's throat, as the Friarmere lot panicked inside the room. Sarah was being attacked mercilessly but still held onto the door so that they could not go outside. Jackie had grabbed one vampires' arms and was strangling another with them.

'Two for one,' Jackie shouted crazily. She pulled, and the first one's arms flew off up the Bandroom, hitting the whiteboard that they wrote their Band jobs on. The other one felt the pressure release. He had not been strangled as he didn't breathe as it was, but he was effectively trapped. Relieved to be free, he turned to find two Moorston vampires behind him. One took out his eyes before the other took out his heart.

Penelope moved around quickly, slashing vampires with her fingernails. Some of these would prove fatal. Others at least would be weakening the horde.

Two of the Moorston vampires had quite a novel way of dealing with their foes. They had taken a Friarmere vampire by the hands and feet they proceeded to bang them up and down. Like putting a quilt in a quilt cover. It seemed like they could not get it straight, so flapped and flapped until they were over a chair back. They carried on flapping them up and down until the vampire broke into two.

Outside, Wee Renee was trying to attack Lynn with her machete while Pat came at her, swinging the club hammer. Ernie had understandably said that he would be keeping out of any attack of Lynn. However, he did understand that it had to be done. He could not bring himself to watch it or to be involved. So, turned to look at the other foes they had to deal with.

Lynn moved one way and another. Wee Renee had to admit that, for a woman in retirement, Lynn had made a surprisingly good vampire. Her eyes darted from Wee Renee to Pat. If they could just catch her, they could get her good.

Luckily for everyone else, Lynn was not looking behind her. Agnes ran around from the side, with her cutthroat razor flashing in the dim lights from the inside the Bandroom, she managed to cut Lynn's face. Agnes was significantly taller than Lynn and had gouged a deep cut just over one of Lynn's eyebrows.

The black blood started dripping into Lynn's eye. Now she only had one to see with. It was hard keeping watch on Wee Renee and Pat with two. Now she had no chance. Plus, there was this new woman with an incredibly sharp weapon.

The Bandroom was a portacabin that sat high on bricks. In desperation, Lynn scrabbled backwards and got underneath it. Now they could not reach her. For the moment she was safe. She growled and watched them with her one functioning eye. The blood had now reached her chin. She would think of something.

Penelope spied something that she thought was an ideal weapon. She didn't really need to use it, but she thought it would be poetic to have it used.

Penelope put a lot of store into memories. Into things that had importance. This was more precious than anything to these Band people. It had to be used. The cycle ended. She laughed a little before picking up the Brass Band Trophy with the sharp edges and walked to the door. The Moorston vampires seemed to have it mostly under control in here. She wondered what was happening outside.

'I'm going out, but I'll be back in a minute,' she said to Sarah, who nodded once and let Penelope through.

Our Doris, Liz, Andy, Danny and Gary were working on the female vampire who was outside now. There was only this female, Stephen, and Lynn underneath the portacabin to deal with on the exterior. For the moment anyway. Andy and Danny both had knives, Gary had his nail gun, which was ineffective at this range.

Sue saw an opportunity to get the vampire at the back and came at her, with a hairspray can and candle lighter. As Sue ignited it, she moved the female vampire closer to the other attacks and away from a small area, where she would be close to the boundary and be able to retreat. There was a patch of land that had not been part of the Bands property, and through this, she could get to a little stile and away.

Sue tilted the angle of the flame so that the female would have to turn away from the area of escape. If she had her back against the portacabin, she could not move.

'Gary, pin her,' Sue said. The female's hand was on the corner of the Bandroom, clutching it as if she was about to push off from it. To spring away to freedom. The vampire continued to back away from the fire and was turned away from Gary, unaware of the weapon he held.

Gary nailed her hands directly to the Bandroom straight away with three quick nails.

'Our Doris!' Gary shouted. The female tried to pull her hand away from the side of the Bandroom. Sue continued to fire the hairspray at her, to stop her from escaping. Sue could feel the can was getting quite empty now.

'Come on someone. Anyone!' Sue said. It's going to run out!' Our Doris arrived now to decapitate the vampire, but in the female's struggles, while she reached to grab the hairspray can, she had set fire to her own blouse sleeve. Our Doris was just in time as the female pulled a chunk out of her hand to free it, and herself from the Bandroom, but Our Doris was already swinging and off came her head.

Her body, complete with burning blouse, fell onto the ground. It fell onto the petrol, so liberally splashed around the perimeter. This ignited, and blue flames ran squarely around it within a few seconds. The men had sloshed it on the walls, on the ground and had even managed to spray some up to the roof with a handy plant spray. Now the Bandroom was very much on fire.

Angela, Jackie, Sarah and the Moorston vampires were caught inside.

29 Senses

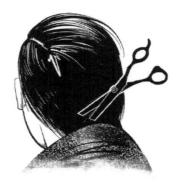

Penelope quickly handed the Friarmere Band trophy to Freddie.

'Use this,' Penelope said. Then she turned straight around and ran back into the flaming Bandroom. Penelope pushed inwards on the door. Sarah allowed Penelope entry as she continued to guard the exit. With the Bandroom getting considerably hotter, and time becoming shorter, Penelope was a welcome addition to join the fight for their lives. But they would all have to be quick.

Freddie looked down at what she had given him. A perfect weapon, in every respect.

Outside the Bandroom, the huge party of heroes did not know what to do. This plan had got out of control. Their friends, the Moorston vampires were now trapped inside. Outside they had two Friarmere vampires to deal with. One who was incredibly vicious and one who was very smart. She had nearly ruined all their plans.

What did they do now? Storm inside the Bandroom to help the vampires? As their enemies came out, perhaps they could cut each one in two with Joe's chainsaw. But as the half-vampires got stacked up, surely that would give the game away. It would be so easy for one of them to escape. They could use the pieces as shields.

Lynn was trapped behind the flames. They could just about see her looking out petrified, from under the Bandroom. Lynn clawed at the gravel under there as she waited to make her escape. She would keep for the moment.

Kathy had a garlic spray. Without warning, she just began to spray this at Stephen's face. Unfortunately for the humans, even though this was very distasteful for vampires. It did not have the same effect as mistletoe in Moorston. That had been a game changer. Just like the Brass Necks.

It did, however, make them physically sick if they had too much of it, and this was too much. It was no mistletoe spray, but it threw a spanner into the works.

'Fuck off, bitch!' Stephen shouted, as he visibly heaved. This was way too much on top of an already queasy stomach.

A group began to form around Stephen. One by one they came, standing beside Kathy. Liz and Andy, Gary, Wee Renee and Pat, Our Doris, Terry, Helen Shuttleworth, Adam, Lauren and Rick, Miles and Freddie. Stephen wasn't going anywhere.

They started to move a little closer, Rick began to swing his chain to trap him, but Stephen dodged and stepped backwards. The chain was great, but it was noisy therefore useless if you knew it existed.

Everything was very loud now, and the smells were extremely strong. The sound of Joe's chainsaw was indeed the worst sound with a strong, hot electrical smell that went with it. The vampire's fighting sounds and screaming was coming from those inside the Bandroom. The rhythmic music of the Brass Band music still blared out. The shouting of the people fighting outside. The smell of petrol - the smell of burning wood.

All their senses seemed to be turned up to the maximum.

Wee Renee moved first. She managed to strike Stephen on his arm with the machete. He swung towards it and momentarily knocked it out of her hands. From the other side, Father Philip ran in with one of Ian's hatchets in his right hand, taking one of Stephen's ears clean off.

There was now a succession of humans running past Stephen from one way or another, each taking their turn as his back was turned.

This was quite entertaining to watch, and some of the others thought this was a spectacle too. Andy ran low and tried to slash Stephen with all his weight behind it, but Stephen's jeans were thick, and he didn't get very far.

Our Doris flung her up her sword and ran as fast as she could, connecting with Stephen right across the shoulder blades before returning into the crowd.

Agnes ran with her scissors high. She made a bullseye, stabbing him in the back of his neck. Leaving the scissors sticking out and quivering. This wound made Stephen very angry.

Bob looked at the scene. It reminded him of something he had seen - a video on the internet and thought that this was a lot like that. The video was about bear baiting. The more they wounded and teased Stephen, the angrier he got. He was turned away from Bob, Agnes's Silver scissors gleaming in the firelight from the Bandroom.

Bob ran forward with Ian's knife sharpener straight through the crowd into the back of Stephen. It entered just above his coccyx, through the gash in the denim that Andy had made, and Bob did not try to take it out.

Now, Stephen, had two objects sticking out of the back of him, but it did not slow him down. He was like a maniac, a wild animal, ferociously trying to grab at least one of his attackers. Something terrible was going to happen soon. Something was going to break.

Pat ran at the back of him, but he knew she was coming as she was too heavy footed, and he was used to them attacking him from the back now, so continuously whirled around. As she struck him with her club hammer around his heart, he grabbed her coat, using it to pull her closer towards him.

His teeth went close to her neck. He would bite her, there was no question. Even with the Brass Neck, Stephen could pinch Pat and make her pass out, just like Colin had with Bob. But if he discovered it, and tore it off, he could be ripping Pat's throat out in a second.

'No,' Wee Renee shouted and ran forward with the machete. Every person, in fact, surged forward to save Pat. Surprisingly, the first one there was Freddie. He held the Friarmere Band trophy and drove it hard into Stephen's heart. It was not wood, it was, in fact, plastic sprayed gold, but with its many spikes, it completely punctured the organ. Stephen struggled backwards, and Freddie hit him again with the spikes. This was making quite a mash of the heart area. Stephen stumbled backwards again.

'Die you bastard murderer,' Wee Renee shouted. Adam moved behind Stephen, who finally let Pat go. Terry grabbed her coat and shoved her behind him, out of danger. This gave Freddie even more of a chance to bash him again in the heart area with the Friarmere Band trophy.

Adam was behind him, looking at the weapons sticking out of the back of Stephen. Adam put his leg out. Freddie lunged at him. It did the trick nicely. This careless trip caused Stephen to fall backwards. Right onto the knife sharpener and the scissors that Agnes and Bob had conveniently left in there.

The knife sharpener pushed through the rest of Stephen's soft flesh coming out the other side, directly through his genitals. After all that, amazingly Stephen was still alive

'Aye carumba!' Bob exclaimed.

Stephen kept his head raised, the scissors did not enter any further. A few of them got down to work on Stephen. Freddie continued to bash the trophy into his heart area, in the end just leaving it embedded half in and half out, the base sticking out towards the stormy sky.

Wee Renee squatted down near the top of him, hacking away at the top of his head for some reason. It looked like she wanted to perform brain surgery. She was also trying to force his head down further, which would embed the scissors into his neck. In the end, the deathly blow came from Agnes, who slit his throat. This sprayed an awful lot of blood all over the diminishing snow.

'That's for ruining my best scissors,' Agnes said. 'I bet they're bent now!'

They were all looking at Stephen. Bob thought the picture should be captioned *'Death by Band trophy.'* The rest of the party were just glad that all the vampires hadn't been that hard to kill. They all breathed heavily. That had really been hard, and most of them had a good amount of Stephen's blood on them. They weren't looking behind them.

Lynn had managed to scrabble out from the underside of the Bandroom. She didn't know what she was going to do, but she was going to make a run for it, she knew that for sure. With one eye working, she wasn't about to tackle this grizzly lot. Lynn was not stupid. What she hadn't bargained on was Joe, Carl, Craig and Darren emerging from around the side of the Bandroom towards her.

30 Sacrifice

Lynn jumped back when she saw the burly vigilantes. She turned to go the other way. From behind her started to come all the others to trap her, Terry, Kathy, Sue, Tony, Nigel, Gary and Danny.

Nigel was up for it in a big way. He hadn't had a chance to work on one of the vampires yet and didn't want to feel useless at the end of the night. Bravely and defiantly he stepped in front of his friends, holding one of his huge kebab knives.

'The game is up, I think,' Nigel said. 'Don't you?'

Lynn was not concerned at all with this silly human man. Even with one eye, she could take him. Lynn had never seen him before. He wasn't local. Who did he think he was? She got into a crouching position. Nigel had a quick knowing glance at Joe.

'Come on then, Mrs Ernie. I don't know your name,' Nigel said.

'It's Lynn,' Gary informed him.

'Is it? She doesn't look like a Lynn,' Nigel said. 'So, come and get it. See if you can take me. I bet you are down before I am!'

Lynn moved towards him, distracted from anything else and not thinking of the people she had seen behind her. Father Philip got in first with one of Ian's knives. He stuck it quite firmly into her back, running right past her to the group that were at the front. Stationing himself now behind Nigel. Father Philip wasn't going to let an injured arm stop him from helping on the very last night that he had a chance. He would never feel that he had done enough.

This had reminded Lynn that there were large men behind her. Men that could be a more significant threat. When she whirled around to them, she saw that Joe's gang were closer than Nigel's crescent of people. Joe only needed to strike properly with his weapon and Lynn would be no more. He just had to get close enough to her.

'Rick!' Joe said. Rick knew what he wanted. He was the one with the chain. It didn't matter about the noise. Lynn would not be able to evade it. The other people were too close. She would leap back into them. They all had something sharp. Something that would make her bleed.

Lynn needed to be secured as far as the vigilantes were concerned. If she was darting around and Joe was swinging his chainsaw, it was bound to connect with a live human rather than her. Lynn thought this was all too much for her really. She had felt ill since yesterday, she had walked from her house, to the Blood Farm, into the Village. From Maurice's house to The Grange, the Primary School and now right over here to the Bandroom. Lynn was exhausted, half blinded and wanted to vomit. She wouldn't surrender though. Never.

Rick flung out the chain towards Lynn, and at first, it did not snag her. She moved to the side away from it, but Kathy sprayed her with some garlic spray. Shocked by the sudden wet and vomit inducing spray, which seemed to come from nowhere. Lynn jumped towards Rick, and it looked like he had all the time in the world to trap her. He shot the chain out again, and she became ensnared.

Joe stepped towards Lynn, his chainsaw tilted to the side and began to aim for Lynn's neck sideways.

Lynn was trapped and surrounded. She did the only thing she was able to. Lynn hissed at Joe. That was all she had left.

'It'll be quick,' Joe said to her. Joe felt a little sympathy for Ernie's wife. He didn't know why. This creature hadn't made a choice for herself. In fact, it was now a hero that had made that choice for her, Mark. In other circumstances, she would probably have been standing with Wee Renee and Pat against the horde. Just another small twist of fate. Yes, Lynn was to be pitied, but she was also to be liberated.

He moved the chainsaw straight over the top of the chain collar that Lynn currently wore. The noise and vibration went through everyone's teeth as the whirring blades of the chainsaw caught the odd piece of metal as it cut through Lynn's neck. Joe yanked it back as soon as its work was done, a few sparks glittered down prettily onto Lynn's sad wellingtons, which would never fart again.

'So long Lynn,' Ernie said from a little distance away.

'Now for the rest of them,' Wee Renee said. She ran up the steps and banged on the door. 'Get out! Her shouting could only just be heard over the noise.

'What's wrong?' Sarah said through the door.

'It's safe out here now. But it's not in there. Come out, we are all waiting to help you? Wee Renee said.

'They've finished outside and want to help!' Sarah shouted to Angela.

'Out! Angela said and immediately Sarah opened the door. The Moorston vampires flooded out. 'Now you Sarah,' Angela said. 'I will hold the door from the outside.'

'No, you will still be in danger from the burning. I've had enough. I don't want to be here anymore. There is no miracle cure for me. My old Mistress is dead. She can't be bled. Who would want to drink that anyway? I think I'll just wait here with these. My vampire line is over with. My vampire line *should* be over with. And I'm over and done. I have atoned for my sins with that Queen of wolves and crows. I have done what I needed to do. Now go outside and live,' she said.

Angela looked into her eyes and could see that it would take a lot of arguing to get Sarah to change her mind. She had decided to sacrifice herself, and she had made her mind up. Angela put her hand gently on Sarah's face.

'Forever *my* child. I won't forget you, Sarah' Angela said, then went out of the door. Once it had shut behind them, Angela caught Wee Renee's eye.

'Now,' she said.

Wee Renee thought that there was always an outside chance that something would happen. Something she couldn't know but had to make preparation for. At one point she wondered if they may be prevented from tipping petrol on the Bandroom, so just in case had filled twenty condoms full of petrol. Pat had tied them all at the top, laughing the whole time.

Helen Shuttleworth, Danny and Lisa had these, and after the Moorston vampires safe exit, threw them as hard as they could at the Bandroom so that they burst. The building was immediately engulfed in flames.

Every single hero stood outside waiting for the next occurrence, their eyes scanning the bright burning Bandroom for any sign of an escape. They expected that some of the vampires would get through the door at any moment and they would have to spring into action. Each held their weapon up, and they breathed heavily.

Sarah had locked her arms through the door handle and a safety rail that was the other side. The remaining Friarmere vampires kicked and gouged her flesh. Sarah now hoped that the door would be burnt first and she would be gone. If it were enough to burn her, then they would not be able to get through it.

As if Norman's vampires knew this exit was useless now, they tried to find another way out. A window exploded with the sound of screaming glass. The Conductors Stand was now on the grass outside, used very effectively to break the window.

The vampires tried making a run for, that hole, the air rushing into them like vines of freedom, pulling them out.

Their dead fingers reached for the night, their eyes black, reflected the firelight so beautifully. All fangs were bared. They had an exit and were going to make the most of it.

The observers the other side of the window saw them scanning the outside for a space. A small opening for them to run into. Hide until all this was over. Just do anything to get out of this burning mass coffin. They edged forward. The flames were around the window frame, but they could leap through there so easily. The room was full of toxic smoke. Some kind of cladding was burning, and it smoked more than it burnt. There was little was left of Sarah, and the Friarmere vampires thought that they were about to become free again.

Alas, Danny used this opportunity to throw in more condoms through the hole, which then brought the flames inside.

The people outside moved closer. If any of them got out of that window, they would gang up on them and kill them. Our Doris watched the other windows, just in case, they found something to smash those with. The Moorston vampires paced the perimeter. Joe's chainsaw still buzzed. Rick waited by the open window with his chain, Agnes with her cutthroat razor, Gary with his nail-gun.

Nigel could see that the floor was on fire, there was a definite light from there. The condoms had fallen on the carpet, burst and the flames were underneath them. The flames were over their feet.

The heroes could hear terrible noises inside. Unholy noises, screams, quivering screeches – unnatural sounds. The odd maniacal shout or yell periodically assured them that the vampires were suffering and, on their way, out. All of them tried not to think of Sarah in there with Friarmere vampires, but she had done what she wanted.

It was only a matter of five minutes before they were all gone. The gang waited outside a bit longer to make sure it was over. The Bandroom was just one big flame, and the crackle and occasional cracking glass were all that they could hear.

Jackie whispered a few words to Wee Renee about something, but the fire was still very loud, and Wee Renee did not know what she was getting at.

'What love. I can't hear you at all,' Wee Renee said to Jackie.

'I said, Sarah, told me earlier what she was going to do. She made me swear not to tell anyone else. This was a final farewell, and she had planned to go down with this sinking ship,' Jackie said sadly.

'She was a good egg, was Sarah,' Pat said at the side of them.

31 Shafted

Our Doris insisted on the pieces of the three dead vampires being thrown on the flames, Lynn, Stephen and the male with the triangle cut under his clavicle. The female was already against the Bandroom, after all, in a way it was her who had started it. Our Doris said it was just to *make it neat*.

Finally, there was nothing more to be done, and it was time to go back to the mill. Wee Renee looked at her watch. It was 10:15 pm.

'Another year we'd be whooping it up somewhere at a New Year's Eve party, wouldn't we Pat?" Wee Renee said laughing.

'Not on your Nellie. We usually spend New Year watching stuff we have recorded over Christmas and having a sweet sherry, don't we?' Pat replied.

'Aye we do,' Wee Renee said. 'Punctuated by the occasional sausage roll.'

'It feels strange, doesn't it?' Bob said.

He was walking along with Adam. Bob was speaking personally to him, but everyone else could hear it too.

'Yes, it's all over,' Tony said. 'And I kind of feel happy, but also…… I don't know.'

'Deflated,' Gary offered.

'Aye well, that's natural. We'll discuss that at another point after we've got over this lot,' Wee Renee said. 'Don't worry about it. Wee Renee's got a cure for all that!'

'Interesting,' Freddie said.

'I'm sorry Sarah died. I liked her in the end,' Penelope said sadly.

'Yeah, my rooftop mates gone. I won't be there either. There's no-one to be on watch anymore,' Adam said, a little worried.

'And there is no need to be, is there?' Terry said. 'No more vampire kids. No more spying because vampires are searching for victims through one another's Villages. No more killing and burning corpses. Life's back to normal.'

'I don't know what I'm going to do,' Adam said. 'I suppose the authorities will have to take me in.'

'We'll take you in,' Sue said. This was news to Bob, great news. But certainly news.

'Really?' Adam asked. He had been hoping against hope that this is what would happen, but he thought they would never take another teenage boy on.

'Yes, we've already discussed it, me and Sue,' Tony said. 'That's depending of course, that you want to come to us.'

'But what about the authorities, won't they have something to say?' Terry commented.

'They might,' Sue said. 'Remember Terry, there are a lot of children to find homes, for now, aren't there? And probably a lot of parents who want children. Plus, the authorities have to sort all this mess out. Can you imagine how much paperwork there will be? If someone is with a friend of the same age, and he is being looked after, I am sure it will be fine. Besides that, these two have only a couple of years more left in School, then it's up to them, and there's bugger all the authorities can do about it.'

Adam had not felt as happy as this for a long time. He had been dreadfully unhappy when he was a vampire, but for a long time before this, Sue and Tony were always the parents he wished he had had instead of Julie. Now he wouldn't become just another orphan. He would live in happiness, having Sunday Dinners around the table with the family, Basil and Sue's other cats. His family.

'What are you going to do now?' Wee Renee asked. They all wondered who she was speaking to and found that she was waiting for Michael to reply.

'I don't know,' Michael said. 'I've got a lot to deal with. Having two girlfriends killed, plus my brother and a lot of my friends. I have to be honest, I feel pretty shafted. I have also betrayed what friends I had before, which is making me guilty too.'

'Good,' Liz said quietly.

'It's a lot to take in, and I'll probably never be over it. I don't know - I might go on a journey of self-discovery. I think that's what I need,' Michael said.

'No-one understands that as well as I do,' Father Philip said to him. 'You know about what I did, don't you? My betrayal. Well afterwards, I went on my own journey of self-discovery. Delving deep into my soul. Alone in that tent, in the quarry. Of course, I had God helping me, but it was still difficult and will always be. We cannot change the facts or the past. In the future, I can only try and be the very best person I can be. My advice to you Michael is that things will look rosier when you don't force it. Let it come naturally, and it will come right. I can assure you, there is light at the other end of the tunnel.'

'What are you going to do?' Wee Renee asked Angela, Marcel, Penelope, Jackie and the other Moorston vampires.

'Well that is down to me to decide, and I have decided that we may go on a little journey ourselves. Take one small holiday to regroup after The Masters death and all this. After that, I would like to return to Moorston. We have Sheila there, we had safe places to rest. We have been there for many years and feel comfortable. Not to mention we have made a lot of human friends that we would miss very much.' Agnes smiled in particular at this statement.

'If I could arrange, like our Master used to, to have our shipments brought in, we could survive and make no trouble. I would like to do that really. I feel it honours Len. Gives praise to how he made us and confirms he was right, as by choice we would live the same way,' Angela said.

'I would like that too, I have to admit it,' Wee Renee said. 'I may have to call on you in the future, and it would be nice to know I can contact you and have you near. I trust you, and I think that everyone here would find it quite acceptable for a nest of vampires to be close by when you are The Mistress.'

'Thank you,' Angela said.

When they got close to the mill, they could hear Haggis and Bambi barking. The two dogs must have heard all the people returning, and Beryl poked her head through the door. She saw them all trooping out of the trees on the donkey path and was so relieved to see them safe.

They stunk of smoke and blood. Not to mention, they were utterly exhausted but so immensely relieved. All were sad at the loss of dear Sarah, but that had been a minimal loss. A volunteered death, not a murder.

'Listen, everyone,' Wee Renee said. 'I planned to have a party tonight. It is New Year and it is the end of our odyssey, but now I feel sad and think it would be disrespectful on Sarah if we did this.'

'Nonsense.' Angela said. 'Sarah did this, so we could live. Those were the last words she said to me. We will live, and we will enjoy it, and that is how she helped make it for us. Tonight, we will not be sad, because the world will actually be a happier place. So yes, let's celebrate. Sarah would never forgive any of us if we didn't.'

There had been food prepared, which was now laid out on a buffet table. Party poppers were placed amongst the plates. A disco and games had been planned. They still needed to make life as normal as possible for the poor children. This would be a celebration of an ending and a beginning more poignant than any other New Year's Eve party.

32 Poaching

Wee Renee looked around at the people enjoying themselves at the party. A few people had found CD's in their homes and Sue had brought her CD player. Jason was doing what he did best and playing everyone's requests. She stood with Pat, both of them with their traditional New Year's Eve drink of sweet sherry. Some of the others had found champagne and were drinking wine, beer or spirits - whatever they wanted because they could. They didn't have to fight tonight, and everyone was free.

Pat was eating a chunk of cheddar on a cracker. Wee Renee was enjoying some nuts and raisins.

'I think we should keep this going. All get together next year, have another one,' Miles shouted merrily from the crowd.

'I think this one will be enough for me,' Wee Renee said to Pat quietly.

'Yes. Oh, for the quiet life. But I tell you what. It's been a blast hasn't it Rene,' Pat said.

'Aye, it has,' Wee Renee said with a sigh. 'Going back to normality - it's going to be hard to do.'

'Don't I know it, Wee Renee,' Gary said. He and Ernie wandered over to the two women.

'What are you two talking all privately about, over here?' Ernie asked.

'Nothing secret,' Pat said. 'Just about going back to normality and what happens.'

'Well I suppose we go back to our houses in time when all the snow is gone,' Gary said.

'That won't be long,' Wee Renee said.

'Yes, this large group will disband, and everyone else will go back to Moorston or Melden,' Ernie said.

'But we'll always friends and will always have what we faced together to bind us,' Pat said. 'Nothing can change that. No adventure will be as big, before or after this one.'

'I can't remember what life was like before, it seems so long ago. This enormous task we had, seems like it has lasted forever, but it only started on Bonfire Night, and we are now at New Year's Eve. These short few weeks have changed our lives. Taken so many. But it could have changed the world,' Wee Renee said.

'Questions will be asked in Parliament, I should imagine,' Ernie mused.

'Damn right they should be,' Wee Renee said.

'Listen, I have a major concern, and it is something that I don't have the answer to,' Ernie said.

'Go on,' Gary said, intrigued.

'Well we've got all the instruments in Maurice's House the majority I would say are there. Do you still have your Flugel Gary?' Ernie asked.

'Yes, I do. It's in Our Doris's back bedroom with Liz's cornet,' Gary said.

'So we have all the instruments. But we have no blasted Bandroom. We just burnt it down,' Ernie said sadly. 'It was perfect for us as well. Miles away from anywhere, we didn't disturb anyone with our music, and there was loads of parking. We have no big premises to practice in now. No-one's house is big enough in the interim. Plus, there would be noise sanctions.'

'It was bloody cheap as well,' Gary said. 'After we built it, the portacabin was free, apart from the utilities.'

'So to solve your problem, Ernie - what we are looking for is somewhere nobody wants. It has to be big enough for the Band. Far away enough so that we don't disturb anyone when we rehearse, with parking. And cheap,' Wee Renee said, gesturing to Gary on this last point.

'Yes,' said Ernie hopelessly.

'Then we have one. I know where we can go,' Wee Renee said.

'Where?' Ernie asked.

'Crikey, think about it. Somewhere that someone has left now. A place that is big. We have played there, so we know they have a room big enough and no questions will get asked. It is paid off, and we will probably be able to find documents to get it over to us,' Wee Renee said, her face animated. They all frowned at her.

'Where Rene? That felt like I was trying to decipher a limerick or something,' Pat said.

'The Grange of course,' Wee Renee said happily. Everyone else gasped.

'I hope you're kidding,' Ernie said. 'Go back there where *he's* been. Where we all got turned? Where all of this started? I think you should have a word with yourself, Wee Renee.'

'There would be a lot of bad memories there, Rene. Come on,' Pat said.

'Are you kidding me,' Wee Renee said. 'He owes us, and we don't have a Bandroom. We can give that place a lick of paint, it won't be like when he was there. There isn't many houses or buildings in Friarmere that have not been infected by him or his kind. What are we going to do? Rule every single one of those out as well? It would be a long time before we would be able to rebuild the portacabin too. I think we should take it. We take it for our own before someone else does. After all our trouble it's the least that the Morgan family can do for us. We have paid for that in toil and heartache and blood. We will change it all. Even outside if we want to. Paint it white or something. I don't know,' Wee Renee said.

'Or Band colours,' said Ernie, who was obviously already coming around to the idea.

'I've changed my mind. I think its brilliant actually,' Pat said. 'He doesn't need it now. No other Band could have a better Bandroom.'

'Do you know what as well,' Gary said. 'We could have our own little Band contests up there. It's big enough. We could entertain and do other things. We could hire out some of the rooms as well. Maybe for functions - get some money into Band.'

'What a good plan. There are a lot of outstanding subs to collect, and a few of them will be hard to get. Like Keith for instance,' Ernie said.

Pat openly laughed at Ernie. Anyone else would have thought he was joking, but she had an idea, she would be getting a knock on the door soon from Ernie with his accounting book.

'Things are looking great for the New Year now,' Ernie said. 'I'm going to go on a wander, to tell a few people about this, see what they think. I am already making plans, and I'm looking forward to the future of the Band. Thanks, Wee Renee, you know, for thinking of that.'

'My pleasure,' Wee Renee said.

Ernie did wander around, and every Bands person who was asked said that not only was it a great idea, but it was another strike back at Norman Morgan. A kind of dance on his grave.

Ernie spoke to Lee to ask if he would like to come and conduct the Band. Lee said he would think about it because the majority of Moorston band were still alive and they would need someone to conduct them. Ernie also tried to poach a few players from Moorston and Melden Band. He spoke to Terry, who played the tuba. Terry said he might actually come and join Friarmere, and that he would give it some thought.

He spoke to Carl who was the Principal Cornet of Melden Band previously and successfully managed to poach him.

Carl said he would love to see the old gang and play Principal, see them twice a week and replace Sophie who had been their last one.

Maurice was still ready to play, as were the others. Ernie put his mind to the percussion section next. He only had one percussionist left, out of five. Bob was still about. Peter had been killed long ago. Laura had been killed in Moorston and Lynn who used to dabble a bit had unfortunately gone. Five, he had just thought of four. Who was the other one? With a start, Ernie realised that they had another vampire, apart from the Moorston ones.

He started running around panicking and decided to grab a select few to ask what had been agreed about Mark. Ernie didn't know if it had even been brought up before.

In an absolute flap, he called Angela, Jackie, Maurice, Adam, Wee Renee, Pat, Gary, Our Doris and Freddie over to one corner. He was breathless and didn't really want to give them the bad news.

'I've just had a bloody terrible thought,' Ernie said.

'What?' Pat asked, her face going a bit grey. They must have missed something.

'Mark,' he said. 'Mark is still about.'

'Oh aye,' Wee Renee said. 'Yes, he is. Good thinking Ernie.'

'What's your take on him?' Our Doris asked.

'Well, he didn't want to be with the others, right from the beginning. And I suppose I've been closest to him than anyone. He has been on the side of the light, and he told me not to tell anyone, but before this, even before us four vigilantes joined together, he had killed some other vampires,' Ernie said.

'That was clear to me too,' Adam said. 'There is no doubt that he has killed wild vampire kids. I could tell from something he said one time.'

'But what's he doing with the blood? Where is he getting it from? He must be getting it from people. What do you know about it, Ernie?' Angela asked.

'I do know a bit, yes. He's getting it from people, but it is kind of ethically sourced. I do know that it is by their consent that these people are giving it up. Norman said he was providing a service, so he let him be free, without questions. I didn't see much when I went to his premises. Just a human lady in a bed giving blood quite happily and she didn't look drunk or drugged. He is a good vampire really, but he *has* drunk human blood,' Ernie said.

The others were silent for a moment, and then Ernie continued.

'I suppose you could say that he is like you really,' Ernie said to Angela and Jackie. That statement probably saved Mark.

'Are you sure that this blood is freely taken? That it is pain-free? We do not want another Anne situation,' Wee Renee said.

'I'm sure that if it meant that Mark could stay alive, he would explain it to you or show you,' Ernie said.

'What do you think, Wee Renee?' Angela and Jackie asked.

'If it is as Ernie says, or has been led to believe, then I see no reason why he should not stay alive,' Wee Renee said. 'Ernie is right. Mark's heart has been in the right place, but he does enjoy a human tipple. Exactly like the Moorston vampires.'

'Yes, this facility needs to be checked out. But what a boon for all of us, if he can supply us with blood. We would not have to outsource it from Eastern Europe. We could work together,' Angela said.

'So, Mark stays alive?' Ernie asked.

'I think what Wee Renee means is, until she checks out his gaff, yes,' Freddie said. 'What do you think Maurice?'

'He's a good bloke, yes. I will stand for his integrity. I don't know anything about his practices up at the Farm, but if Wee Renee checks it out, then I think he should be kept alive.'

'Listen though, heed this warning. It is no-one else's business, and they may take things the wrong way. Don't go discussing this with anyone else. They won't see things like us. I will check it out. As long as that is satisfactory, then he will remain, for as long as we want him here and he wishes to be here. Provided he does not cause trouble. Reverts back to Normans ways,' Wee Renee said, winking at them.

'And another matter we have to deal with,' Wee Renee continued. 'Sooner or later, Michael Thompson has to take the cure. The anti-biotics. He needs to get Norman out of his system for good. That is very important.' They had all forgotten that too. Yes, that was important.

Jason put on *'Stayin Alive'* by the Bee Gees.

'Come on Pat, this is my song, I told him to play this. We are going to have a dance. Our Doris are you coming?' Wee Renee asked.

'Try and stop me,' Our Doris said, who was in her tights, the bunions clearly visible. Her cowboy boots were drying on the top of a pallet.

At about 2 o'clock in the morning, everyone was so tired that they decided they would call it a night. All the people, even if they still had homes said they would stay here tonight just for one last night of being together. The mill held them safe while they dreamed sweet dreams and waited for the morning of the New Year.

33 Dull

On the morning of the 1st of January, while it was still dark, a group of men on the outskirts of Friarmere worked. The snow had retreated so much that the whole side of the double-decker bus was visible from the outside of the Village. The men hacked away at the wet snow until the bus was free and able to be moved. As there was now a path down the front of the bus, the first couple of men walked into Friarmere. The first ordinary people - not warriors or vampires or werewolves that the Village had had in over a month.

'What's it look like?' One of them shouted from the back. 'Why did they block it off?'

'I don't know. It looks pretty normal to me. Dull in fact,' he said. 'Let's move the bus.'

Wee Renee woke up earlier than everyone else. Something had woken her. Some strange noise. Wee Renee sat up with a start. It was still dark. She looked at her watch it was 6.15. What had she heard?

She couldn't make out the sounds exactly, not in her bleary state. They were sounds that she recognised and had not heard for a long time. She put her boots and coat over her clothes and walked out of the door. Even Haggis didn't wake up this morning. Most of them had only just had just over three hours sleep, including the dogs.

The air was fresh, and she breathed it in deeply, as she walked away from the mill. This was so refreshing. Wee Renee listened. She listened hard. The noise wasn't there anymore. She yawned. It was a kind of slow continuous sound. A bit too far away from her bed. It was familiar though. But what was it? Perhaps she had been dreaming. She considered getting back to sleep, then she heard it again, and she made it out straight away. She was no longer sleepy, her eyes shot open.

She rushed inside to tell Pat what was going on. Wee Renee fumbled around in the dark for a while trying not to disturb anyone else as she found her friend. She began to shake Pat, who mumbled. *'Pull my nightie back down,'*

'Pat, it's not Dennis, it's Rene, love. Come outside, it's really important,' Wee Renee said.

'What! Another git to mutilate. Right! Let me get my hammer,' Pat said.

'No, no, it's nothing like that. It's something wonderful. Just get your coat and boots on and join me outside. And don't wake up anyone else,' Wee Renee said before dancing towards the door and disappearing into the winter morning.

She stood in the same place where she had heard it before. The noise was not there anymore, but Wee Renee had already heard it twice that morning. She waited for Pat with a smile on her face. Wee Renee continued looking out towards the trees at the road, the other side of the donkey path.

'What's wrong love?' Pat said at last.

'Nothing. Nothing at all,' Wee Renee said, who by her tone, obviously knew something that Pat didn't.

'Why are you out here then?' Pat asked.

'I heard something,' Wee Renee said, 'and came out to investigate and make sure I was right, and I was right. So now we will wait until we both can hear it. I promise you, Pat – it is exciting.'

Pat could only use her ears and listen hard. Wee Renee wasn't going to give it away. Pat could hear the constant melting snow dripping and nothing else.

'What was it, Rene? I'm not getting it,' Pat said.

'Wait it will come. I want *you* to hear it,' she informed her friend.

Then it came, a shooshing sound, far away, then close, then far away again. It had been a long time.

'What is it?' Pat asked.

'Cars driving through Friarmere,' Wee Renee said. Pat beamed at her.

Adam heard the two women go out. He felt warm and comfortable. This was his first morning as a human again.

He sat up hugging his legs. With no distractions, he began to think of the last few weeks. He couldn't believe what he had gone through. What he had done and had to do, especially in the Primary School. How had he got through it?

Now life was going to be back to normal, better than the old normal too. It was the 1st of January, a beautiful day. All the baddies were gone, all the goodies had triumphed.

As the others got up one by one, the first thing that everyone was talking about was that cars were driving through Friarmere. Some went outside to listen, and within five minutes, they would hear one.

The other two Villages had also successfully been cut off. But there, Anne had organised that Council diggers should be placed at the exits. She had even orchestrated the ones that had cut off Moorston. Her long fingers of blackmail reached very far into the Council on that side of the Pennines.

The people from those two villages thought that if this had happened here - and today, perhaps the Council had removed their blocks too. That their Villages would be free.

They started to pack their possessions into their backpacks. Several people who lived in Friarmere who had cars said that they would try to get the others back home as quickly as possible. Leaving everyone else was sad. However, they could not stay in the mill forever. They had fought for normality, and here it was. To be enjoyed or endured.

Freddie, Gary, Tony, Ernie and Andy all had cars and offered to take groups of people over as long as they still worked and had petrol. Gary's Land Rover was the first to be tried and instantly sprung to life. The plan was to take Carl and Terry over first, who had cars themselves and could help in the transportation too. So that is what they did.

Freddie said he felt like contacting the police.

'After Stuart and Keith, you don't really trust them to come and sort everything out,' Brenda said.

'I suppose your right, Bren,' Freddie said.

'Yes. I'd keep out of it,' Our Doris said. 'You don't want to go through the last few weeks, blow by blow, do you?'

'No. It was bad enough the first time,' Freddie said.

'Wipe it off your boots and unless they contact you, leave it,' Brenda said.

'It's finally time to say, *I'm all right Jack!* Let someone else have the headaches of it all,' Our Doris said.

'Fair enough,' Freddie said.

The road over to Melden was totally clear. They looked across at the Moors, where they had been hunted, and the snowmobiles had carried the vampires. It didn't seem real already, and yet it had been real only last night.

Soon most people were back in their homes. Families took the orphaned children in ones and twos to live with them until everything got sorted out.

The first people to be taken over to Moorston were Lee, Miles and Graham. They had forgotten how bad it was here. The authorities certainly could not cover this up. There were still dead bodies littered everywhere, near the Church and the Bandroom. They sadly looked down at the most recent victim, Stuart, found in two halves, either side of some snowmobile tracks.

'What shall we do?' Graham asked. 'We can't leave Moorston like this.'

'Bloody leave it. We have done enough. Let everyone else sort that out. Where are we going to put them all anyway? Where? Besides that, they will have our fingerprints on them then, and we didn't kill any of these. The authorities will be after a scapegoat, and I won't be it,' Lee said.

'I am unanimous with him,' Miles said. Graham had to agree with Lee there, he had made some good points. Especially with the statement, *where?* They went back to their homes and shut their doors, hoping for the shops to open quickly.

Inside the mill, Wee Renee had waved everyone off. She had to make sure that everyone had homes to go to. First, as the departures had started, Pat and Wee Renee had made a list of where every child was placed and with whom. Then she just took everyone else's addresses anyway in all of the three villages. She and a few others said she would be checking that all involved were okay in due course. Terry said he would check on the Meldener's, Graham said he would check on the Moorstoner's.

Beryl was one of the last to walk back to Friarmere, under her arm she carried her new and beloved pet, Bambi. Joe, Rick and Lauren walked back with her, bringing her doggy possessions.

Finally, it was time for Wee Renee and Pat to go back home and Our Doris was with them. She said she would go back later when everyone else had gone over, with Jennifer and Beverly, who were at Freddie's house.

She wasn't ready to say goodbye to her new best friends yet, so ventured with Pat, up to Wee Renee's house. They needed some kind of a debriefing – a period of normality. To just be friends, who had no enemies. Brenda and Freddie would take all the Melden ladies over just before tea.

The only inhabitants of the mill now were the Moorston vampires on the second floor, in a cave they had made themselves. The ladies and Marcel would make their way back over to their Village and their secret place when it was nightfall and safe to do so.

34 Hidden

In the afternoon Wee Renee, Pat and Our Doris sat around Wee Renee's kitchen table. Wee Renee had put her hot water on, and Pat was going to be the first to have a bath. Wee Renee said she would have one later when everyone had gone. She wanted to get in her pyjamas and have a nice relax in the armchair.

They all were drinking a cup of tea and breaking up another wheel of Scottish shortbread

'You know the shops will be open tomorrow in town. It will be the 2nd of January everything will be getting back to normal,' Wee Renee said.

'Good because I've got a big shop to do,' Pat said.

'Don't forget to put some of that other stuff on your list,' Wee Renee said.

'What do you mean?' Pat asked.

'Well, kitten food and stuff. The rescue centre will be open. Me and Our Doris will go with you and get you your kitten. We promised you that, when all this was over, didn't we?' Wee Renee said.

'Don't be silly,' Pat said, 'There is plenty of time for that.'

'Yes and there's plenty of kittens that need homes right now, and you need a little one of your own. The buses will be running tomorrow. We can catch one into town and bring it back on the bus,' Wee Renee said, taking a bite of her shortbread.

'Sod that,' Our Doris said. 'After all this, I'm doing anything I want. I'm driving again. We'll go in the Jag. It's not staying in the garage any longer. I'm going to live my life to the full!'

'I didn't even know you had a license,' Wee Renee said.

'Oh, I have, and I used to drive it when face-ache wanted a drink and expected me to drive him home. We will go out in style, fill the boot with the shopping and pick up your kitten Pat,' Our Doris said plainly. They both waited for a response from Pat.

Pat looked at them both. She would definitely have a lovely sleep tonight, looking forward to her new friend tomorrow.

'Oh, go on. Yes please, you soft pair,' Pat said. For the first time in all these weeks, Pat had let her guard down. She had a tear in her eye.

Michael had decided he was setting off on a new adventure. He had nothing to stick around here for and had decided that he was a survivor could tackle anything. He had plenty of money in his holdall. He had siphoned it off all the folk that had either become vampires or had been murdered. After all, they didn't need it. It had been something to do in the daytime, he had been very bored on his own. He didn't really know if it would come in handy. If Anne and Norman had had their way, it wouldn't. Now he was glad he had had the foresight to do it.

In the holdall, he also had some clothes and one spray of deodorant. On his back, Michael also carried a backpack, which clicked and clinked as he walked, but he was not bothered by the sound. It comforted him to hear the bones of the dead Master banging together inside it. He had never intended to take the cure.

On the roof of the Standedge Tunnel, on the way to Moorston, something crouched. It pressed in against the wooden rafters of the roof, next to the black bricks. Outside it was light, and this creature needed darkness. There had been three of them left, but he had been forgotten. Forgotten by his friends. Overlooked by the heroes. The other two had gone now and had not joined him. Soon he would find others to play with, he was very friendly. Vampire children were like that.

He could wait for a long time up here. This little monster had had a massive feed in the Civic Hall. He could wait until summer for the right type of friend. A friend that would make him happy.

The End

Printed in Poland
by Amazon Fulfillment
Poland Sp. z o.o., Wrocław